ALSO BY AMIE BARRODALE

You Are Having a Good Time: Stories

TRIP

TRIP

A Novel

AMIE BARRODALE

FARRAR, STRAUS AND GIROUX
NEW YORK

Farrar, Straus and Giroux
120 Broadway, New York 10271

EU Representative: Macmillan Publishers Ireland Ltd, 1st Floor, The Liffey Trust Centre, 117–126 Sheriff Street Upper, Dublin 1, DO1 YC43

Copyright © 2025 by Amie Barrodale
All rights reserved
Printed in the United States of America
First edition, 2025

Grateful acknowledgment is made to Dzongsar Khyentse Rinpoche for permission to reprint his short quote from a talk given to Dharma Gar students; Rabjam Rinpoche for permission to quote from Kyabje Dilgo Khyentse Rinpoche's Maha Ati Pith Instructions; and Robert Thurman for permission to quote at length from *Tibetan Book of the Dead: Liberation through Understanding in the Between*.

Library of Congress Cataloging-in-Publication Data
Names: Barrodale, Amie, author.
Title: Trip : a novel / Amie Barrodale.
Description: First edition. | New York : Farrar, Straus and Giroux, 2025.
Identifiers: LCCN 2025005383 | ISBN 9780374617349 (hardcover)
Subjects: LCGFT: Novels.
Classification: LCC PS3602.A777543 T75 2025 | DDC 813/.6—dc23/
  eng/20250403
LC record available at https://lccn.loc.gov/2025005383

Designed by Gretchen Achilles

The publisher of this book does not authorize the use or reproduction of any part of this book in any manner for the purpose of training artificial intelligence technologies or systems. The publisher of this book expressly reserves this book from the Text and Data Mining exception in accordance with Article 4(3) of the European Union Digital Single Market Directive 2019/790.

Our books may be purchased in bulk for specialty retail/wholesale, literacy, corporate/premium, educational, and subscription box use. Please contact MacmillanSpecialMarkets@macmillan.com.

www.fsgbooks.com
Follow us on social media at @fsgbooks

10 9 8 7 6 5 4 3 2 1

This is a work of fiction. Names, characters, places, organizations, and incidents either are products of the author's imagination or are used fictitiously. Any resemblance to actual events, places, organizations, or persons, living or dead, is entirely coincidental.

For R. A. M.

TRIP

I

THE HOUSE WAS SHAPED like a child's drawing, a triangle on top of a square. The exterior was tin, the interior cedar, pine, and glass. We never did anything with the yard. It was just dirt, empty except for a concrete tube the builders left behind.

My ex-husband had called to ask for help getting our son to school. As I pulled up, I saw him out front with his dog on a leash. Broad shouldered, almost pudgy, his collarbone-length blond hair going gray, he stood beside a fake-grass rug I hadn't seen before.

I got out of the car. He exhaled a cloud of smoke and slipped his vape back into his pocket. "Sorry," he said.

I shrugged. "What's with the Astroturf?"

"It's for house-training." He gestured toward Misty Two.

I made a face, and the dog growled softly.

"Hey, that's not nice." Vic frowned at his dog.

He brought Misty Two with him to his apartment on my weeks. We hadn't intended to do nested custody—where the child stays in place, and the parents alternate weeks in the home—but it had sort of taken shape around us. He reached down and scratched the dog's ear.

"So, you really have to go?" he said.

"I mean, yes. If I want to keep the job."

"Can they hire someone locally?"

"How many times are you gonna ask me that?"

Vic squinted. "It's 'Death and . . .' Remind me?"

"'Death and Denouement.' It's a conference for people who study death. They're going to present their work. I think Robert Thurman will be there."

"Oh, I know Bob."

He rocked back on his heels, and I could tell he wanted me to ask him about his work. He was a sculptor. He had been hung up on one piece, *The Gaurea*, for twenty years. It was a sixty-foot yellow blown-glass vessel full of oblong holes that he kept on its side in the garage. When we first met, he'd just had a solo show at an important gallery, but things hadn't turned out the way everyone had predicted.

"Let me see those new glasses you bought on the internet," I said. "Trip said they're bold."

He reached into his pocket for a pale yellow case, took out his glasses, and put them on. They were hot pink, with a heavy bridge that made him look sleazy and disoriented.

"You don't like them."

"They're okay."

"They're stupid. I'm going to return them." He took them off. "The house is messy. Sorry. The cleaning ladies are coming tomorrow."

I let myself in and walked past the eleven-foot urns and mold-blown bottles in the shape of fish, up the stairs, past a row of overwatered succulents, to my son's bedroom.

Trip was lying on his futon, his chin-length blond hair covering his face.

"I'm sick," he said. He opened his eyes and pushed away his hair. "Don't even touch me."

I touched his forehead. "You don't have a temperature."

"Dad says I'm sick."

"No . . . I just talked to your father."

"He said, 'I'm sorry you're sick.' That means he thinks I'm sick."

"No, it doesn't."

"Uh-huh. He said so."

"He says you refuse to get out of bed, which is true."

"I just don't understand anything. I'm not smart." He covered his head with the blankets.

"You are smart. I'm sorry that it's hard."

I pulled the blankets down, uncovering Trip's phone on the mattress beside him. I picked it up.

"What are you doing?"

"I'm taking your phone. You can have it after school."

He snatched it back and turned away from me. Abruptly, I lost my temper. I grabbed his ankles and dragged him out of the bed.

He was fifteen years old, but small for his age. He dropped the phone as he slipped off the mattress and onto the rug.

I had never done something like that—yanking him out

of bed. It startled me. I was worried about how he would react.

He put his palms to the floor and crossed his legs and looked at me.

"I'm sorry," I said.

"That's okay." He crawled back into bed.

"We still have to get to school."

He took hold of either side of his headboard. "You don't understand me," he said. "I don't need school."

"Everyone goes to school. I went to school. Your father went to school." I picked up his phone.

"You guys aren't autistic." He let go of the headboard and crossed his legs. "Anyway, it should be my choice."

"Here's a choice: Get up or I'm taking the router."

"You can't take it. It's Dad's. It's Dad's week! Legally, it's Dad's router."

"Whatever."

"That's the law. Do you think I have an internet addiction?"

"No."

He lay down, turned to face the wall, and flipped a sheet over his head. "Do you think Aristarchus of Samos was wrong?"

"I am so far past the point of being able to discuss Aristarchus of Samos right now."

"I know."

I turned and walked out of his bedroom. In the hallway, I heard him repeating his question.

I called back to him. "I'm leaving, but I want you to

understand that you are making a choice right now. You are choosing—"

"Do you think Aristarchus of Samos was wrong?"

"—to leave us with no options."

"Do you think Aristarchus of Samos was wrong?"

I walked down the stairs, stepping over piles of books, thinking about taking the router as I set his phone down.

"I left your phone on the landing. Trip? Did you hear me? I said I left your—"

He spoke over me. "Do you think Aristarchus of Samos was wrong?"

"I love you."

"I love you, too," he said.

Outside, Vic was standing in the driveway, talking to the young couple from next door. I could never remember their names.

I started to tell him I couldn't get our son out of bed, but he looked up and nodded, and I knew he understood.

2

My office was small, with wooden floors, a narrow desk, and a yellow, laminated-glass wall that let in light from the windows on the other side of the hallway. When they'd interviewed me a few months earlier, I'd worried that the color would give me migraines, but I barely noticed it.

I was preparing for the conference in Nepal by reading the memoirs of a fellow at Cambridge who said she was frequently possessed by spirits. She called herself a horse, because the spirits rode her.

My phone rang, and Vic told me that Trip had smashed *The Gaurea*.

"Okay," I said. I got up and went down the hall and let myself out into the fire-escape stairwell. "When you say he smashed *The Gaurea*, you mean he broke part of it off?"

"He broke it into a thousand pieces."

"Like, it's gone?"

"I spent the past few hours sweeping it into Glad bags. It's out by the curb if, uh . . . but no, not salvageable. It's gone. He's quite thorough, as you know."

In the crack between a light fixture and a halogen, I noticed the polarization around the bulb and thought of my mother. Before she died, she had mentioned the rainbows wildly circling incandescents, and I sometimes thought about that, wondering if she had gone her whole life without noticing the effect of the light, or if she had been seeing something different.

"Can you meet with me and Cathy before you leave?" Vic said.

"Sure." Cathy was Trip's therapist. I pushed the door handle and felt it give under my hand. "I'm sure I could do it by Zoom."

"I made an appointment tomorrow morning at Spin."

"Why at Spin?"

"I'm allergic to Cathy's cat."

"When did she get a cat?"

"She's always had a cat."

Spin was one of a handful of restaurants Trip liked. He could sometimes eat two orders of their breadsticks.

It was a chain, with high ceilings and concrete floors. You ordered at a counter and a server brought your food to the table, but you bused your own tray. Even though it was empty, the loud music bouncing off the hard surfaces made me feel crazy.

Vic got Trip set up in his own booth on the other side of the restaurant, then came to sit down with me. I could tell from the way he walked that he thought I would be angry with him for bringing Trip along. When he sat down, he said, "He wanted to come."

I nodded. "The breadsticks."

"Exactly. I put him over there. I think there's no way he can hear us. Not that it would matter much, I guess."

"How are you doing?" I said.

"Oh, okay." He picked up the happy-hour menu. "I wasn't sure if I should order food for our table or not. Are you hungry?"

"Not really."

Vic looked pained. He got out his phone, murmuring about canceling it. I didn't understand what he meant, but before I could ask him, Trip's therapist put her hands on the tabletop.

She was still wearing her sunglasses. Her short hair freshly blown out, she wore a pale blue sweater and white jeans. She sat and took a notebook out of her purse, wrote the date, then glanced up and said, "Trip outdid himself this time."

Vic burst into tears. "I'm sorry," he said. "I'm sorry, Cathy. Sandra hates it when I cry."

Cathy took off her sunglasses. She reached into her bag for a package of tissues and gave it to Vic. "Feeling some big emotions!"

Vic glanced up.

The waiter had come to the table with a large pizza. "Online order?" he said, and I understood that Vic had put in his and Trip's orders through the app.

Vic nodded, gesturing back and forth between the two of us. He turned to Cathy. "I'm sorry. I guess we aren't doing food."

"And who had the root beer?"

"That's me." Vic turned to Cathy. "I feel guilty. I shouldn't have ordered ahead."

"That's okay. No biggie."

"I'm not even hungry." Vic sipped his root beer. "Help yourself, if you'd like some. There's more than I can eat."

I took a piece, but Cathy shook her head.

"Just one slice," Vic said.

"I have an event tonight, so I'm saving room."

"Come on. Take a small one."

"No. Thank you."

"Oh, sorry. I didn't mean to be forcing it on you." Vic took a slice of pizza.

"That's all right."

"You're not forcing it on her," I said. "She's just saying no."

Cathy looked disoriented. She made a face, revealing complicated bridgework, and said, "Vic, can you tell Sandra what you told me yesterday?"

Vic set down his slice of pizza.

"Okay, yes. So this isn't easy. I don't like saying this." He took a napkin from the dispenser and wiped his fingers. "Sandra, I feel like I'm pushing myself beyond what is safe. I don't think I'll be safe, with myself, if you go."

I frowned at Cathy.

"What are you feeling, Sandra? Let us in on your thoughts."

"I'm feeling angry. I was a filmmaker, you know. Before all this."

"Here we go," Vic said.

"I mean, I'm less than two months into—"

The waiter set down a basket of breadsticks. Vic raised them in the air. "These go to my son." He pointed to Trip.

"—less than two months into this job, about to go

produce my first segment, and he tells me I can't go. I mean—okay, look. Forgetting all the rest. The job is arranged. The conference starts in four days. I leave day after tomorrow."

Cathy cleared her throat. "I'm afraid I'm playing catch-up here. Sandra, could you tell me a little more about the assignment?"

"I'm going to Nepal to produce a segment on a death conference."

"And what is a death conference? Is it like morticians?"

"It's academics, neurologists, and mystics—people who study consciousness after death."

"Okay. Sure. Assuming there is such a thing." She smiled at her own wit. "Now, I'm not intending to imply anything, but is this something only you can do? They don't have another producer . . . ?"

"I can't! I can't do it," Vic said.

Cathy reached across the table and patted his hand. "Sandra, how long will you be gone?"

"They need me to go ahead of the crew and host, to get to know the conference participants and the location. I have to figure out who we want to talk to, where we're going to shoot, what story we're going to tell, how we want to tell it. They're known for going in depth."

"Five weeks," Vic said.

"It's one month."

"Thirty-three days."

"We can agree that it's a relatively long time to parent solo," Cathy said. "Do you think you could ask your work about leaving sooner? Maybe if you explained you're in a crisis at home?"

I shook my head. "Not really. No. Not when they're just getting to know me."

"I'm sorry," Vic said. "You need to stay home. I need you, and so does Trip." He turned to Cathy. "Cathy, can you back me up here? Please?"

Cathy took a breath. "Sure. Well, as you know, Trip destroyed some artworks and supplies of Vic's yesterday and screamed at Vic."

"He screamed at you?" I said.

Vic nodded. "He said to me, 'It's your fault I'm having all these problems, because you're a *this* and you're a *that* and you *did the other*.' It's not the meltdown. Meltdowns aren't a big deal. What is a big deal is that I'm reaching a point where I'm having suicidal ideation."

I sighed.

He said, "I know this has been ongoing. It isn't because of Trip. It's my own psychology. But the suicidal ideation is becoming more particular, and more concrete, turning into secret behaviors. I mean, this meeting isn't about me. I know we agreed that I would have him while you're out of town, but I am saying now that I don't think I can do it."

"I talked to you. I said, 'Can you handle this?' and you said yes."

"Okay, time out," Cathy said. "Vic is saying he needs time to focus on his own well-being. Sandra, you're saying that your work trip can't be canceled. Am I hearing you both correctly?"

On the other side of the room, Trip dipped a breadstick in marinara sauce and ate it without looking away from his phone.

"I think we need a new approach," Cathy said. "Vic and I discussed a summer intensive. Sort of like a summer camp, at the Center. This is a facility I've told you both about, you'll recall. It's a good place, where they're trained to work with teenagers like Trip."

"No. I don't want to do that, and neither does Vic. But even if we were going to do that, it's not a decision we'd make at Spin pizza because I had a trip coming up."

"I'm afraid there's no road map," she said. "Particularly in a situation like this. We can't consult the mages and sages. All we can do is come together and decide what we think is best for your son. Now, I made some calls, and we're lucky. They have a bed opening up, and I held it for Trip. I also found out they have equine therapy, so I put that on hold, too."

We went back and forth for twenty minutes, with me saying I couldn't stay, Vic saying he was a danger to himself, and Cathy saying the Center had horses.

Across the restaurant, Trip used a breadstick to wipe up the last of his sauce. The painting on the wall above him was a field of blue with what looked like a round incandescent lamp on one side, a set of steps on the other. I wondered what it was, if it was supposed to be the view from underwater, in a swimming pool at night.

"Sandra?" Cathy said. "Are you still with us?"

"Yeah, sorry. I got distracted for a second. So . . . how would we go about this?"

Trip stood on the landing, his headphones around his neck, his phone in hand.

"They won't let you have technology," Vic said. He was on the ground floor, looking up.

"Whatever. They can confiscate it from me."

"Don't you want to bring anything else? You need clothes."

"Oh right." Trip turned and went to his room.

I looked past Vic into the backyard and noticed the neighbors were trying to line up a large plastic barrel under their rain gutter. "What are they doing out there?" I said.

"Oh, Vickie and Bill? I think they're setting up some rainwater-harvesting thing. It's all local, or native, or . . . what do they call that kind of garden?"

"Ramshackle."

"You think so? I like it."

Trip came back out onto the landing holding a Gucci shoe bag.

"What's in that?" Vic said.

"My skincare and my telescope."

"Don't you want, like, a backpack?" I looked around and saw his bag by the steps. "Like your school backpack."

"It has Dad's blowtorch in it."

"What?" I picked up the backpack and saw Vic's Shimadzu inside. I set it on the floor and looked at Trip. He shrugged and gave me two thumbs-up.

I went upstairs to pack his suitcase.

3

WE DROVE A COUPLE HOURS, then turned off the interstate and took a double-lane highway through miles of desert scrub into the woodlands, where we took a country road over the mountains into the forest.

The Center was at the end of a long gravel lane. It seemed to have been designed and built by a minor genius in the seventies. It was a low concrete building with darkened windows and a geodesic-dome-shaped greenhouse surrounded by elaborate juniper hedges that were trimmed so they appeared to undulate away from the facility.

Vic clicked the button on his car keys, and his headlights flashed. He clicked it repeatedly as we approached the smoked-glass doors.

I pushed the intercom button and after a few moments someone buzzed us in.

It was clean and bright inside. Skylights over the waiting area filled it with natural light, and two twelve- or thirteen-year-old boys were running around, playing some kind of game with paddles.

We sat on a Togo leather couch. A television showed

the weather, satellite images of an approaching hurricane. I asked the receptionist where the other campers were, and she said, "The patients are in group."

It was not what I'd expected. Trip didn't need to be at a place with patients. I wanted to put a stop to it right then, but I was so angry with Vic that I sat there thinking that he would do anything to hold me back professionally, and that if he wanted to play chicken, we'd just see who would blink. I was thinking this kind of ridiculous stuff when a woman called Trip's name.

She was short and stocky, with dangerous, glittering eyes and a runny nose. She said, "Usually what I'll do is I'll take him back, then after we talk, I can talk to Mom and Dad." She turned to Trip. "Sound okay, buddy?"

Trip glanced into his shoe bag and gasped. "My cologne bottle broke."

He held out the drawstring sack. Vic took it and walked over to a wastepaper basket. He removed the telescope and the toiletries, lining them up on an expensive-looking acrylic end table, then turned the sack inside out over the trash and shook it. He picked the remaining tiny shards of glass from the cotton with his fingers, then turned the bag right-side in and returned the products one by one, saving the telescope for last. He handed it back to Trip.

The intake nurse watched all this carefully, then led Trip away.

After half an hour, the intake nurse came back. "You think we could talk briefly out here? I've spoken to Trip, but I want to hear from you."

She slid sideways down onto a lounge chair and sat with her legs draped over the arm. She bent forward, her clipboard wedged between her chin and thighs, and wrapped her arms around her knees. She sat there like that, like we were college chums.

I frowned, and she turned and sat in the chair properly. She cleared her throat. "Now, apparently, he's not going to school. How does that happen?"

"He refuses."

"He refuses," she said as she wrote the words down. She looked up and tapped her pencil. "He's depressed. I can see that, and he's anxious. He's OCD. I knew that, took one look at him, course you get more familiar with the tells."

Vic and I traded looks. Trip was not OCD, but we let it go.

The nurse looked up at me. "I hope it's not too presumptuous of me to say that I see autism spectrum disorder is in the family on Mom's side."

"Excuse me?"

"You get to where you know the outlines." She smiled. "See, I'm fifty-fifty on this one. I don't know if it merits a six-week stay. We don't just hand beds out for asking. But then I'm going, Well, he seems happy to be here. I guess he thinks it will make a change."

"I thought we had, like, a reservation," I said. "A bed or something."

She tapped her pencil and frowned. "I knew he was OCD after talking to him for about three minutes. He's a perfectionist. And he's smart. He's too smart for a psychologist. Psychologists have their place, but not with smart kids like that. Smart kids like that talk their way around it. He needs medication."

"That's something we've avoided."

She frowned and made a note. "Medication can be helpful."

"He has outbursts," Vic said. "Meltdowns, screaming. Breaking things. Sometimes I worry he'll hurt himself. And I don't feel safe. I mean, not from him, he's not the least bit violent, but the effect it has on me. Is unsafe." He paused, looking embarrassed.

The nurse lit up. "Thank you! That's all I needed. I'll use that." She looked at her clipboard and murmured, "Dad does not feel safe." Then she smiled back up at us. "Okay! You two want to come on back and say goodbye?"

She led us through the waiting room, past a locked door, down a hallway, pausing to press her ID card to a pad that opened a set of swinging doors. She spoke freely as she walked.

"He's a good-looking kid. Course he doesn't know it. I said that to him. I said, 'You should be out dating girls, driving cars. You don't even know how handsome you are, do you?' No idea. I said, 'You could be having the time of your life.' But he has no desire. That's typical with ASD. You add OCD, and that's what I call the introvert's cocktail."

"Trip isn't OCD."

She stopped abruptly and looked me in the eye, as though I would backtrack under the heat of her gaze.

"He isn't OCD," I said again. I shook my head. "He's just not. He's not. Not at all."

She held up her palm. "I hear what you're saying. He's your baby boy. You've been loving him since before he was born, but as a PhD nurse practitioner with two decades' clinical experience working with these kids, I can say it was about as clear-cut a case as you get. He told me about rituals, routines, a fear of Satan."

Vic burst out laughing.

I shook my head. "None of that is true," I said. "He lies to people. He tells lies when he thinks it'll endear them to him."

Her pride was wounded. She could see the truth of what I was saying. I knew I should leave it alone, but I couldn't control myself.

"He lies if he doesn't respect someone, like a harebrained administrator."

"Sandra," Vic said.

"Or sometimes if he thinks they are stupid. You should hear the things he's told his guidance counselor."

"Sandra?" Vic was pleading with me.

"Sorry, but she should know," I said. "Someone has to tell her, otherwise she'll go around thinking she's able to diagnose. He thinks it's funny. He likes to see the effect it has on people. Most people don't believe the stuff he says."

"Sandra!"

The nurse started walking again, like she was done with me. She used a card around her neck to open another unmarked swinging door. On the other side was a long corridor. She used her card to let us into a small room.

TRIP

Trip was sitting on a bed. He glanced up when we came in, then looked back at his phone.

"Are you getting service in here?"

"She gave me the password to the Wi-Fi."

"That was nice of her." I looked up at the nurse, but she wouldn't meet my eyes. "What are you playing?"

"It's this game where you go inside people's bodies. You can help them."

"What is it, like *The Walking Dead*?"

"No, it's not zombies. It's like you're a psychologist. You get to help someone. And you can chat with other people who are playing."

"What, like adults?"

"No. God. It's other kids."

"How do you know they're kids?"

"Jeez, Mom."

"I think it's time we say our goodbyes," the nurse said.

Trip stood and gave Vic a hug. He held out a hand for me. I wanted to push it aside and enfold him in my arms, but I didn't want to be overbearing. That's not true. The truth is I was taken by some strange shyness, some imaginary feeling of being watched and evaluated that had come over me intermittently since becoming a mom. I felt like someone was judging me for what I was doing, dropping him off at this horrible place he clearly didn't need to be, so I could go to Nepal, and I took his hand.

4

I FLEW OUT the next evening, feeling sick. I even started to go back home. In Paris, I got up out of my seat while they were still boarding my connecting flight and made my way up the aisle, past all the enraged people who were just getting on.

I called Vic on the jet bridge. "I'm coming back. I can't leave him there. It's wrong."

"No, go. We need to take care of ourselves, too, or there won't be anyone to take care of him."

The reversal was ordinary for us. When we were angry, we staked out our territory, and once we settled down, we wanted to surrender it. So, I felt guilty and wanted to come home, and Vic felt guilty and wanted me to go to Nepal.

"Get back on the plane," he said. "Don't come home."

"What if it's a mistake? Like when we took him out of Lowell."

"Taking him out of Lowell wasn't a mistake. You can't always pore over the past, looking for how you are to blame."

I thought about canceling the trip and possibly finding a new job, and the idea of doing that irritated me.

"Well, if you don't want to go, just come home," Vic said.

"No. I need to go," I said. "I have to get back on the plane."

"Okay . . ." He was confused.

I had trouble getting to sleep, because of the whirring of the privacy divider beside my ear. It was all the way down, but the button must have been depressed, causing it to repeatedly roll over and click, making a sound like "I know I know I know" and "Riot Grrrl Riot Grrrl."

They'd put me in business class. I was feeling terrible, in a lie-flat seat with a small cubicle for my feet, *Yotsuya kaidan* playing on a fifteen-inch screen, noise-canceling headphones on the floor, cord still jacked in the armrest. It was dark. I lay there under a twisted quilt, unaware that I was beginning to dream, the privacy divider saying, "Back whore back whore back whore." I closed my eyes, and the whirling blue at the center of my vision briefly and almost imperceptibly switched to an image of long columns of aluminum pipe on a white wall, then I saw a matrix of brilliant blue and white triangles and opened my eyes. The flight attendant walked irritably toward the rear of the plane, shaking her head, loose hairs coming undone from her bun.

I got into Kathmandu late at night and took a car to the Hilton.

Three conference participants and I were sharing a car up to the site. It was before sunrise, and the lobby was empty except for the hotel staff and a man around my age who looked like a pygmy bear. He had a single white patch in his beard and wore tinted glasses and gray jeans. He pulled a silver trunk across the lobby to an early-bird coffee stand, where he separated a paper cup from its stack fastidiously, as if he was afraid a coffee-stand attendant would jump out and scold him. He pressed the lever on top of the coffee urn a few times, then took a sip before adding cream.

The revolving door beside him jumped to life and he startled, then noticed that I was watching him. We recognized each other as conference participants. He looked back down at the coffee station, squinting at the packets of sugar, and I turned away from him, then went out through the revolving door.

It was already warm, even though the sun hadn't risen. A bleary-eyed man in a blue-and-white cotton button-up shirt stood smoking at the curb. He had white hair that was stained yellow, maybe from smoke or a henna job that was a few months old. Someone coughed, and I noticed a young woman in a long skirt and a lightweight denim jacket sitting on a bench flush with the hotel's glass exterior. I went and sat beside her.

She moved slightly away and hunched over her phone. The man in the blue-and-white shirt turned to gaze at the night sky, and the bear man came out of the revolving door.

By this time, we all knew we would be sharing a car. The two men started talking. The bear man introduced himself as Donald, and explained that he worked in AI and was trying to create an intelligence that feared death. He was precise in his speech and manners, explaining that we didn't know how to define *sentience* exactly. "Maybe it's the point where a computer program has preferences for favorable things. Actual desires—not just being able to convince us of that. I don't know."

The bleary-eyed man, Larry, had an Australian accent and said he specialized in natural law in the afterlife. When we started to probe him about his field, he interrupted us, asking Donald if he knew anything about the hotel where the conference was being held.

"It's a heritage property in the middle of nowhere," Donald said. "It was formerly the queen's summer palace. A fantastic place. The Nepali government can't touch it. It's a long drive, though, on bad roads."

Our SUV pulled up and the driver let us in and piled our bags in his trunk.

As we drove out of the city, the woman, Linda, explained that she worked on dirge and threnody at the University of Chicago, and I told them I was a documentary news producer for PBS.

"Where is your crew?" Linda said.

I told her they were coming in a couple weeks, around the middle of the conference, that they would be flying in from Australia, and she burst out laughing.

"Why's that funny?" Larry said, and she shook her head.

"It just is."

I sighed. The freeways and concrete buildings with rolldown doors began to give way to pastures. I bundled my backpack up in the window and rested.

When I woke up, we were on a winding road in a forest of semitropical-looking trees, and they were arguing about self-awareness. Linda argued that consciousness was permanent, and Donald that it was momentary. They agreed that the forms we perceive belong not to external objects but to consciousness, but then Donald, irritably, made some distinction about even that. I was not really paying attention. I tuned out, and when I tuned back in, Larry and Donald were arguing about a jar of mayonnaise. Larry told Donald it wouldn't keep after he opened it. Donald argued that it would keep, because of the preservatives, and Larry seemed to remain angry about that until he fell asleep, snoring loudly.

The landscape changed again. It started to look more like a pine forest. The roads got rougher. Sometimes we had to pass over fords. We came to a stop at a rockslide, several feet of shale covering the road, and waited while a single crane cleared it. We got caught in the mud, and the driver spent twenty minutes inching forward and back, then gave up, and we all had to get out and look for rocks to put under the tires, to provide traction for the SUV.

We made it out of the mud, and had been driving in silence for a while when Donald said, "This experience, this life that we are experiencing right now, this experience of life, so-called *life*, is just one out of billions and billions and billions of thoughts and projections and hallucinations. And this fleeting, temporary so-called life is totally under the influence of all kinds of influencers."[1]

"I'm feeling a little carsick," I said.

"And then us thinking that this is all we have, and when we die, that's the end. That is how narrow and childish we are. At the moment we have perceptions of our friends and enemies. I don't know, perceptions of security, food, insurance. That's just our perception."[2]

"I'm going to try to get some more sleep," I said. I balled up my jacket and put it between my head and the car door.

In a few minutes, I opened my eyes, and he was looking out the window, wearing a disposable mask.

"The road is bad," the driver said, and Donald laughed for a long time.

Close to nightfall, the driver pointed to the ditch. He turned in his seat, waggling his eyebrows and smiling.

We were confused.

The driver pointed again. Then he pulled over and jumped out of the car.

He ran down the road, dove into the ditch, and dragged himself along the ground. Then he stood, holding a baby bird. He jogged back toward us.

"What is he doing?" Donald asked.

"He's running toward the car with a bird in his fist," I said.

"Oh, hello." Donald turned to me and smiled. "You're awake."

The driver knelt and picked up a stone. He threw it at a bush.

"What's he doing now?" Donald asked.

"He is throwing rocks at the mother."

The driver threw a second rock, and a large bird flew straight up out of the bush toward the sky.

He walked over to the bush, bent forward, then ran back toward us and opened the car door smiling, a baby bird in each of his fists. When he saw our expressions, his smile fell. He threw the birds down into the dirt, flung himself back in the car, and drove in offended silence.

"Maybe we're in some other realm," Larry said.

We pulled through an iron gate and drove down a muddy road to a brightly lit chalet. It was built at the edge of a cliff and connected by stairs carved into the mountainside to cobblestone walkways that led through the forest to the newer buildings—a dining room, some accommodations, a conference room building, a swimming pool, and an unrenovated barn. The main house, the heritage building, was four stories tall, with an angled slate roof and dozens of long windows that glowed in the night.

A hotel employee came out to greet us. He wore a khaki uniform and was bent forward, moving with deference, but when he saw us, he slowed down, stood straight, and scowled.

"The scholars are having dinner," he said. He pointed to a building about a quarter mile away. "I suggest you leave your bags here and go to the dining room."

We followed a path through a mango grove, past a marble shrine to Kali. As we got close to the dining room, we could hear the conference participants. A man's voice rose over the din. "Yes, yes, seeing everything as an illusion is fine," he shouted angrily. "But it's for beginners!"

The dining room had high ceilings and marble floors and was lit with incandescent lights. Brocade curtains hung in the windows, and long wooden tables were set in the center of the room, with smaller round tables in the corners. French doors opened onto the garden, where several two-tops overlooked the valley.

A buffet was laid out in steam trays on a sideboard. I took a plate and opened a lid and scooped some rice. Behind a large rectangular serving hatch, a busboy in black trousers and a maroon vest scraped plates and loaded them into an autoclave. I opened another tray, frowned, and closed it, then looked around the dining hall, hoping to see an empty table, somewhere I could discreetly sit alone and eat quickly.

Most of the tables were full. A group of women in brand-new salwar suits and creased pashmina shawls—things they had probably bought at the airport or in the hotel gift shop and didn't quite know how to wear—called to Donald, and he brightened and waved and went over to say hello.

Larry was behind me at the buffet, scooping rice onto his plate, when a man in an Oxford shirt and a new hill-country wool vest that bunched at his shoulders came up to him to say hello. He poked Larry in the chest. "Hey, hey," he said.

I looked back down, opened another lid, scooped some curry, and made my way down the buffet, to the end of the table where there were condiments—yogurt, lime wedges, mango pickle, and hot peppers.

"I'm not talking about that," the man in the vest said. "I'm not talking about that. I'm talking about something altogether different. Okay? I'm talking about something else."

I squinted to read the man's name tag, thinking he might be a good person to interview, but I couldn't make it out.

"I'm talking about projecting my consciousness out of my body and into a corpse."

"Really?"

"Yes. I got a vessel and placed it on a platform marked with the particular diagram. I think I have it here." The man wiped his fingers on his pants and reached for his phone. "Yeah, here it is." He turned his phone toward Larry. "You can set the vessel down like a cup and write this word here inside it with a piece of chalk, or you can flip it over and write it on top. Six of one, half a dozen of the other. Then what you do is . . ."

A waiter brought out a plate of steaming parathas. He opened a steam tray lid and scraped the fresh bread in with tongs while the man in the hill-country vest explained the procedure for inhabiting another body.

"Of course"—the man picked up a piece of paratha and took a bite—"you test to see if you're ready. I'm working on the corpses of small animals, trying to revitalize them."

Larry shook his head.

"Sometimes I can get one to warm up a little," the man said. He looked at the paratha. "This is too spicy."

Larry opened a steam tray and heaped fried ramen onto his plate. "No one does that anymore. It's too dangerous."

I spooned some yogurt onto my plate and walked over to a table laid out with glasses and urns of tea.

A man with bushy eyebrows shouted, "Donald? It's me, David Bercholz. We met in Kenya."

Donald nodded. "Of course," he said, and excused himself from the women in salwar suits and pashmina shawls.

At the drinks station, two women were filling their glasses. One was impish and wore a pale yellow cashmere sweater and matching trousers. The other was in her thirties and wore sweatpants and an old concert T-shirt.

"The title of your talk," the younger woman said, "is it *orgasm* in Spanish?"

"I mean, yes. But nobody is going to think of that."

"*Orgasmo*?"

"What's your title?"

"'Narrative Structure in End-of-Life Care.'"

"Hmm. A little dowdy."

I got a glass of tea and walked out among the tables, heading toward an empty one. Before I could get to it, Larry caught up with me and said, "Sandra. Come and join us. Everyone, this is Sandra. I'm not going to tell you their names, because you'll just forget."

We sat at the table. An animated man with a Santa Claus beard paused mid-sentence, then continued his story. "The person I'm touching turns, and I'm eye to eye with Robert Pattinson."

"Who?"

"A famous young actor. He says, 'Can I order for you? Do you want something to drink?' and my mind goes blank. Just—nothing."

"I'd faint if he tried to buy me a drink."

"Didn't he jack off as Dalí?" a woman asked. She was middle-aged and tightly wound, with light blue eyes and a copper-colored bob.

"What?"

"I think he was in a movie as Dalí and masturbated on camera or something."

"I've got to see that," the man with the Santa Claus beard said. "Remind me to have a look."

"He doesn't drink, right?"

"It was 2017, so to be honest I do think he was still drinking at that time, not that it really matters. The point is, the lips move, and the words come out of my mouth: 'I'll have the Pappy Van Winkle.' It was kind of a strange thing to order," Santa Claus explained. "In addition to being exorbitantly expensive and served in a snifter . . . it just wasn't the right thing in the moment."

I reached for a container of chili oil.

On the other side of the table, a man said, "Every ten thousand years, the pigeon takes a silk scarf in its claws and flies up to the top of Mount Everest, where it brushes the peak with the scarf one time."

"I see where you're going with this," the woman who had been talking about Dalí said. "A moment is the amount of time it would take, proceeding like that, to wipe the mountain away."

The man laughed.

"A moment is brief, Albert."

"Let me ask you a question, Jody, and I want you to really take some time to consider it. In your entire life, has this moment ever ended?"

"Yes, Albert. In fact, all of them end!"

"Hmm. I'm surprised at you."

"Okay, Albert." She did the finger-winding-by-her-ear gesture.

I took a few quick bites of my dinner and wrapped some paratha in a napkin and said good night, and stood.

On my way out of the dining room, I passed the serving hatch, where a man with crazy hair was holding a packet of ramen and talking to the busboy who had been scraping dishes.

"You add a quarter cup of tahini at the very end," the man said. "Supposedly it's like the most insane broth you've ever tasted."

The busboy nodded, handing the man a teapot of boiling water.

"I'm a vegan neurologist," the man said. "I always bring my own food."

I went back to the check-in desk, and a bellhop took my bag and showed me to my room.

It was on the ground floor of the heritage house, a long, rectangular space with an antique-tiled floor and screened windows overlooking a small interior courtyard. A queen-size bed was at one end and a sitting area at the other. I thanked the bellhop, apologizing as I handed him a few American dollars.

I went to the bathroom. It had celadon marble floors,

a boxy marble sink and counter, and a tiny, opaque oval window.

I reached in past the plastic curtain to turn the shower on. The nozzles weren't marked, so I ran both to figure out which was hot. While I waited for the water, I looked in the mirror.

My hair lay flat against my head, but I didn't want to go into my suitcase to find my hairbrush, so I opened the hotel's little plastic-wrapped comb and started working it through the ends. It was like a lice comb, just a tiny little thing, so I went out and got my brush and brought it back to the bathroom.

I was brushing my hair when the phone rang. In my rush to answer it, I dropped my hairbrush on the marble bathroom floor, but I made it out in time to catch Vic.

"These floors are so slippery."

"What?" he said.

"Nothing, sorry. Hi."

I asked if he'd heard from Trip. He said he hadn't, but that that was to be expected, that we shouldn't worry.

When we got off the phone, I noticed some texts from the office. I glanced at them, and saw that the host of the show wanted to come to Nepal a little sooner than originally planned. I replied, saying that was great, then showered and went to sleep.

5

I HAD JOINED the conference participants on a hike to a local naga cave, guided by Gail and Horace, a married couple from Sarah Lawrence. At first, they took the lead, but when Horace turned beet red and gasped for air, they fell back, and Donald and I led the group.

The way was mostly flat—sometimes grassy and open, sometimes wooded. It looked like any pine forest, except for the one- or two-story boulders resting beside the path as if set there by giants.

We had walked for more than an hour when we came to the sadhus. They sat beside a mud hut, quietly watching us. One was naked, with broad horizontal strokes of white ash smudged across his forehead and a large enamel pin in his topknot. Something in his manner seemed to ask what impression he made. The other wore a T-shirt and a sarong printed with marijuana leaves. His outfit was not so good, but his gaze showed indifference to our thoughts, and that made him the more formidable of the two.

"You think that's it?" Donald said. "That hut."

"I think it might be."

I smiled lamely as I walked past the sadhus and peered

in. The hut was empty except for a rustic shrine. A picture of a snake was nailed to the wall, and offerings were arranged on a table beneath it. I walked through the room, down a narrow earthen hallway to a round room with a ladder coming out of a pit in the floor.

I looked over the side. It was about fifteen feet to the bottom. I felt disoriented by the lack of museum context—ticket takers, guards, ropes. Thinking, Maybe this is just what you do, I got onto the ladder.

Halfway down, a rung bowed and snapped, dropping me neatly onto the rung below. I gasped, then lowered myself carefully the rest of the way, putting my feet on the edges of the rungs, close to the rails, until I got to the bottom of the shaft, where I saw the entrance to a cave.

The light was dim. A vine grew from the floor all the way up the wall. Little round fruits grew on the vine. I recognized them from a holiday Vic and I had taken to Thailand before Trip was born. I picked one.

"Sandra?" Donald said.

I looked up and saw him peering down from the top. "Uh, be careful on the ladder. It's rotten."

"Wait there while I get the others, okay?" He ducked back out of sight.

I heard the scholars up above, their voices overlapping. It sounded like they were arguing about whether or not to take off their shoes.

I looked at the fruit I'd pulled from the vine. I peeled some of the skin off and touched the flesh to my tongue. It had the texture of a plum but the flavor of a grapefruit. I took three quick bites.

"Are you eating the plant life?" Donald was looking over the top of the pit again. "You've heard the myths, right? *I took food in the dark realm.*"³

"Burmese grapes."

"Hmm. Anyway, the shrine keeper took charge up here. Everyone has to take off their shoes and prostrate." He lowered his voice and stage-whispered, "If I were you, I'd ut-pay away-ay the uit-fray. This man is very serious."

A barefoot man in a headlamp and shorts put a hand on Donald's shoulder and looked down at me with a smile. "Ma'am, yes. Take off the shoes."

"I need the shoes."

"Ma'am? Okay, okay." He climbed down the ladder, pausing to inspect the snapped rung, then glanced up at Donald. "Come."

"Oh," Donald said. "Okay." He called to the others. "Guys, he's taking us down now."

I watched him begin to climb down the ladder, then turned and followed the shrine keeper through a hallway and into a small cave the size of a barbershop. It was dry, the ground rocky but mostly flat.

The shrine keeper said, "Here," and slipped through a tall, narrow crack in the wall.

I turned my shoulders to the side, glancing to make sure Donald saw me, then went in after him.

The shrine keeper and I were in a passageway. The floor tilted sharply to the left, toward a dark, narrow opening that ran parallel to the tilted pathway, like a gutter. I pressed myself up against the right wall, stepping carefully.

Ahead of me, the shrine keeper lowered himself into a hole in the floor and gestured for me to follow.

"Don't want to fall here," I said. "Can't fall here."

Donald slipped in behind us. He noticed the gutter and picked up a rock and dropped it down into the chasm, counting to three before it hit the ground.

"Does this seem safe to you?" he said.

"Not really." I lowered myself into the hole, following the shrine keeper, who led us down a winding maze of narrow passages, lit only by his headlamp. He moved nimbly, without any trace of hesitation, hopping up and over boulders and sliding between cracks. He had obviously led people in and out of the cave many times.

He lowered himself onto his hands and knees.

"Follow, Aunt," he said, and slipped inside a rift.

I crawled after him, into a gallery where we could stand.

He pointed at a long crack in the wall, just where it would have met the floor.

"You go," he said. "Go, Auntie."

I knelt and peered in. The passage was narrow, about two feet high, but the walls were twenty feet apart, so it was sort of like a bedroom with a very low ceiling.

"Will I fit?" I said.

"Only sinners cannot pass, Auntie."

A bat flew silently into the strange bedroom. I crawled in after it. The rock under my hands was scratchy and dry. The ceiling got lower, and I had to lie on my stomach and drag myself, but before I could get too claustrophobic, I came to the other side and stood.

It was a different section of the cave. The walls were moist and the rock rippled all over like the surface of water.

The shrine keeper followed me. When he slipped out of the crack, he seemed energized. "River surface room," he said, gesturing around.

He pointed to another crack near the floor on the opposite side of the gallery and said, "Crystal room. Very special. On the stomach and drag." He held out his headlamp. "You go ahead, Madame. Like this. Take the light. Like the snake. Like Superman."

Donald had caught up to us. He was right behind me, and he could tell that I was afraid. "Let me go first," he said. He took the lamp and slipped into the darkness, grunting, making his way slowly.

"It's intense," he said.

Then he gasped. After a few moments, he called from the other side.

"Come on, you have to see this."

I looked at the shrine keeper and he nodded. I got down on my knees and looked in. It was like the previous space, but the ceiling was low enough that I would have to squeeze in, my back and stomach touching rock the whole way through.

I could see Donald's light reflecting off the ceiling.

I slipped in and started to make my way forward.

It was not as difficult as I'd expected it to be. I dragged myself into the crack on my forearms.

"You doing okay?" Donald said.

I turned my head to the side and closed my eyes. "If I try to tilt my head, my mouth brushes the rock."

"You just gotta get through to the other side. Just keep dragging yourself until you get to me."

"If this rock moves an inch, I'm crushed like a bug. I'm dead." I closed my eyes and started to inch forward. I had the thought that the crack seemed to be narrowing. "Got to keep pushing it," I said.

"What's that?"

I grunted and felt my shirt rip against the rock.

"Are you okay?"

I extended my arms in front of me and dragged myself forward twice, then paused to breathe.

"It's longer than I thought," I said. "It's getting lower."

"You're a little off course."

I opened my eyes.

"It'll be fine," Donald said. "Just come to me."

"Donald?"

"Don't be scared."

"I think I'm going back."

"What?"

"I need to get out. If I want to move my head forward I can't. I have to keep it to the side. I need to get out."

I pushed myself backward. I released all the air from my lungs and pushed again. I breathed in and found myself wedged in more tightly.

"This is not good. I can't move. Donald?"

"Yes?"

"I think I'm stuck."

"What? It can't be. Just take a second and get your bearings."

I noticed a place at the far end of the crack where it

got wider. "Okay, no," I said, "I got it. I can see where it opens up."

I pushed myself to where the ceiling was higher. Even though I was off course, I wanted to breathe for a second. A pebble was wedged under my breastbone, and I reached under myself to move it, and then dragged myself two times quickly.

Donald moved his headlamp, and I realized that the ceiling was not any higher where I was heading, that it had been a trick of the light.

"Oh my god," I said. "I thought it was going to get wider, but now that I'm over here I'm realizing it was just an illusion. The way the shadows fell, it made it look like it was wider over here."

"Come to me."

"I can't. I can't move."

"That's not possible."

"It just looked like a way bigger space. I'm going to shove myself back."

"I remember a scouting book I read as a kid. It said if your head could get through a space, then technically your entire body could."

I was frantic suddenly. I started straining, trying to find a way out. Grunting, I exhaled and turned my head to the left, resting my cheek against the rock. "Oh my god. I think I'm stuck," I said. "It's not a joke. I think maybe yeah, I'm stuck."

"What? No. I got through fine and I'm bigger than you."

"I'm going to be sick."

"Try again."

I tried to rock forward. I managed to wriggle half an

inch, wedging myself tighter. "I may need some help." I couldn't twist onto my side.

I felt someone behind me reach into the crack and tug at my feet. My head was wedged in, turned to the side. I worried that someone would jerk my legs without warning and dislocate my spine, or paralyze me.

"No!" I kicked my legs.

"Stay calm." I recognized the voice of the man who had been talking about ordering an expensive drink from Robert Pattinson the night before. He said, "You're the news lady, right? The producer? Your name is what? Cheryl. I'm Bart Diamond. I'm going to ease you out."

He pulled, popping my neck.

"Stop! Now!"

"Sorry. Cheryl? I just need to give you a . . ."

"Stop! Don't fucking pull my ankles. Don't touch me."

"Sorry." He let go of my feet. "Sorry."

"Just you go, ma'am. Just you go through."

I took several deep breaths, feeling my rib cage corseted by rock.

"Sandra?" Donald said.

The breccia was settling in around me. The cave felt alive and angry, like it was holding me close, telling me it was over.

"Sandra?" someone said behind me. "Sandra, it's Benito Cruz. We may have seen each other last night at dinner." He cleared his throat and took off my shoes.

"Don't touch my feet!"

"Yeah, don't touch her feet," Bart said. "She doesn't like that."

"My head is caught here," I said slowly and carefully. "If you pull my feet hard enough, you will break my neck."

"Are you hurt?"

"My head is wedged in here somehow."

"Can you turn it?"

"No."

"I see your feet." Benito put a hand on either of my heels and squeezed gently. "Maybe I could—"

"Benito?"

"Yes."

"If you touch my feet again, I'm going to go crazy."

Benito let go of my feet. "I apologize."

"Would you please put my shoes back on."

Benito said, "I'm going to touch them now, just to put your shoes back on." He slid my shoes onto my feet and called back to the other scholars, "No one touch her feet!"

"What?"

They were piling up behind me now. Some understood that my situation was potentially grave, but others didn't.

"Sandra? My name is Jody. I don't think we met ever. But we're supposed to take off our shoes. I think you should keep them off. Also, if you don't mind hurrying, we need to get in to see the cave and then head back. A lot of us are jet-lagged."

"Listen," a man's voice said. "If you can get your head through a space, then technically your whole body will fit. So, all you have to do here is stay calm."

"Everyone," Larry said. "We can help Sandra by—"

I started to lose my temper. "By leaving me alone!"

"The problem might be because you have shoes on," Jody said. "The shrine keeper said take them off."

"Jody, please."

"Well, Larry, I'm just—"

"Madame, you come back. Just you come."

"She can't!"

"Everyone," Donald said loudly through the passage. "Everyone, please settle down and listen. What Sandra needs right now is to relax. When you are relaxed, you are smaller, and you are able to think more clearly. What I propose is that you all go back, give us some space. The shrine keeper can lead you. I'll stay here with Sandra."

"We need the headlamp, Donald."

"Madame," the shrine keeper said. "You come to see cave? Yes, you go."

"She's stuck," Donald said. "We need help."

"Sir?"

"Donald. My name is Donald." Donald let his fear for me show for a moment, and then he got hold of himself. "Stuck," Donald called. "My friend is stuck. Trapped."

The other scholars echoed what Donald had said, until the shrine keeper understood, and then he took out a second light and led them out of the cave. When it was quiet, Donald crawled back into the tube with his hand over his lamp so the light was dim.

He scooted in so we were eye to eye, like kids hiding under a blanket, and said, "I see what happened. Actually, let me just reach."

"No."

"Shh. Let me just . . ." He took a hold of my right hand and slowly began to tug. "Let's just . . ."

"Stop!" I said. "Please, stop."

6

"Sandra, I knocked. What's your deadwood?"

The straw from Donald's thermos started to tip over his cup. I thought, Grab it, get the cup, but my hand didn't move in time, and the whiskey spilled. It pooled, then dribbled toward me.

We had the shrine keeper's headlamp pointed at the ceiling and a pack of playing cards. A migraine extended from my head down into my chest, and though I could breathe, an unlocatable pain came with every inhale, then settled in my right hip.

Water moved deep down in the cave, a spring or an underground stream. I kept hearing a noise like a gurgle or a whisper. It sounded like words, and I could almost understand what it said. If I could make it out, it would let me get free, I thought. And then I thought, You're letting your fear get the better of you. Pull yourself together.

Donald picked up the cup, wiped the liquid away as best he could with his hand, and poured more whiskey. He pushed the straw awkwardly toward my mouth. I parted my lips.

"Here, I'll count for you."

He turned the cards over, keeping score with a pencil and a tiny notepad.

"The shrine keeper said they were sending men from the village with spades. That's only about ten miles, but it's dark outside, so they'll be going slowly. I think the group should be getting back to the hotel by now, and they're going to call in everybody they can. Jody has family in the embassy in Delhi, so I think by morning we'll have this whole thing figured out. Until then, our only job is to keep our cool."

I let my eyes close, wondering if the embassy in India would be able to help an American in Nepal. I tried to lift my head, then tilted it back to rest it against the rock.

"I'm sad," I said. I was sort of joking, not expecting it to make sense to Donald.

He exhaled from his nose, sort of laughing.

"And I need to pee."

"Just go. It's all right. I went too. Just on the other side of the cave."

I felt embarrassed. I wouldn't have thought I could still feel embarrassed in this kind of situation. I would have thought that was an emotion for different circumstances.

I peed. Then I must have fallen asleep for a while. I woke up when something skittered up my back.

Donald had formed his shirt into a pillow and rested it under his own head. It irritated me. Why couldn't he make two pillows, one for each of us? His snoring grew louder. I was suddenly terrified. I wondered, Why is this happening to me? And Trip! The insect stopped, turned, and began crawling down my side.

I heard something on the other side of Donald's feet. It sounded like an animal landing on the cave floor.

A bright light flashed behind him.

"He, murkharu! Uniharu yahaan chhan. Maile timiharulai bhaneko thiyeu!"* It was the voice of a boy speaking Nepali.

I heard a group of men who sounded like they were far away. I didn't know it at the time, but they were the rescuers from a nearby village. One young man had rappelled two hundred feet, down a hole in the ceiling of the gallery on the other side of the crystal cave. The others had followed the shrine keeper's route.

Donald startled awake, knocking his head on the rock above.

"Hello?" the boy said. "Ma'am?"

"We're here," Donald said. "One minute."

He backed out and explained to the boy that I was stuck.

The boy shone a flashlight into my face. He held it in place for a moment, then lowered it. "But her hand is there, sir," he said.

On the other end of my body, the rescuers gathered at my feet. One clutched my ankle and tugged.

"Unko khutta nachhunu!"†

"Samatna arko thau nai chaina. Yo aapatkaaleen awastha ho. Ma unko jyan bachaaune kosis gariraheko chhu."‡

---

* Hey, idiots! They're over here. I told you!

† Don't touch her feet!

‡ There's nowhere else to grab. It's an emergency situation. I'm trying to save her life.

"Kati asabhya!"*

"Excuse me," I said. "Please don't touch my feet."

The man took his hand away. He said, "Okay, okay, ma'am. Sorry, sorry. It's okay."

"Don't pull her feet," Donald called. "She's wedged in there."

"Okay, sir. Okay, okay."

"Ahile uniharule ke bhaniraheka chhan?"†

"Sambhavata, 'Unko khutta chhuna banda gara, murkha' bhaniraheka chhan."‡

The man who had been touching my foot said, "Uniharu prashna sodhiraheka chhan. Ma bhandai chhu sabai thik chha. Tyesbhek, videshile khutta chhoyera narisauncha. Tyesko chinta nagar."§

"Usle 1994 ma Dutch mahilasanga coffee khaeko thiyo, aba u bigya bhaeko chha."¶

"Sathiharu, shaant ho. Chup laga!"** the boy shouted at the rescuers. He shone his flashlight at me again. "This is dangerous, sir. Why did you come here without a guide? I could have been your guide."

"The shrine keeper was our guide."

"*Mangel?* Mangel guided you. Sir, Mangel is not suitable. This is a holy place, sir."

---

* So rude of you.

† What are they saying now?

‡ Probably saying, "Stop touching her foot, asshole."

§ They're asking questions. I'm saying that it's all right. Besides, foreigners don't care if you touch their feet. Don't worry about it.

¶ He had coffee with a Dutch woman in 1994 and now he's an expert.

** Guys, settle down. Shut up!

TRIP

On the other end of my body, the man who had touched my feet said, "La, gayera heraun. Ma unlai taandai chhu."* He took hold of one of my ankles and twisted it back and forth, then tugged angrily.

"Rok. Rok. Saachchai, unlai yasari nagar. Videshile maane pani, timile ta ramrosanga jannu parchha."†

Someone lit incense. Another man reached up and clutched at my crotch. Several of the men shouted at him, and he pulled his hand away.

The boy looked down. "Her hand is there, sir," he said again. "Did you not try pulling her?"

"She said she was trapped."

The boy called out, "Yo 'brain surgeon' le unlai taanna khojeko pani chaina. Uniharu tala basera whiskey piudai ra patte kheldai chhan."‡

The men laughed.

The boy wiggled into the tube and grabbed my hands.

"Oh," I said. "I'm wedged in here pretty good."

He yanked my hands before I could say any more, pulling until some breccia snapped and I was unceremoniously drawn halfway out and he fell onto his butt.

"Oh my god," I said.

The boy laughed and turned to Donald. "Easy-peasy lemon squeezy, sir. Just had to pull."

---

* Fuck it. I'm pulling her out.

† Stop. Stop. Seriously, don't do that to her. Even if foreigners don't mind it, you should know better.

‡ This brain surgeon hasn't even tried to pull her out. They've been down here drinking whiskey and playing cards.

I put my hands onto the floor of the cave, and Donald and the boy helped me out.

Only then did I notice the small cavern we were in. It was like we were sitting inside a geode. The walls, the floor, the ceiling—the entire cave was made of sparkling crystals.

"Yes, take a moment, ma'am," the boy said. "Very beautiful. Holy place."

"You want to stay for a minute?" Donald said.

"Fuck no."

The boy looked offended. Donald laughed nervously.

"What do we do now?" I said.

"The men will go out and haul us up with ropes," the boy said. He pointed to the corner of the cave. "Sir, you urinated here?"

When we got back to the hotel, I was too exhausted to open my suitcase. I took off my clothes and got into bed and fell asleep.

A few hours later, I woke up to pee. I walked across the room in the darkness. I had taken a few steps on the bathroom's marble floor when my feet gave out under me, and I was falling through the air.

I saw the sharp corner of the marble counter in the pale moonlight just as I heard my skull crack. My vision went white. It was more of a surprise than anything else, until the pain started.

I was on the floor. I couldn't lift my head. I opened my eye and saw that I had slipped on my hairbrush. "Lift me up!" I said. "Lift me up!"

I felt overwhelmed with heaviness. There was a crushing weight on my chest. The walls began to waver, like a calm sea, then they picked up into choppy waves, and I wondered if I could swim out, reach help. Then it appeared as though everything—the bathroom, the tub, the little window—was swept away. I shut my eyes. A mirage twisted to life in the black field of my vision.

I began to tremble and twitch. I lost control of my bladder and bowels. I felt embarrassed again.

Blood, drool, and snot pooled under my face. I lifted my cheek, then gently eased it back down against the marble floor.

I tried to remember how I had gotten to this point. There had been a conference, geodes, a headlamp. I closed my eyes and saw a smoke-filled sauna, an arm ladling water onto rocks, a gust of steam.

I was cold. My mouth and nose were dry like twigs, my breath cold on my forehead and cheeks. I dry-heaved. The bathroom floor burned. My hands and face were freezing. It was difficult to distinguish my face from the floor. I closed my eyes and saw smoke, like a wildfire. Sparks, or fireflies.

A maelstrom blew away the bathroom, me, even the past. My breathing was labored—short and ragged inhales, long faint exhales. I regretted all the mental energy I had spent justifying selfish impulses. My mother sat near me, on the other side of the shower curtain, doodling on a yellow legal pad.

I leaned my childhood banana-seated bicycle against the brick exterior of the convenience store and pushed open the glass door, turning shyly away from the man behind the counter as I went down the aisle to the Marathon candy bars. I picked up the long red package with its yellow stripe and tore it open. Milk-chocolate-dipped caramel lattice. The toilet was braided like the candy, woven to itself, chocolate-dipped, saying something to me about water. I wanted to close my eyes or open them. I didn't really care. Candlelight flickered in my mind's eye. It was fine.

I saw a bright, clear moon, and felt my emotions peel away from my perception. It was a bit like all the complicated ideas that had been Sandra seemed to be drifting further and further away, becoming slightly ridiculous. All the time I had spent justifying myself. Wouldn't it have been easier to have been gentle? The hotel cat was licking up a pool of liquid close to my nose. And the subtler parts of myself disassembled. Detachment, medium and intense. Engagement, disengagement. Sadness, peace, fear, craving. The thought of Trip. They came apart, leaving whiteness. Then red. More subtle emotions crumbled. Amazement, vigor. Shamelessness, lucidity, and understanding. Then blackness, the last traces—the moment of medium desire, forgetfulness, being confused, weariness, and doubt. Some perceiving, overcome for a moment by the intense suffering of the interruption of life, and then a primordial experience of black.[4]

7

A BLACK LIZARD sat on a rock in the sun. It was as big as a cat, with several orange stripes down its back. Trip wondered what it ate.

He had slipped away from his cohort while they headed from group to the cafeteria. It was hectic during mealtimes. He didn't think anyone would notice until medications at two.

He picked a dandelion. It was floofy, with dark hairs. He knelt and held it under the lizard's nose.

The lizard didn't move.

He had been at the Center for two days. He didn't like it. His roommate had shit his pants on purpose when the registered behavior technician on duty took his guitar, and then he'd threatened to eat a battery. The RBT gave him wipes and a garbage bag and a twist tie and said it was his job to clean himself.

The lizard took a slow step toward the flower, then darted forward and bit Trip's thumb.

Trip dropped the flower and pressed his hand to his chest.

The lizard looked embarrassed. It climbed down off the rock and crawled away.

Trip sat down on the gravel road. He pressed his hand between his thighs. He thought maybe he should go back to the Center to get help. He imagined catching the cohort as they finished up, and then struggling to tell the story. Jesse would take him to the infirmary. They would fix his hand, but they'd probably put him in the trailer. Deescalate him in the cool-down room, as it was called.

The pain was growing, spreading through his palm. He took off his T-shirt and wrapped the hand. He decided to walk to the freeway. He had hitchhiked in his own neighborhood. The highway wasn't so different.

He came out of the forest and stood on the shoulder of the road, crying, unsure what to do. A white Toyota Camry drove past. He imagined the RBTs finding his corpse on the freeway, swollen and blue. The Camry slowed, eased to the side of the road, and began backing up toward him. The pain was okay if he focused on it, but he couldn't do that for long before he got carried away, thinking about how it was going to fill his whole body and then kill him. He would lose his arm. He would be paralyzed in a wheelchair.

The Camry came to a stop several feet from him. The driver lowered his window. "You okay? You need some help?"

He was middle-aged, neatly dressed, with cropped hair

and bulging eyes, his shoulders slightly rounded. Though he had a potbelly, Trip could tell he lifted weights.

"You okay?" he said again.

Trip raised his hand. He wanted to tell the man what had happened, but he was too upset.

"Whoa, easy," the man said. "Show me."

Trip held out his hand.

The man got out of the car. He gently unwrapped the T-shirt and looked. "Not too bad. Something definitely got you. Not an insect. Not a snake or a rodent. Was it a lizard?"

Trip nodded.

"Sit down," the man said. "I have some peroxide in the first-aid kit in back. It will sting, but you won't get infected. Actually, you might not even feel it, given . . . the pain level you're experiencing. Hold on."

Trip stayed where he was.

The man came back with a brown spray bottle. He unscrewed the sprayer and asked Trip to hold out his hand.

"Okay, brace yourself."

"No!"

"Close your eyes and breathe."

Trip closed his eyes. The man poured peroxide over the bite. He expected to feel his hand lit up by flame, but instead it just felt like a cool wash.

"It must have been a Gila monster. They're poisonous, but not deadly. You may wish you were dead. Extremely painful. I got one on my toe a long time back. You're handling it well."

Trip felt his legs buckle, then caught himself against the door of the car.

"That's why I suggested sitting," the man said. "I could give you a lift, take you to Mom or Dad."

He shook his head.

"Maybe some water? You can get dehydrated out here. I have some alkaline, some sparkling. I have a diet soda, too, though that won't help much with the dehydration. You want to come sit?"

Trip thought the situation was a little weird, but the man seemed nice. His car was sparkling clean, still cool, though he'd let out some of the AC. Trip had seen a photograph on the internet of Ted Bundy's kidnapping kit, which was just a few different kinds of rope, some trash bags, and an ice pick. He began to hiccup through his tears.

"Whoa, whoa," the man said. "The bite itself is not so bad. I know it hurts, but look at it. He barely got you. Just gave you a warning tap."

Trip peered down, expecting something like the monkey-attack pictures he'd seen online once, extremely deep claw marks and disturbing swollen skin. But it was nothing, just a little semicircle of dots the depth of a scratch. It was less severe than a stapler injury, the kind some of the tough kids used to give themselves in fourth grade to show they didn't mind the pain.

"A friendly bite, I think. He wasn't angry. Maybe just confused. Should we pour peroxide on it one more time? I always like to do it twice. Maybe not so close to the car. Just step back a bit. Here, I'll let you."

Trip accepted the bottle and tried to wash his hand, but he was so jumpy he missed.

"That's okay, I got you pretty good on round one. You live nearby? I could take you home."

Trip covered his face and sobbed like a baby.

"You could use my phone, if you'd like. Maybe call a friend." The man held out his phone.

Trip didn't answer. He knew he couldn't explain. He walked away from the car. The sun was still high in the sky. He imagined sleeping by the roadside, sleeping in the forest, being bitten by more lizards or eaten by hogs.

"I think I have a shirt back here somewhere you can wear," the man said.

He reached in back and rummaged in a bag for a navy T-shirt, which he held out to Trip. It said VANCOUVER MANNERS in white letters. "It may not smell the greatest."

Trip put it on. It smelled like woodsmoke and soap.

The man looked around. "I want to help you out. It might be getting dark here soon. I could take you to the hospital or the police. Maybe a shelter. No, that's not a good idea."

Trip sniffed.

"How about this? You can ride with me a bit. I'm not asking you the details of your situation."

Trip nodded. He went around and opened the passenger door and sat.

"Okay," the man said. "I can drop you at home, or someplace safer than this. You know, let me drop you at a hospital."

"No, please." He closed the door.

"Okay." The man frowned. "I get it. I'm Anthony," he said. "Like the saint. Saint Anthony. I have a son not too much older than you. I'm heading down to Florida now."

They drove to the interstate. Anthony got into the passing lane and set his cruise control at fifty-five.

8

Beautiful multicolored patterns of light, electric, strobing, then scintillating, indescribable shapes moving.

The patterns of light began to be intercut with images, brief and unrelated. A bottle of Sprite, its surface beaded with moisture. A beautiful young man in a fur hat. A typewriter made of bread. An old woman with red pantyhose over her head, a hole torn for her mouth: "I am protected by the various spirits of the delta. I am covered, as you can see. A barrier between me and anything that pierces or can tear the body."

Men in monochromatic cotton jackets shouted back and forth on the stock market floor, flashing hand signals. A man in a yellow jacket raised two fingers. Three women in red cotton jackets shouted back, palms in, three fingers up. A dog ran past a tree, and a young man told a girl with an envelope opener in her hair that he could only have sex without a condom. Two young men climbed from the ocean onto the transom of a yacht, a snake wound its body around a lizard, and an analyst folded his hands across his stomach. "It's like changing your oil. Say what's giving you pain." A loud boom, followed by a whoosh, the sound of showering glass.

I was standing in the hotel lobby in front of a portrait of a woman who had posed with her hair down. She was looking away from the camera, over her shoulder, with a rude expression, and she wore ropes of carnelian beads around both her wide wrists.

Outside, the air was cool, the perfectly flat lawns dotted with white mushrooms. I walked down a stone path, under the arched boughs of two cypress trees, their soft feathery leaves electric jade in the moonlight. I sat on a wrought-iron chair several hundred paces from the hotel and tilted my head to look at the sky. It was empty. I couldn't find the moon. A winged insect landed on the chair, and I leaped up and shouted. I sat on the grass.

I lay down on the lawn and looked up. I searched for Mars but couldn't find it. A dog barked. I had a song stuck in my head.

A woman was lying beside me with the tail of her sari flipped over her face. Probably in her early thirties, with stern lips and small eyes. Beside her was a jade bowl of chocolate almonds. She picked one up and smelled it through the fabric of her sari, then put it back with the others.

"You're making fun of me," she said.

"What?"

"You think I'm a joke. I don't matter to you." She stood up and adjusted her sari. It was worn cotton the color of a clementine.

I sat up. "You're a guest at the hotel?"

"A *guest*," she said. "No. I am not a *guest* here. A guest."

She pressed her face into her hands. Beneath her fingers, I could see that her cheeks were bright red. I didn't understand if she was crying or laughing. She bent to pick up her almonds. I thought she was going to storm away, but she didn't. She blew a lock of frizzy hair off her forehead.

"How are the almonds?" I said.

She sniffed one, then put it back in her bowl. "They're almonds."

I frowned up at the sky.

9

"I'M IN A HURRY, so I'm going to keep pushing," Anthony said. "You tell me where to drop you. Until then, I'll assume we're staying on the road. I should make time while I can."

He drove down into West Texas, passing through Dallas and Fort Worth in the evening, then Louisiana, where his exhaustion began to show. He yawned and sighed and grew agitated, snapping his head around when 18-wheelers passed him.

Trip pointed out hotels, but Anthony shook his head no. He said he had several places in the Florida Keys that he needed to board up before the hurricane hit land.

"My caretakers are all college students. They didn't do anything a week ago, and now that the storm is a murdercane or whatever, their parents have flown them out. It's all noise. Getting clicks. You watch, it will change direction, or get recategorized. They always do."

Trip nodded.

"I am not a remainer," Anthony said. "I am not a person who stays in place when the government says to go, but in the eighties, during Hurricane Alicia, I happened to be stuck in place due to some substance abuse. It was one of the most beautiful experiences of my life. That was before I met Bill." He glanced at Trip. "Bill W., you know? *The Big Book*?"

Trip looked at Anthony out of the corner of his eyes.

"Were you running from a treatment center when I picked you up?"

Trip was quiet.

"For alcohol, or?"

Trip nodded.

"Alcohol." Anthony waited for him to say more. After a minute, he said, "I'm sorry, it's none of my business. It's Alcoholics Anonymous, not Alcoholics Nosy Nelly. I was just saying that I was a bit of a party animal back in the day, and some of the government warnings blew past me."

He kept talking. Trip was distracted by the pain heading toward his chest. He wondered if he would keel over and die in the passenger seat, and imagined Anthony driving across the country with his corpse, talking about his substance-abuse problems.

An ambulance that had been riding their tail flashed its brights, then swung out and accelerated.

Anthony made a hissing noise, like he had bitten into something hot. "Go on," he murmured. "Kill yourselves." He glanced at Trip. "I don't like it when people drive that way."

Trip nodded, feeling queasy, wishing that Anthony would be quiet.

"I do contemplative meditation," Anthony said. The ambulance pulled back into the fast lane, and he shook his head. "Mindfulness. I have chronic back pain, but no painkillers. I'd like it if I were a woman and could give birth naturally. I would like to have a baby in a blow-up kiddie pool. Women waste it, of course, with their epidurals, fentanyl, and Stadol. When my wife was pregnant, she took all three, and begged for more. Spent the whole of the birth repeatedly saying, 'I feel like I'm going to poop.' Even got a bikini wax for the doctor." He glanced at Trip. "Right now, as we speak, I have a cavity. It's moderately painful. I hope it's not affecting my breath. The point is, I'm aware of it. When I get home and have it filled, I'll refuse anesthesia and numbing. I always do. I regard it as an opportunity."

Trip nodded, feeling like he might throw up.

A Chevy Cavalier was riding Anthony's tail. He glanced at it in the rearview. "Go around," he shouted at the mirror. "Go around!"

The Chevy pulled closer.

"I have this random word generator," Anthony said. He fumbled around for his phone, looking in his pockets, then found it in his glove compartment.

"Generate word," he said. "Hey, Siri, generate word for me. Generate word. Generate—"

"*Cocaine*," his phone said.

"*Cocaine*," Anthony said. He glanced at the Chevy in his rearview. "That takes me places."

The Chevy pulled out of the fast lane and accelerated. When it was alongside their car, a blond woman in a black fleece flipped her middle finger. Anthony nodded and smiled. "Very nice," he said, as the woman slotted herself in the fast lane just ahead of him.

"Where were we . . . cocaine . . ." Anthony narrowed his eyes and drifted off, seeming to savor some memory, then snapped back to and said, "You get an ordinary mindfulness app, it's going to offer you a lot of garbage. Don't get me wrong, those breathing techniques are wonderful, but this really . . . I'm sorry, how can you do better than that. Contemplate cocaine."

Anthony took a few loud breaths.

"The storm is days away. I know it's not great to drive exhausted, but that's the situation we're in."

Trip must have dozed off. When he woke up, it was after midnight, and Anthony was road-hypnotized, in the middle of leaving a long message for someone on his phone.

"It wasn't your fault I misunderstood the letter, though it was a bit unclear. I got carried away, and I embarrassed you in your professional environment. Again. Please, if you'll just talk to me, I think we can work it out. If you'll just answer one of my calls."

His head swiveled to look at Trip and he dropped his phone, then scrambled to find it and switch it off, veering out of his lane, across the next one, and onto the rumble strip, before he darted back into place, still reaching around on the floor.

Trip fell asleep again. When he woke up, Anthony's head was tilted all the way to the left, resting on his window. Before Trip could say anything, Anthony's eyes opened and he blinked and sat up. After a moment, his head began to tilt to the side again.

"Maybe we should stop." Trip pointed at a billboard for a roadside motel at the next exit. "What about that place?"

"Yes," Anthony said. "You're right. A quick nap. Three hours max."

He exited the freeway. Trip thought he would sleep in the car, but Anthony reserved two singles, one for each of them, saying it was the least he could offer.

Trip settled into his room, but he couldn't sleep. He went out and walked away from the little light in the motel hallway to see what stars he could make out in the sky. He found Orion, Ursa Major. He found the Big Dipper, then followed Megrez and Phecda, the inner stars of the Big Dipper's bowl, to the sickle shape. Regulus, the brightest star, at the base of the sickle, was the lion's heart. He felt himself beginning to relax as he followed Regulus and Denebola, the lion's tail, to the galaxies in Leo.

He wondered if he could make out Leo Minor. Praecipua was just visible, but nothing else. Merak and Dubhe, the outer stars of the Big Dipper's bowl, took him to the North Star. He stayed up for several hours, until the sky began to lighten, and then he went inside and fell asleep on top of the hotel duvet.

When he woke up, his thumb didn't hurt anymore. He started to go back to sleep, then got out of bed. He reached to check his phone and remembered he had left it behind at the Center.

A thought occurred to him, and he pulled back the curtain to make sure that Anthony's car was still out front. The sun dazzled his eyes.

The white Camry's nose was pulled all the way up to the motel's aluminum fence.

Trip got dressed. He went downstairs, past the hotel's liver-shaped pool, to the lobby.

Breakfast was set out. He made a plate and carried it back past the pool, where several old men in bathrobes had gathered, to an old-fashioned playground with a metal slide and a rusty jungle gym.

He climbed the monkey bars and sat for a while, soaking up the sun and drinking his apple juice, wondering if Anthony was coming on to him. He imagined telling Anthony that he wasn't really in college, that he was just in high school, so any kind of romantic relationship between them was not possible. He pictured Anthony nodding and looking sad. He climbed back down and threw his juice box and muffin wrapper into a trash barrel and roamed to the edge of the playground, to a fence made of two stretches of barbed wire. On the other side of the fence, tall grass blew in the wind, bowing in strange whorls and patterns.

In his mind, he explained the situation to Anthony again: that he was a teenager, that he wasn't even gay. This time Anthony pleaded a little. He let Anthony talk. He gave him the space to suggest that age was just a number. He was about to counter, saying something about how numbers are important, when he heard a grunting sound.

He looked down and saw a small feral hog staring up at him from the grass. Hogs were dangerous. A minor serial killer had used them to murder people, he was pretty sure. The hog scratched the ground with its nose, considered Trip, then ran in the other direction. Trip tried to remember what he had been thinking. He put a hand down and touched the grass, then turned to head back to his room.

Anthony was pacing in front of the car. He spotted Trip from a distance and held his keys in the air and shook them, looking annoyed but not angry. Trip ran over and climbed into the passenger seat.

Anthony took his time getting in, muttering about the cost of a bag of cashews he had purchased from the lobby.

"That's fifty cents a cashew," he said. He pulled out of the parking lot onto the feeder road, still grousing about being overcharged.

Trip felt vaguely like Anthony was blaming him for the cost. He said, "There were a lot of stars out last night."

Anthony grunted.

"You could see the Great Diamond."

"Oh?"

"Arcturus in Boötes, Spica in Virgo, Cor Caroli in Canes Venatici, and Denebola in Leo."

"That right?"

"The asterism has two shared vertices."

"Mm."

"With the Spring Triangle, formed by Arcturus, Spica, and Regulus. You can find Arcturus and Spica with the Big Dipper's handle. Alioth, Mizar, and Alkaid take you right there."

"That's interesting. I'm going to focus on the road now."

"Sorry."

They were quiet for a bit. Then Anthony told a story

about renting a catamaran and nearly drowning off Key Largo because the sail was broken. "It was missing whatever it needed to be able to tack," he said. "If you can't tack, you can't sail into the wind. I hadn't noticed it while sailing out, with the wind at my back."

He'd spent the afternoon, and into early dusk, slowly tacking back and forth at wide angles. The story was long. Trip did not really understand the geometry of sailing, nor did he consider a few hours on a catamaran sufficient material for a lost-at-sea narrative, but he was moved by Anthony's evocation of the ocean.

He said, "I wish I was going with you all the way to Florida."

"The evacuation warning went out this morning. We'd never get you in." Anthony stared forward. He tried to keep his tough-guy expression, but he was obviously having second thoughts. After a few minutes, he said, "Maybe you could come in with me. Maybe you could go in the trunk?"

Trip was quiet.

"Or we could say you are my son. I suppose I could use help battening down the hatches."

Trip looked out the window, a slight smile on his lips.

Anthony said, "But I don't want you saying, 'We need to leave, Anthony. Drive us out.' None of that."

A U-Haul swerved into oncoming traffic to pass them, and Anthony suddenly lost his composure. He laid on the horn and shouted at the driver, then resettled himself in his seat several times, like a person who has recently put on weight.

"The traffic leaving the Keys is going to be substantial," he said, glancing in the rearview at an SUV speeding toward him. "And I have a regular Narcotics Anonymous group down there. They will be wanting to see me—I expect a number of them will stay behind—and we ought to be able to pull a group together. So, if you're worried about your sobriety, please don't. Though I do think any Zoom meetings will be canceled, just due to the possible lack of electricity."

Trip's eyes widened.

"Oh yes, we'll likely lose water, gas, cell service. We won't even be in touch with our sponsors, but we'll have each other—a small community of addicts, hunkered down in the storm. We will be in charge of our own sobriety."

Trip looked at his hurt hand, stretched his fingers.

"That hand looks like it's pretty much better," Anthony said.

Trip glanced at him. They didn't discuss the logistics of Florida again. They would go together. It had been decided.

They drove east, coming into Pensacola near nightfall. The sky was clear. Northbound traffic was heavy. Police had set up checkpoints on the southbound side.

Trip was talking about the stars. "You can find the Kite between the Big Dipper's handle and the curved line of the Northern Crown."

Anthony pulled off the freeway, grumbling irritably.

"Cor Caroli is the faintest of the stars in the Canes Venatici constellation. Its brightness varies due to magnetic fields around the star."

Anthony turned into a gas station and angled himself in at the pump.

"But you can find it to the right of Alkaid, the star at the tip of the Big Dipper's handle."

"Trip, could we take a tiny break from astronomy class?" Anthony cracked the door and peered out. "Shit," he said.

He restarted the car and pulled around to the opposite side of the pump, then switched the car off.

"The night sky itself is associated with Kali, goddess of death and destruction." He turned to Anthony. "But then they also say she is love itself."

"Use the restroom now, if you don't mind."

"I looked it up once, and read that it is a mistake, thinking that life is about being happy—that it is much more interesting than that."

"Trip? If you need to use the little boys' room, now would be the time. I'm a wee bit tired of pulling over for 'pee on a tree.' Frankly, on the highway, it's unsafe."

"Oh, right." Trip sat a little while longer, then hopped out and headed toward the convenience store, repeating the conversation back to himself as he walked through the aisles and pushed open the men's room door.

The bathroom was large and clean, with a dozen stalls stretching back. Two old men stood a few feet apart at a long steel urinal.

"Kind of a sad night for the single drunks of Wesley," one said.

The other nodded. "Some twenty-eight-year-old genius cop maneuver."

Trip peed, then stood daydreaming, staring at the deep orange tile on the gas station wall as he imagined cats and dogs fighting in the place where the rain hits the sidewalk.

One of the old men zipped up and washed his hands. He bumped the air dryer with a fist, and its howl brought Trip back to the gas station bathroom. He zipped up and went to the sink, where he rinsed his hands.

Outside at the pump, a few police officers were gathered around Anthony, whose arms were folded tightly across his chest. Trip drew closer and heard Anthony say, "I understand that, Officer."

"He says he understands that." The officer closest to Anthony traded looks with the others. "You see the traffic going out, sir? You are aware of the possibility of getting stranded? No water, sheltering in school basements, and that's the good stories. I've seen other stuff. Help me out here?"

"Try poison gas, crocodiles," a tall officer said. "Islands of fire ants. Do you know what a rat king is? It's a technical term for when a bunch of rats get their tails tied in a knot."

"These things blow across land now. Wildfires. People drowning in their own homes. Families beaten and left for dead. Waving for a helicopter from your rooftop, using your pants as a flag, talking about God."

"You're a pain in my ass, you know," the tall one said. He poked Anthony in the chest.

Anthony smiled. It was the dumb, angry smile of a man who is about to get into a fistfight.

"All grit if the hurricane blows by. But if it hits you?" The officer closest to Anthony turned back to the others.

"Squeal time," the tall officer said.

"Yes, sir," Anthony said. "As I said, I need to close up our rental properties, and then we—my son and I—will immediately evacuate."

"Go down to drown?"

"I believe I'm within my legal rights, officers. I could consult my attorney if that would help clarify matters."

The tall one made a sudden aggravated barking sound and walked away. "Jackass," he said. The other officers glared at Anthony, then looked confused. They turned and walked away, too.

Anthony pulled the nozzle out of the tank and set it back in its hatch, then went around to sit in the front seat. He reached into the glove compartment and pulled out a glass jar of gummy bears. His hands were trembling. He popped the metal latch top and put two into his mouth, then offered the jar to Trip.

Trip didn't move to take it.

"For nerves." He shook the jar once. "Try one."

Trip took a gummy and popped it into his mouth. He looked out the window.

"CBD gummies," Anthony said. "Strictly speaking, off limits. I bought them last week. A lot of the people I know in AA use CBD. It is calming but doesn't cause a high of any kind. I don't count it as a relapse."

"Oh!" He winced in pain and pressed his cheek. "Got my bad tooth there. Very sensitive to pressure. I usually chew on the other side."

He latched the jar and set it at his feet. "Hey, Siri, give me a word. Hey, Siri. Generate word."

"*Balustrade*," his phone said.

"*Balustrade*," Anthony said. "Not a good one."

He started the car.

10

IN MY HOTEL ROOM, two housekeepers were dividing up the things in my suitcase. The man looked like a Nepali David Cross. The woman was small, with crow's feet around her wide-set eyes.

"I know how to type, so I should get it," the man said.

"Okay, Mr. Typist. Listen. You have the laptop. I keep the credit cards and the purse."

I cleared my throat, but they ignored me. I said, "May I help you?" but they continued to argue. I went to find a hotel manager and ran into the neurologist with crazy hair—dark and smooth, except for a wiry thicket on the top of his head.

Somehow I got turned around, involved in the things the crazy-haired neurologist was thinking.

He was envisioning a man. The man was at the buffet. He reached out and took a big serving of bacon. The suddenness of the motion, like a snake's strike, made a beautiful young woman laugh. The laughter wounded the neurologist, even though he wasn't grabbing bacon, because he felt he had served himself a lot of food, and suspected he was the secret object of the woman's derision.

The filmstrip played over and over in the neurologist's mind as he walked into the dining room, where people were milling around, speaking in soft voices.

Donald was red-eyed, bent over a cup of coffee.

"Have we let the family know?" Larry said.

"We're working that out."

A waiter tiptoed around, quietly refilling coffee cups.

"I can't find my phone," I said.

Vic stood in the living room, trying to lay our rug down. He held it by two corners and flung it open, then bent to straighten the ends, pulling one corner and then the other, trying to cover the rug mat. As he worked, I could see the carpet, his hands, everything in the room in detail.

"It shrunk in the dryer that time," I said. "It's never going to cover the rug mat now."

Vic bent over and jerked the corner of the rug.

"Okay." I went upstairs to the bedroom. I opened my laptop to do "find my phone," but the cloud wasn't accepting my password. I came back down to the living room. Vic stood in the middle of the rug.

"I can't figure out how to do that 'find' function," I said. I went back to looking. I checked on top of the refrigerator, on the windowsill by the toilet.

I turned, and Trip was sitting naked in the bathtub.

He had his back to me, a toy car in either hand. It was just after his first haircut. He was three years old.

"Trip?"

Vic brushed past with a small plate of cheese and

crackers. He sat on the bathroom floor beside the tub and held the plate out to Trip, who reached with wet fingers and gingerly took a saltine. Vic set the plate down on a step stool. He picked up *The Encyclopedia of Animals* and pointed. "What's that?" he said.

"Axolotl."

"What's that?"

"Eagle."

"What's that?"

"Toucan."

"What's it doing?"

"What's it doing?" Trip said.

"It's flying. How about this one? What's it doing?"

"It's flying."

"I think that one's more like slithering. Point with this finger." Vic demonstrated. He held up the plate of cheese and crackers, then paged forward. "What's that?"

"Sri Lankan green pit viper."

"What's that?"

"Banded sea snake."

"Good." Vic took Trip's hand. He tucked in his middle, ring, and pinkie fingers, and uncurled his pointer. "Point like this," he said. "What's that?"

"Timber rattlesnake." Trip pointed with the okay sign.

A woman in knee boots gestured toward a three-story rock-climbing wall. "Preschoolers can use this as soon as they're big enough for the harnesses. I think that's forty pounds."

She pushed open a door and stepped out of the gymnasium into the sunshine. Vic followed her, pausing for a moment to turn and squint at me.

"C'mon, weirdo," he said.

He walked ahead, falling in with the admissions coordinator, who opened the doors to the quad. I jogged to catch up.

It hadn't changed since Trip was a student, when he was three and a half years old. The interior windows of the building looked out on a playground, and the exterior walls were lined with cubbies full of rain gear.

"When it rains," the woman said, "the friends put on their rubber boots and go outside and stomp in puddles. Let me show you where Trip would be next year."

She led us down the hall and knocked on a classroom door as she pushed it open.

"Mr. Nitgo? These are some prospectives. This is Vic and Sandra. They're thinking of enrolling their son, Trip, in the fall."

A young man with a beard looked up from his desk and stood.

"Remind me, Mr. Nitgo," the woman said. "What is your project?"

"Sticks," Mr. Nitgo said.

She nodded. "The students do a project each year, based on whatever the class is drawn to as a whole."

"Your class project is sticks?" Vic said.

"Tight, right?" The teacher led Vic to a bookshelf lined with labeled twigs and got down on one knee. "All their doing, of course."

Vic got down, too, and read aloud. "Pine, fig, birch." He noticed two sticks that were unlabeled. He held one of them out. "This one is nice. What is it?"

"Man, you know your trees. That's a manzanita branch. I want to say Sage brought it in."

"And this?"

The teacher took off his glasses and squinted at the stick. "These should be labeled." He ran a hand under the shelf and withdrew two small squares of construction paper and read them out loud. "Manzanita, this we know. And cherry." He went to his desk and put Scotch tape on the backs of the labels.

"Oh, hold up. You guys gotta see these."

He moved his desk and pointed to the floor. Against the wall he had stashed several twenty-foot pieces of bamboo.

"Is that a stick, though?" Vic said.

"Technically it's a grass." Mr. Nitgo shrugged. "They're gonna go nuts."

I wandered over to a window.

Out on the lawn, the children enrolled in extended-day programs played in small groups. Several had set up a car wash. They were dirtying and washing their cars while a woman with a frizzy ponytail looked on.

Brown plumes of smoke unfurled from nothingness, covering the sun.

The woman turned, and I saw her eyes were blackened. Her curly bangs were clotted with blood, and her cheek was torn from her nose down to a large pit in its center, the size of a cherry.

"Beat," she said. "Kill." I felt my stomach drop. She nodded her head.

"I think we need a new wiper blade."

I was sitting beside Vic in our old car. It was raining, and he had the wipers going furiously, but the glass kept fogging up. He rolled down the driver-side window and reached out to wipe the windshield with his hand.

We were in what appeared at first to be traffic, but then Vic inched forward through a set of wrought-iron gates, and I recognized the long line of luxury cars leading to the pickup spot in front of Trip's first school.

His teacher stood waiting with him under an umbrella. Trip was almost four years old. He still had his shoulder-length blond hair, his physical ease.

We pulled forward, and his teacher opened the car door. "Climb on up into your car seat," she said.

Trip stood still.

"Use those muscles!" she said. "Climb on up."

Something bounced off the windshield. Vic leaned forward. "Oh, I think that was hail."

Dozens of hailstones struck the car.

"Climb on up, sweetheart."

Trip stood, staring forward.

His teacher propped the umbrella on her shoulder and lifted him into the car seat, knocking his head against the doorframe. I turned and touched his knee.

"How did he do?" Vic said.

"That's something I wanted to talk about," the teacher

said, buckling him in with shaking hands. "Trip punched me today."

"Punched?" Vic said.

"Pinched."

"Oh—pinched!" Vic smiled with relief, then noticed the teacher's face and erased his smile. "Still, I'm surprised."

A hailstone hit the windshield, leaving a hairline crack.

"Whoa!" Vic said. "I'll email you. We can set up a meeting."

A pandit was doing a puja, filling the bathroom with smoke. Donald coughed and fanned the air with his hand, and the two maids prayed, waving the smoke toward their faces, passing a dish of oil. The maid who looked like David Cross, who had taken my laptop, handed the dish back to the pandit, thinking, Please watch out for my daughter. Please protect her. Please let her get well.

I was sitting on the edge of the tub. I opened my eyes and closed them.

Trip's preschool teacher greeted us and gestured for us to sit at a heavy white table.

"Oh, this is a cool table," Vic said. "Is it a lightboard?"

"It is, in fact." She flicked a switch and the tabletop lit up.

She took out a basket of translucent acrylic shapes and demonstrated, laying a red circle over a blue rectangle.

"This is so cool," Vic said. He started to make a shape

out of blue and red triangles and diamonds, then caught himself. "Sorry. You didn't bring us here to play with the kids' toys."

"No, go on ahead." She got out a list of questions and cleared her throat. "I can talk while you explore."

Vic shaped a mountain running into the sea. A green boat floating in the middle of the ocean.

Trip's teacher said, "What does mealtime look like for Trip?"

The truth was that we sat at the dining room table while Trip circled us in his toy tractor. Occasionally one of us would reach down and stick a piece of chicken into his mouth.

"He has a chair," Vic said. "One of those chairs that goes onto the table."

"A baby chair." The teacher nodded and made a note. "Does he eat with utensils at home?"

"Yes," Vic said. "He'll sort of switch his spoon back and forth between his left and right hands."

"Hmm. He uses his hands to eat here. Does he cut with scissors at home?"

"We haven't really given him scissors yet."

The teacher widened her eyes. "What does using the bathroom look like?"

We had a system called "pee on a tree," and a kid's potty next to the table where he played.

"He has a kid's potty," Vic said, adding a mast and sails to his green acrylic boat. "It is in the bathroom."

"What does walking look like? Does Trip have a stroller, or . . ."

"No! God no. We just kind of follow his lead. Like at the park, we stay behind him."

"I love that you give him that independence. But what do you do when you need to get him somewhere? Is he able to walk beside you, or does he wander off, or maybe come to abrupt stops and sort of stand there?"

"We pick him up."

The teacher frowned.

"It's true," Vic said. "Whatever it is in all of us that likes praise, Trip doesn't have it. He doesn't like those performing poodle activities. We call him the Little Emperor."

"I've seen that side," the teacher said. "He'll dismiss me. He'll just say, 'Bye.'" She tilted her head. "But I don't think it's about being a performing poodle. Let me tell you what I'm seeing. Trip subitizes. He knows his planets, letters, and numbers, and he recognizes and creates patterns and symbols. He does not cross the midline." She moved her right hand to her left side. "He has not chosen left- or right-hand dominance. His pencil grip is not what we would expect to see at his age, and his expressive language is also somewhat behind."

"Hmm." We had noticed similar things. We had even felt these things before he was born.

"I asked Trip to identify simple images, like a house or a dog, and while he was able to do it, his responses often included echolalia. I would say, 'What is that?' and Trip would reply, 'What is that? It's a house.' When I showed him a picture of a rabbit driving a tractor and said, 'What's the rabbit doing?' he said, 'What's the rabbit doing?'"

"Okay, well, we can work on that."

"There is also the matter of his pointing. He uses the rake." She held up an okay sign. "Which is not what we'd expect to see."

She dropped the okay sign. "What I am trying to say is that I'd like to recommend Trip do a little coaching, offered through the school."

"Meaning . . ."

"Oh, it can be all different things. Let's see . . . We had one girl, when you touched her, she'd go rigid." She demonstrated, locking her elbows and straightening her back. "So the therapist had us put her in a body bag. We'd zip her up in her body bag, then everybody in the classroom would run at her and hug her all over."

"You want to put Trip in a body bag?"

"It's a therapeutic tool—just an example of what we're able to achieve with these kiddos when we get them in therapy early."

This was the moment when I was separated from my son. I was told that something was wrong, and that I should address this by changing him. The message was given that if Trip pointed with a different finger, it would be all right. I was made to understand that my son needed to be a different person, and it was my job to change him.

The hotel maids who had divided up my things were cleaning the bathroom countertop and floor.

Donald sat on my hotel bed, reading aloud from a book he had on the Kindle app on his phone.

"Hello, Sandra," he said, filling in my name in the place where his text said "[insert name]." "This is Donald. I want to share a few things with you. As you know, no one on this earth is permanent. We all change, we all die. So it's not just you who will die. Also, we don't know when death will come. But no matter what, death will come. And this so-called death has come to you. So maybe it is important that you hear some of these messages."[5]

"Better you don't disturb her with this," David Cross said. "Let her be in peace."

"Do not consider this death as an end." Donald frowned and closed the bathroom door. "Instead, think that this is just the beginning. Yes, there is going to be change, but there is also a continuation. Now it is time to take the bodhisattva vow, no matter what—in this life, next life, and the bardo. Take a vow that you will do all you can to awaken sentient beings. Generate this determination again and again.

"And sometimes think of the people who inspire you, the historical saints. You can do it even more vividly than in the past. So take this opportunity and make some effort."[6]

David Cross opened the bathroom door. "Sir, are you religious?"

"You should not feel that you have things that you need to finish." Donald shifted, turning his back to the housekeeper. "You have done everything in this life. There is nothing to worry about. There is nothing to complete, nothing to finish. Do not be attached to your surroundings. Instead, look forward to a greater endeavor."[7]

"This is not right, sir, you reading from a phone. Let me call the pandit. Pandit Beshan is a very good man."

"Hey," the small maid said. She was on her hands and knees, scrubbing the floor. "Come help. Quit shirking."

Donald said, "When the time of separation between your body and the mind comes, everything will become different. Everything will be vivid. Therefore, everything may appear to be abnormal, not normal. Probably you will experience extreme light, extreme sound, or many other uncertain, myriad visions of beings, of environments, such as a cliff, such as typhoons, such as thunder. No matter what, just remember that this is all a projection of your mind. All this experience is due to the separation of your body and the mind.

"Instead, keep on taking the bodhisattva vow, that you will never rest until all sentient beings are awakened, again and again. Generate love and compassion toward yourself and toward everyone. Take this opportunity. Take this opportunity to look into yourself. This is one of the most precious opportunities. So make use of this opportunity fully."[8]

Donald began reading again from the start.

David Cross put on a pair of gloves. "She was from the conference. It's bad luck in here."

"I heard we won't have movies now," the woman said.

11

AT THE FERRY, a handful of sunburned Floridians had set up a tailgate by the dock. They wore neon plastic ponchos and drank hard seltzers and shouted cheers. Two were pretending to shoot each other with rifles and falling to the ground, rolling in the dirt, cracking up.

Trip was looking at his thumb. It didn't hurt at all, the bite just two tiny purple scabs, like strokes of a ballpoint pen.

A teenager knocked on the driver's-side window of Anthony's car. He did the cranking motion. Anthony pressed the window-lowering button with an expression on his face like, "You idiot."

"You meeting somebody coming in?"

"We're going out," Anthony said.

"Going out?"

"I need to close up some properties."

"If you want to go out, you need to go show ID inside. Cops are only letting residents take the ferry out. Everybody's coming in!" He pointed to a ferry two hundred yards out. "You better hurry up. That's the last one."

Anthony nodded but took his time getting his wallet from the glove compartment.

The Floridians were still doing their stadium calls as Anthony slipped out of the car and walked up to the pink kiosk, bent forward against the wind, his hands in his pockets. The gusts ballooned his shirt and then flattened it against the front of his body.

"One, two, three, four, who were they cheering for?" the Floridians shouted. "Donnie! That's who!"

A man, presumably Donnie, looked shy. He took a sip of his seltzer and fingered the skulls embroidered on the pockets of his pants.

"Someone on the bus shouted hooray for Sharon!"

The others took up the cheer.

"A guy made a fuss, said hooray for Sharon!"

"One, two, three, four! Who were they shouting for? Sharon, that's who!"

Sharon rolled her eyes. "Oh, please," she said.

The pratfallers with their rifles tumbled in increasingly dangerous ways.

The ferry bumped against the slip. A couple of teenagers in ponchos frantically tied it up at its apron.

Anthony came out of the kiosk and walked back to the car.

Frightened drivers began to move off the ferry, eyes wide, gripping their steering wheels.

Anthony sat. He was behaving strangely, muttering under his breath about peasants.

A driver coming off the ferry noticed Trip. A moment

after their eyes met, she shook her head and looked away, as if his recklessness were airborne.

Anthony eased the car up across the apron and onto the ferry. He idled, looking for the best spot. He chose to park on the other end, so he would be the first to get off the ferry when it landed. They waited in silence for the other cars to board. Only one joined them. Outside, the ferry employees gathered by the boat, looking out at the sea. One kid with long hair tucked his hands under his armpits as he talked to the others.

Anthony popped the lid to his gummy bears. He took two, then offered the jar to Trip, who also took two.

The ferry slipped away from the coast. Anthony opened the windows, filling the car with violent wind.

"Ah!" Anthony said, in pain. He touched his cheek and frowned. "This tooth is a wonder."

Seeing the coast recede, Trip felt himself getting upset. He clenched his fists in his lap. He breathed in, held it. Then breathed out. Held it. Then he gave up. He huddled over, wrapped his arms around his waist, and rocked gently back and forth.

The ferry slowed imperceptibly, then reversed course. It returned to the dock. Anthony looked around, confused. The teenagers tied it up at its apron. A worker with long hair ran to Anthony's car doing the slashed-throat gesture with one hand. He tapped the window. Anthony lowered it a few inches and raised his eyebrows imperiously.

"Coast Guard shut us down," he said. "Closed the roads, governor just now put through the order: no ferries."

Anthony gunned the engine and turned the car in a circle. As he pulled away from the ferry, his phone rang.

"Glad to hear your voice," he said, raising the car window and smiling.

His smile fell. He stopped the car. "I didn't realize you were such a fan of my previous attorney."

The person on the other end spoke.

"The motions have all been routine," Anthony said, "and I do think your father's lawyers can handle them. It is a tough process, and there's not any getting around that, but surely you can agree that we'll both be happier if we can go through it respectfully, without name-calling. Hello?" Anthony put his phone back in his pocket. He bent forward over the steering wheel and didn't move.

The single car behind them honked.

This seemed to change everything for Anthony, who sat up straight and waved in the rearview. "Go," he said. "Go!" He opened his car door and got halfway out of the car. "Do you really want to go?" he screamed.

He got back into the car and turned to Trip. "That was my wife on the phone. The Big Boss. She says I'm deliberately slowing the divorce. So . . . plan B." He cradled his cheek in his hand. "I'm going to their place on the mainland, near Saint Simon. My father-in-law's place."

He brightened. "You can come if you want. You'd be most welcome."

12

PHYSICAL FORM SAT holding a mirror, the top of her empty hand resting on her thigh. Her partner, Visual Consciousness, was sitting apart from her. Past Events sat with her hands on her thighs, her lap full of flowers. Apparent Phenomena was holding something that looked like a chain or a rope, and was turned away from me, looking over her shoulder at Olfactory Consciousness, one of the guys. Objects of Smell was burning incense. It smelled woody and clean. Objects of Sound was playing music. She had a sash tied around her guitar. Mental Constructs Associated with Future Events held a lamp. Mental Constructs Associated with Present Events held perfume. Mental Objects Associated with Taste had a plate of exquisite food. They had eight guys with them: Olfactory Consciousness, whom I mentioned, as well as Visual, Auditory, Gustatory, Tactile, Mental, Ground-of-All, and Dissonant. All of them were watching me, inviting me, but the brilliance and the splendor made me feel meager. I turned away.[9]

13

AT THE FRONT of the room, Larry stood at a lectern, a film still of an art deco bathroom projected on the slightly crooked pull-down screen behind him. Across the bottom of the PowerPoint slide in purple font was the title of his talk: "The Body-Mind Complex and Stephen King's *The Shining*."

He wore khaki trousers and a wrinkled flannel shirt. His eyes were bloodshot, his hair wet. On a desk beside him, a cup of coffee steamed. He looked down at his lectern, shuffling his printed notes.

Thirty participants sat at round wooden tables, between white pillars supporting Mughal-style arches. On the far side of the room, alone at the end of a single row of chairs set against the windows, Gary the neurologist had taken off his shoes and sat grasping the serape-patterned turquoise carpet with his toes.

Larry checked his watch and began to make the motions of starting. One of the conference participants stood up to adjust the pull-down screen.

"Thank you. That's great. You can just. Thank you," Larry said. "Much improved."

TRIP

The participant nodded and sat back down.

Larry paused. "These are not the conditions under which I had planned to be speaking to you, but last night the group decided that naturally we must go forward with the conference, and Gail asked that I start."

The pattern on Larry's shirt lifted and moved in three dimensions in the space and light around him.

"So just by way of getting us going, this project started with a class I taught in, what, I want to say 2008. It may sound frivolous, but I've found it's an effective way to get the students engaged. They always want to talk about the hotel, or whatever that's about—*the evil*—but I find that's an effective window into a discussion." Larry pressed the clicker to change the slide, and an image of an old woman covered with sores appeared on the pull-down screen. "The old lady in the bathtub."

Jody leaned over to Albert, a young man who provided hospice care for homeless addicts. She whispered, "Next slide, rabid Saint Bernard: the eschatological mind."

Albert smiled but kept his eyes on Larry.

"The schemes we need to understand here are those of the three levels of gross, subtle, and extremely subtle body and mind . . ."[10] Larry snapped his clicker again, and a picture of Shelley Duvall sprang up.

"Before describing them, we should bear in mind that all such schemes in Buddhist sciences are heuristic devices, patterns easy to remember . . . Conceptual schemes are like lenses in a camera. A scene with a hundred-and-five-millimeter lens looks different than it does with a thirty-five-millimeter lens. There is no need to argue over which is more true to what is out there. They are merely different levels of magnification."[11]

The woman in the orange sari lay on the floor, smelling little pieces of round chocolate she had in a bowl. "The tiles under this carpet are so hard," she said. "They're, like, beyond hard."

"Beyond hard," I said.

She laughed. "Seriously." She propped herself up on an elbow. "It's not like sleeping on the grass. It actually hurts."

"You shouldn't sleep in the conference room."

"Whatever."

Larry sneezed. "The three levels of the body-mind complex are used to provide a framework for Buddhist practitioners to integrate their subtle contemplative experiences with their ordinary experience. This enables them to alter their habitual self-identification process, in order to enter usually unconscious states consciously. Thus, when we see something or feel a sensation, we are normally conscious only of the surface level of the experience, the tree over there or the ache in here. We are not conscious of the photons of light striking the neurons of sensitivity and the microscopic workings of the optic nerves. We are not aware of the neurotransmitter chemicals flashing signals through the central nervous system to let the brain know there is an ache in the stomach. But the Buddhist inner scientist or psychonaut seeks to become conscious of such normally unconscious processes. She thus needs the equivalent of a microscope for this inner exploration. So she develops a subtle model of the self with which she trains herself to identify, in order to experience directly the subtler inner processes."[12]

Jody tried to engage Albert again. "Is this Stephen King now?"

Albert frowned and kept his eyes on Larry.

"The body-mind complex is analyzed into three levels: gross, subtle, and extremely subtle. The gross body is the body of flesh, blood, bone, and other substances that can be further analyzed into the five main elements of earth, water, fire, wind, and space."[13]

The neurologist raised a hand. "Yeah, sorry. Just a quick question. Why not use the periodic table?"

"Good question. Further analysis down to the level of modern elemental chemistry is considered too fine for this context, reaching a level of differentiation that is out of touch with the self-identifying imagination."[14]

"Yeah, okay. I think I get that."

Larry nodded. "Good. So . . . The gross mind that corresponds to this body is the mind of the six sense-consciousnesses, the five that correspond to the physical senses of the eyes, ears, nose, tongue, and body, and the sixth, mental sense-consciousness that operates within the central nervous system coordinating all the input from the senses with concepts, thoughts, images, and volitions.

"The subtle body roughly corresponds to what we think of as the central nervous system. It is not as much the wetware, brain matter of the system, as it is the pattern structuring it into a vessel of experience. The nerve channels are a structure of energy pathways that consist of thousands of fibers radiating out from five, six, or seven nexi, or nexuses, called wheels, complexes, or lotuses, themselves strung together on a three-channel, central axis that runs from mid-brow to the tip of the genitals, via the brain crown and the base of the spine.

"Within this network of pathways, there are subtle drops of awareness-transmitting substances moving around by subtle energies called winds. The subtle mind corresponding to these structures and energies consists of three interior states that emerge in consciousness the instant subjective energy is withdrawn from the gross senses—"[15]

"Larry," Jody said and stood. "I have a question. What does this have to do with Jack Nicholson ax-murdering people?"

"Touché." Larry laughed. "In my summer program, we watched the movie before the discussion, so it just kind of happened on its own. I opened my mouth, and Jack Nicholson examples seemed to spring out. If we spent the time to watch the—"

Jody cut him off. "Okay, but what does it have to do with anything? I mean, the NEH paid us to come here, to a seminar. I feel like we've gone off topic or something."

"There is a concrete practical goal, Jody." Larry was visibly annoyed. "To achieve conscious identification with this body-mind, to experience reality from this extremely subtle level of awareness, is tantamount to attaining Buddhahood, and this is the real goal of *The Book of Natural Liberation*."[16]

"That's the correct title for *Tibetan Book of the Dead*? See, that's interesting to me," Jody said still standing. "I wonder what it's like to be dead. Iñárritu says if you want to know, look at your life now. So I guess . . ." She looked around the room.

"This is the contemporary Spanish filmmaker?"

"He's Mexican."

"Well, Jody, about your question: what it's like to be dead. I'm not speaking from memory, here, of course . . . From what I gather . . . When we are dead, we will not have a body, but we will have the habitual memory of one. It will be like our existing body, but made of light. If there was any kind of injury, such as an amputated limb, the limb will be restored. Likewise for any kind of mental impairment. Because we will not have a body, we will be able to travel anywhere by thinking of that place. We will be able to read the thoughts of the living. We will understand foreign languages we've never studied. But it will all happen so—"

"See, I always wondered about that," Jody said. "Like when I'm dead, will I just be forced to experience other people's sexual fantasies?"

Albert cleared his throat, and she sat down.

"It is a reasonable question," Larry said. "From what I gather, anything can happen, so . . . maybe . . . ? I don't know. Everything will be quite vivid, the senses no longer constrained by the physical body. That said, most of us will be totally terrified and confused, because it is all so new. And then, of course, that terror will manifest itself, and you will want to remember that it's all a projection. What did Borges say?"

"'In dreams . . . images take the shape of the effects we believe they cause,'" Albert said. "'We are not terrified because some sphinx is threatening us but rather dream of a sphinx in order to explain the terror we are feeling.' Forgive my hasty translation."

"Wow, yes, exactly," Larry said. "Albert. Always full of surprises."

Albert shrugged. "An occupational hazard."

Gail raised her hand. "After we die, will we remember who we are, according to this? Will I know that I'm Gail?"

"Okay. So, somebody like . . . uh . . . Gary . . . Can I use you as an example?"[17]

Gary nodded.

"So, during his life, he's often thinking about ramen. He's planning where to get noodles, and thinking he needs to open a vegan ramen shop. And he often feels anxious, thinking about people saying bad things about ramen, saying it's overpriced, or it appropriates flavors from different cultures. And he's plotting, how to sell this ramen. I think it's all organic, right?"

Gary nodded.

"Stuff like this. He has this really strong, you know, like, plan. Okay? Then he goes through the bardo of dying. Maybe there, he may go through some agony of seeing Mount Meru the size of a betel nut. And he will think 'What is this!' You understand? So all of that. Now he hits the bardo of luminosity—blank. Okay? Now he's rising, okay. So generally . . . it's very general. For the first twenty-one days—it's very complicated now—but for the first twenty-one days, he will still have this fear and hope surrounding ramen—"[18]

Albert raised a hand. He said, "I left out the Coleridge part because it doesn't really make sense in a quote."

"Sure," Larry nodded at Albert. "Thank you. So, let's say I'm here after Gary dies. I can say, 'Remember, you had a plan to open a vegan ramen shop? Now listen to this. I'm going to fulfill your wishes to open this ramen shop, and I will make five hundred bowls of vegan ramen and distribute them to five hundred people. That way you will accumulate merit, so on and so forth. I can do that because he will still understand what I'm talking about.

"After twenty-one days, everything will end. Now this is the part you need to make note of: There is karma. Say, five hundred lives before, maybe Gary was a parrot in the Amazon. Flying everywhere, beautiful color and all of that.

"After twenty-one days, Gary will still try to put on socks, but his feet will have changed. He will feel that his claws are not really working with socks. It will feel a little awkward. I am just giving you this as an example.

"This is why Tibetans go bananas with this forty-nine days business. The first twenty-one days are considered really important, because the bardo being still has a good reference. After twenty-one days, when Gary's papagallo parrot chemical hits him, talk about ramen doesn't mean anything. Nothing. I can't talk to him about ramen anymore."[19]

Jody raised a hand.

"Yes, Jody."

"You said when we're dead we can go to a place just by thinking of it. If we can go anywhere, can we go anytime? Like, could I go to see Jim Belushi at the Chateau Marmont?"

"Yes," Larry said. "But will you have that control?"

Jody shrugged. "I don't know."

"Do you know when you're dreaming?"

She shook her head. "Sometimes."

"Then probably not."

Jody sat back down. "I'd like to meet Jim Morrison. You know, I heard when Val Kilmer recorded Doors songs for that OIiver Stone movie, some of his bandmates thought it was Jim Morrison singing."

"Okay," I said. "That'll do."

The woman with the bowl of chocolate said, "They can't hear you." She snapped her fingers in front of Larry's face. "See?"

"It is not as bizarre as it sounds," Larry said. "This is happening all the time in our lives, but it is slowed down by matter. We have the thought of going to Bermuda, but in regular life we have to go through a lot to get there: get the funds, make arrangements, buy tickets, get on a plane, so it takes longer. We are also always having thoughts that are setting something in motion, and we are often surprised by the results."

Jody stood back up. "So, like, Belushi is in cold storage, and people with control can see him."

"More like everything is a projection—"

Gary raised a hand.

"Yes," Larry said. "Maybe you can help us."

"I'll give it a try," he said, and told a long story about seeing Bob Dylan play live a few times and crying a lot.

"Is there a question?"

"Oh, yes. I'm asking: I notice I always cry when I see Bob Dylan live. Are those tears a projection of my mind?"

"Who is noticing the tears?"

The neurologist swallowed.

"I'm asking you: Who is noticing them? Are you

noticing your tears, or is somebody else noticing them? If somebody else is noticing them, it's their perception. You understand? Your question is your answer. You said, 'I notice my tears.'"

"The tears are a projection?"

"Of?" Larry lifted his coffee cup halfway to his mouth. "Basically, you are almost saying, 'This is my coffee, whose coffee is this? I'm holding my coffee, whose is this?'"

There was a knock at the door, and the hotel manager peered in. "Excuse me, Dr. Larry, I'm very sorry to interrupt. I have some urgent news about the producer, Ms. Sandra."

Larry nodded. "Yes, please. Come in, Jaswant Paul. Tell us."

"Mmm." The manager hesitated. "Maybe it's better if we talk outside."

"Oh, of course." Larry turned to the group. "I'll just be a moment. If anyone needs to go out, let's say we reconvene in ten?"

Some of the scholars stood to stretch, and others excused themselves to the bathroom. I stayed with Larry. He didn't seem to mind. He and the manager and I stood outside the door, but when the manager started to speak, he thought better of it. He strode down the hall and let himself into an un-remodeled conference room. Larry and I followed.

"The body is not on a flight," the manager said, switching on the lights and glancing up nervously at an insulation tile that had slipped out of its drop-ceiling grid. "Ms. Sandra's body is not on the flight."

I was startled. "Ms. Sandra's body?"

"Okay . . . ?" Larry said, talking over me.

"I am afraid it is my responsibility to tell you that there was a miscommunication. The body—Ms. Sandra—has been cremated in Kathmandu."

Larry removed his glasses and passed a hand over his eyes. His shoulders shook. The conference room filled with fog, and it began to rain.

"I apologize, I barely knew her, but this is all a bit much for me."

"Naturally, sir. I understand. The staff is also very upset."

Larry got ahold of himself. He blew his nose into a handkerchief.

"What has happened to me?" I said.

The two men ignored me.

The manager reached into his breast pocket for an envelope. "I'm afraid there is something else. I need a signature, sir."

Larry started to sign the papers, then hesitated. "One minute, ji. I will sign these, of course, but I might need a moment."

"Of course, sir, of course."

"What's going on?" I said.

The woman in the orange sari passed through the closed door and said, "Ms. Sandra be like," and mimed shooting herself in the face with an imaginary gun.

14

THE WEATHER IMPROVED as they drove across the state and north up the coast, away from the storm.

Anthony stopped at a house on the ocean. It was white stucco, built to resemble a colonial mansion, but small, with a terrace overlooking the sea, and dirty shuttered windows.

A Land Rover sat under a rusty carport. On the beach, thirty yards down, a handful of people in shorts flew an enormous, multitiered box kite.

Anthony turned off the car. He walked the perimeter of the house, pausing to fret over a loose rain gutter. "I think there's a drill inside," he said. "Don't worry, I'll do this. You can shower and relax, go swim in the Atlantic. Come on."

He got a house key out of a fake rock by the back door. He unlocked the house, went inside and switched on the fans. He unbolted the beach-facing double doors and began opening the shutters.

It was clean inside, but it felt abandoned. The light was dim. There was no furniture, and the floors were white marble. It was echoey and strange, every surface painted the same eggshell white.

"This place is a dump," Anthony said. "We won't stay here. We'll stay on one of the islands."

Trip's eyes adjusted, and he noticed outlines of black mold. It had shot through the cheap drywall, and it bloomed up from behind the baseboards, flourished in the corners, was a specter on the walls. On closer examination, he recognized that the walls were not painted white. They were coated in white Kilz.

"Don't worry about the mold, we won't be here long. Take a little time for yourself while I do some odds and ends, and then we'll get the boat out on the water."

Trip squinted.

"Go and shower. I'm going to secure that rain gutter."

Trip looked up the stairs. It was dark, all the windows shuttered.

"Go on. Just open the shutters like this." He demonstrated. "It's fine up there. You'll see!"

The staircase led to an interior balcony overlooking the foyer. Trip went past it, into one of the bedrooms. It was furnished with low shelves made of raw timber painted white with more Kilz, and a queen-size bed improvised out of white moving pallets. The futon mattress was made up with cotton sheets, a bath towel folded at its foot. Trip opened a door on the far side of the room and found himself standing on the flat roof. He walked outside onto the roof to look at the ocean and noticed a rough outdoor shower, really just a low privacy wall, a showerhead, a pressure-balancing valve, and a weathered old bottle of shampoo and body wash.

The wind was strong but warm. On the beach below, Anthony threw a large stick for a few stray dogs.

Trip went back into the bedroom and took off his clothes. He wrapped himself in the towel and went back out on the roof and pulled the shower handle, then turned it. The water was immediately warm.

He showered, dried himself with the worn towel, and went back inside. He put on his old T-shirt and boxers and lay down on the bed, swatting a starving mosquito, wondering if the Center had spoken to his mother and father. He heard some commotion outside and went back out on the roof.

A group of adults stood in a close circle on the beach, staring at something on the sand between them. Trip went out to the edge of the roof and saw a ray suffocating at their feet.

He didn't think he had time to save it. He imagined running down the stairs, through the yard, and out onto the beach. He tried to figure out how he would grab the ray and run into the surf. He wasn't sure if he'd need to get it past the break, or if it might hurt him in its panic. He flinched a little at the memory of the Gila monster's bite.

The ray was showing signs of deep distress. It flared and rhythmically pumped its gills. It pulled air in deeply. Trip tried to be brave, to go down to it, but he was embarrassed. The ray was surrounded by people who weren't helping. If he went to help, they would be insulted, and look on him with derision as a tree hugger, a child. The gasping grew even more desperate. He felt sick. The ray had longer periods between gasps. It lay still in the sand and gasped in a sad and helpless way. Trip saw that he would have had time to save it, had he gone down earlier, and he recognized that there might still be a chance, but he didn't move. It was tremendous, the moment when it was doomed.

The creature was inert. Its gills opened and closed a few more times. Then it was dead. The stray dogs started sniffing around it, curious. An old man found a rock and threw it, hitting one of the dogs in the side. It jumped and snarled, biting the rock in the sand.

Trip went back inside. He felt that something powerful had shifted, and his life as he had known it was over. Then he wondered if he was being dramatic.

He went downstairs to the kitchen. He thought they would be getting back into the car, but Anthony was prepping lunch with pantry ingredients. "Do you know how to make rice?" he said.

Trip shook his head.

"That's all right. Go out! Enjoy the beach. It's never like this. Usually it's completely full of people. This house is normally booked year-round, five-fifty a night. We'll go and get the boat this evening. Or tomorrow at the latest."

Anthony started whistling.

Trip let himself out. He walked through the gate, along a path growing with inkberry vines, onto the shore. The wind was strong. He felt like he could hold his arms out to his sides and get carried away. But he held them out shyly, and nothing happened. He noticed that a dozen dogs were trailing along behind him, hoping he had food.

He had walked a ways when he came across a small group of teenagers. They were shouting back and forth at one another in French. The girls were shy. They traded glances with him when he walked by. It seemed like they were wondering if they should speak to him but didn't know what to say. Neither did Trip, so they all sort of smiled and looked away from each other. Unable to handle passing them again, Trip stepped into the water.

He went as deep as his thighs, but when the waves came, they were up to his chest. He swam toward the horizon, thinking about the French girls. Why hadn't they left already, like everyone else? He pictured Anthony's boxy chest, and the strange, swollen cuticle on one of his fingers.

He turned and looked at the beach. He was farther out than he'd realized. The dogs were still following him, prowling in a circle at the shoreline. He decided to swim back in.

A wave overtook him, and the dogs barked and howled. He swam with the current, parallel to the coast. The dogs formed a loose semicircle and jogged alongside him. He moved toward the shore, thinking the dogs would disperse. As he got closer, they waded into the water. They were emboldened, a wild energy gathering in them. They had strange smiles, like they knew he was beginning to feel afraid he would die, like it was hilarious. He swam back out into the water. He swam with the crosscurrent forty yards, thinking he could get away from the dogs, but they tracked him onshore, smiling. He was dragged farther out and struggled to touch his feet to the bottom.

He swam back toward the shore. He had seen Anthony

throw a stick for these dogs two hours earlier. They were normal dogs. They weren't dangerous. He began to step out of the water, but when he was upright, walking, the dogs swam into the surf. As he walked up onto the beach, they circled him, growling.

He shouted, "Bad dog! Bad! Dog!"

The dogs loped around him. They got lower to the ground and growled as they walked, not taking their eyes off him, distracted only by the water, which occasionally rose, threatening to sweep away one of them, who would then yip and run for the sand, only to rejoin the circle. Then they were quiet. It was too late to get back into the water. If he moved, they would attack. They were waiting for it.

A horn honked. Trip glanced up and saw Anthony driving the Land Rover. He honked again and drove the car at one of the dogs, dispersing the group. The dogs tried to surround Trip again. Anthony honked and drove into one of them, hitting its side. It yelped and ran.

Anthony leaned over and opened the car door. The wind swept it out of his hand, jerking it open.

"Get in."

Trip got in and closed the car door. Anthony laid on the horn and accelerated, digging the jeep into the sand. He paused a moment, then gently touched the gas and the car eased forward. He drove toward one of the dogs, who growled and stared at the grille, giving ground only at the last minute. He laid on the horn again, and the dogs, as if using one mind, recognized they had lost and ran off into the distance at top speed.

"That was a bit careless of you, Trip. Lucky you have a guardian angel."

He wore an unbuttoned dark linen shirt and matching slacks. His skin appeared clean and luminous. "We've been invited to a party on Saint Simon. I brought you these"—he gestured to the back. "If you want to wear them. We have to sail there, so I'm heading over to the marina."

15

THE WOMAN WITH the carnelian bracelets watched me when she thought I wasn't paying attention.

We were in a small half room in the attic. It had three walls and some extra encaustic tiles piled on the floor. Someone who had lived here in the past had curtained off a fourth wall. It was very dusty and dark, with piles of wood and rubbish, and a little raised area that was not long enough for a human body.

The woman said, "This is boring."

I was in my bedroom at home, sitting on Vic's side of the bed with the door closed, listening to Donald talk about the peaceful deities. He was telling me to avoid the smoky light that was familiar to me, and to go toward the dazzling bright light.

I liked to sit on Vic's side of the bed during the day. It was my favorite place to be. I could hear him downstairs, shouting on the phone. He always spoke too loudly on the phone, a habit from his childhood. It sounded, however, like he was almost crying.

TRIP

I was there in the living room, where Vic was pacing and yelling.

"Yes! Why isn't there an Amber Alert? I know! I know! Don't say that again, it's only for when there is a clear case of abduction. I'm telling you, this is an abduction. He would not . . . No. No. No, I have no knowledge about the abductor's vehicle or description. I have already done that!"

The person on the other end spoke. Vic nodded. He wore a threadbare white T-shirt and stained green corduroy pants. He hadn't shaved.

"I filed a report locally and with the police station near the Center, and they told me to reach out to you."

"What's going on?" I said.

He ignored me and stormed into the kitchen, still shouting. He threw open the back door and walked out into the yard, shouting, "I've filed a report with NCIC, and several local watch groups are already out looking. But what I need from you—my son is autistic. He has special needs, he can't be out like this, wandering. He has hitchhiked in the past."

"What's going on?" I said again.

Vic kept talking over me. I asked him several times what was happening, but he seemed to me to be ignoring me.

An old orange wolf sticker on the car bumper caught my eye. It was the mascot of Trip's kindergarten.

I was in the parking lot, in the shadow of the two-story school building. It was full of dusty SUVs, overdressed children, and parents who were a little giddy from a single cup of wine.

It was the school where we had enrolled Trip after withdrawing him from his first school. It was expensive, but not elite.

Trip was holding my hand. He was five years old.

"I want a snow cone."

"We'll get one on the way out," Vic said. "Right now, let's go see your classroom."

My phone vibrated as we walked past the playground's net climbers, goblet drums, and warble chimes.

We had spent the summer in meetings with the principal and the school's learning services specialist, arranging to pay out of pocket for private therapists to come in and support Trip in the classroom part-time. We had asked if we should include the kindergarten teacher, Mrs. Stradlater, in the planning, but the school principal had laughed softly, as if we'd said something naive.

I got out my phone and listened to the voicemail from the school's assistant principal. "Mrs. Stradlater is feeling overwhelmed by the number of adults you're planning on sending into her class. Four different therapists, four times a week, is quite a lot. She asked if you could hold off on sending anyone until we've had another meeting."

We were walking through the cafeteria. On the right, a picture window overlooked the indoor basketball court. I followed Vic up the stairs, down a hall, to Mrs. Stradlater's room.

It was the smaller of two kindergarten classrooms. I suspected it was for the children of new or less-favored families, but it was reasonably cheerful. Clean, colorful, some kind of HOW TO USE CRAYONS poster on the wall: "In the lines, with realistic colors." I didn't care for it, but these kinds of refinements were from a different lifetime.

Trip's teacher stood behind a lectern in the corner, trembling all over.

Vic showed Trip different interesting features of the classroom, and I went to say hi to Mrs. Stradlater.

She was in her forties, thin and pretty, but extremely anxious. I asked her where Trip's supplies should go, and she pointed wordlessly at an itemized list projected on a whiteboard.

"Oh, right. So, you prefer that I read it."

She nodded.

"Sure." I skimmed the list until I got to a line instructing parents to go around the room and put their children's school supplies in labeled baskets. It was only then that I noticed them. In the unfamiliar environment, they had been invisible at first, just a part of the landscape, but I understood they must have been blindingly obvious to Trip's teacher.

"Ah yes, of course, the baskets." I started dropping in the supplies one by one—scissors in the scissors basket, watercolors with watercolors—lost in the experience.

Other families filtered in. Vic and Trip got out a bin of superhero figurines, and Trip set them in a line.

When I was done distributing Trip's supplies, he and Vic gathered the figurines back into their bin and put it on the shelf.

I wanted to say goodbye to Trip's teacher, but she was talking to another family.

In the hallway I saw a friend of mine, another special-needs parent. She wore a brick-colored dress with a tangerine cardigan and ate an orange snow cone. She saw me and smiled, covering her mouth with a hand, and I remembered that she had been the one to persuade us to diagnose Trip. She had even recommended the doctor, a young woman at the local children's hospital.

Dr. Jovanovich was attractive and bright. She led us down a hallway, making small talk with Vic and me, tacitly observing our son.

In the office, Trip climbed up into the sealed window and lay on the ledge, which was about eight inches wide. He teetered on the edge of falling. He liked to do that. We understood what he was doing, but later in the meeting, when the doctor glanced at him, I realized how it looked. He had been up in the windowsill, deliberately seeking the sensation of almost falling for about half an hour while we talked like nothing unusual was going on.

She said we could do an assessment or we could do a general evaluation. We chose the more formal assessment.

A couple of months later, we came back, and she and another doctor assessed him. They began with an IQ test. The doctor said, "I have a couch, a table, and a chair. What do I have?"

"I don't know what furniture is!" Trip screamed. "I don't know what furniture is!"

"Furniture is right. Furniture is the answer."

"Oh, of course!" He relaxed and smiled. "Of course."

The test continued, and he seemed to be getting all the questions right.

It took four hours, with a few breaks. It shifted at some point to activities and conversation. He seemed to be doing very well, so well we thought he wouldn't be diagnosed. During a round of imaginary play, the doctor made a birthday cake out of Play-Doh and presented it to a doll. Trip sang "Happy Birthday," blew out the candles, and went around the room, making eye contact and smiling at everyone, delighted by the silliness of the game. But in the end, he was diagnosed with autism.

"I don't recommend he ever do clinic-based ABA therapy, because his social skills are strong. I recommend enrolling him in a regular kindergarten class and bringing in an ABA therapist when problems arise."

Our eyes met and she stopped. She raised one enormously swollen hand. It was red and green with black necrotic patches.

"Are you okay?"

"This is no big deal," she said, smiling strangely.

Trip sat playing with the Bluey app on my phone. We were on couches in a small waiting room in the middle of a Volvo dealership, a glass box with concrete floors. We were waiting to sign some papers. Our salesman occasionally walked past and showed us a mouthful of yellow, plaque-y teeth.

"That's enough phone," I said. "Trip? Time's up."

"No," Trip said. "I'm not done."

"You've had it long enough. Pass me back the phone."

He turned away from me, gripping the phone tightly in both hands.

I slipped it out of his fingers. "Let's play something," I said.

Trip groaned.

"Let's play catch," Vic said. "We can use one of these pillows."

We took an accent pillow from the couch and went out onto the middle of the salesroom floor and tossed it back and forth. After a few minutes, Vic and I started to lose our minds. We threw the pillow higher and higher, trying to hit the insulation tiles in the ceiling to amuse Trip and annoy the salespeople, whom we blamed for making us wait. I got sort of carried away, throwing the pillow high enough to really knock the ceiling tiles, and I wondered if I would knock one out of place. Vic started to throw the cushion lower, and I realized I had been going too far.

We went back to the couch and I looked at my phone. Trip's teacher had written to request we meet with the principal and the assistant principal to discuss the curriculum. I knew what this meant. It meant that Trip was on probation.

I felt the need to test him on something they were doing in class. Maybe I was living in denial, I thought, and he just needed to be in a special school. I knew they'd been learning counting for the last week or so in Mrs. Stradlater's class. I was being crazy—he'd been counting since he was two—but I wanted to confirm to myself that he could do it. I set out seven napkins and said, "Can you count those, Trip?"

TRIP

Trip looked at the napkins, then looked at me and irritably counted to ten.

"Could you count the napkins? Not just count to ten, but count how many napkins there are."

Trip was quiet.

"I'll let you look at pictures of Mount Rushmore on my phone if you count these napkins."

Trip scowled at me and counted the seven napkins.

I handed him my phone.

He woke up in the middle of the night and couldn't get back to sleep. I got in bed beside him and rubbed his back.

"Turn on my night-light," he said.

I flipped over the small cube night-light on his bedside table.

"I need a one-eyed nickel."

I sighed and got up. I went out to find a one-eyed nickel in the Tupperware we kept in the hallway for this reason.

I came back in and handed him the nickel. He sat up and inspected it in the light.

"When do we die?" he said.

"Not for a long time."

"That's the only way out of this."

He opened his mouth like a person silently screaming. He held it that way for a while, then said, "Get me a Lincoln Memorial penny."

I got up and went to the Tupperware container. I couldn't find one there, so I went down to the stuff drawer in the kitchen and dug through it. When I came back to Trip's room, he was pressed against the side rail of his bed. I gave him the penny.

"Scoot over," I said.

He twisted onto his side.

"Scoot," I said gently, scooting him to make room.

I got into bed beside him. "Cuddle up."

He tucked under my shoulder. I put my arms around him and tucked my face into the top of his head. "Do you want to hear a song?"

"No."

"Do you want to talk about what's going on at school?"

He nodded once, like a solemn bow, against my shoulder.

I thought for a minute. I said, "Your mind is a little different. Some things are easy for you, like your memory is very good. And some things take practice, like drawing." I was quiet. He clutched my arm. "In my opinion, you are smarter and more sensitive than the other kids. You understand things that they only feel."

Too vague, I thought. But true.

I said, "Also, I don't think Mrs. Stradlater is a good teacher. And I don't think it's a good school." I was quiet. I felt his heart racing against me in terror. I said, "Do you want to talk about this anymore?"

He shook his head no. "I want to snuggle."

I wrapped my arms tighter around him.

A few minutes later, he began softly snoring, and I went back to bed with Vic, who lay watching a movie on his laptop. He'd watch a movie while waiting for me to come back to bed, and then often we'd both watch it for a while. It was a good time for us just to be together, next to each other.

"We need to get him out of that school," I said.

Vic paused the movie. "Let's give it time."

I held out a hand, and he passed me an earbud. He unpaused the movie.

Peter O'Toole turned to Omar Sharif.

"If none of Lord Auda's men harms any of yours, will that content the Harith?"

"Yes."

The assistant principal and the principal were speaking to Trip in a conference room adjacent to the front-desk area.

The principal was mid-sentence, talking about the founders of the order of the Hieronymites.

I understood that the two administrators were trying to determine my son's verbal comprehension, his ability to articulate his thoughts. Basically, they were seeing how autistic he was, by speaking to him in a long and ornate way about a fifth-century hermit and biblical scholar. It made me very angry. I felt hurt for my son, who was confused. He had a dawning fear that something separated him from others. It also made me angry because it seemed like the principal did not know how to speak to children. She didn't even know much about Saint Jerome, but she cobbled together what she did know and spoke in a tone of mighty learning.

When she was done talking, everyone looked at Trip. He was five. There wasn't much to say. I wouldn't have known what to say if the onus had been on me to speak. I probably would have said, "Neat."

Trip said, "Did Saint Jerome die on the Fourth of July?"

"No, Trip, he didn't." The principal looked concerned. The assistant principal mimicked her expression.

She and the assistant principal stared at Trip, waiting to see what he would say next, how autistic he was. I wanted to explain that Trip was interested in presidents. A handful of early presidents had died on that day, and one—I couldn't remember who—had been asked if he wanted medications to keep him alive a day or two more, so he could also die on the Fourth of July, but he had declined. I didn't have the communication skills to explain it all.

I said, "Principal Davidson doesn't know the day he died," and took Trip's hand. "She doesn't even know his last name."

She snapped up her phone.

"She knows how to google it," I said. "A lot of adults know how to spend time online. They like to pretend to know other things, but most of them don't." I turned to the two administrators and said, "Thanks, guys," and led my son out.

Trip and I walked out the school doors, down the steps.

I was happy because I had humiliated the principal. But I knew it wouldn't go well. When I was a kid, I'd thought I could get away with that kind of thing. But as an adult I knew that it would be given back to me, magnified in some way, and I would taste defeat.

The principal had her Skype camera turned off. In place of her moving image was a studio portrait of her in some kind

Japanese Noragi jacket, her hair perfectly blown out, her makeup professional and pretty.

Vic and I were sitting downstairs in our living room, the bookshelf behind us.

The assistant principal, Angela, was not the sort of person who would have had any power over us in a former life. She opened the meeting by saying, "Well, Sandra and Vic, how do you think it is going with Trip in kindergarten?"

"We only hear positive things," Vic said. He spoke at length, quoting the good things that he could remember off the top of his head.

The assistant principal stared, a sour expression on her face. She kept her body stock-still.

Vic trailed off, losing steam. He said, "Trip's therapists feel like the school isn't contributing anything to his support."

Angela lit up. She nodded. "Vic, I think that I agree. I'm not sure we have the resources here to support Trip. He just needs so much support."

"Sandra and Vic," the principal said. "I want you to know I'm not being rude, with my camera off. I have had a measles exposure, and I'm isolating due to that."

I didn't see the connection between the exposure and her camera. I guessed what she meant was that she had stayed home from school that day, but as we talked, I kept batting away the thought that she didn't have her teeth in.

"We've gotten to know and love Trip over the past couple of years," the principal said. "He really is a dear boy, but now that he has transitioned into kindergarten, we're wondering if this is the right place for him."

Vic was so desperate and out of his depth that he turned to optimism, to the things the internet advises us to say in these moments. He actually said, "How can we all work together to solve this?"

Angela's features changed ever so slightly, as though Vic had farted. It seemed like she felt sorry for and slightly repulsed by us.

"We don't have that one-on-one," she said, "to pull him out of the classroom and work with him individually. And Mrs. Stradlater isn't trained in special ed."

I rolled my eyes.

Angela looked down and made a note.

The principal said, "Sandra, if we look down, or if we pause, it's not because we're being rude, or not listening to you. It's because we're both taking notes."

Angela nodded and looked up. "And next week, we're doing MAP testing, so we don't even know if he can do that."

"He can," I said.

She looked like I was the one doing the farting now.

"He can do the testing," I said. "He's done it, when he was assessed. He can answer the questions."

"This was one-on-one?" Angela was openly skeptical.

"Is the MAP testing conducted one-on-one?"

Angela looked startled.

"Do you know?" I said. "You don't, do you?"

She made a note.

"It's not about the test," the principal said. "We can see you're unhappy with us. I could see that you were unhappy with us the other day when you came in to get your son. I said, 'She's unhappy with us.' It can be hard, hearing these things about your child, but when you care about someone, you tell them what's going on. We care about you. We've really come to love Trip over these past two years, and that's why we're telling you what's happening here."

She spoke like that at length, talking gobbledygook, some boilerplate about the school, sending me into a fog.

"We are a little different from the other Catholic schools in the city. We're a part of the parish. What that means is that we take the tithe, so we don't have to fundraise. We pay our teachers a little less, but we allow them to create their own curriculums. We like to celebrate—"

Abruptly she went quiet.

"You were saying . . . ?" Angela said. "Beverly?"

A soft exhale.

"Okay," Angela said. "We've lost the connection to Beverly for the moment." She looked uneasy. She wasn't sure what to say. "I'm curious to know what you're thinking, Sandra."

A bloated figure with a blindfold over his eyes, his wet gray clothing clinging to his limbs, stumbled into the room behind Angela. His mouth looked like a puffer fish, his skin pink like bubble gum. Angela said, "This is just a meeting between the administration and the parents to discuss what it is we are seeing in school."

The bloated figure held a finger to his lips. The skin hung off the bone in places, like a torn rubber glove. He reached down and wrapped his fingers around Angela's face and squeezed.

Her eyes widened. Her hands went up to his.

"Hey," she said.

He dug his fingers in deeper, penetrating her orbital sockets.

She tried feebly to bat his hands away. She tried to stand. "Hey," she said again.

Her camera switched off. The video was replaced by a studio portrait. Her hair curled and sprayed, lit from behind, making visible the outline of her skull.

16

ANTHONY HAD THE LAND ROVER AC turned up full blast with the windows open. His thick, wavy hair blew around like a crazed villain's.

"The sea air," he said to Trip.

He turned down a private drive and stopped in front of a gate and punched in a code nervously. When the gate didn't open, he assumed an innocent and bored expression as he dug through his wallet.

An attendant ran out.

"Of course." The attendant smiled. He punched in a code, and the gate swung open. "Welcome back, Mr. Garabedian, sir."

"It's Langley."

"Mr. Langley, yes. It's nice to see you again. How long has it been? A few years?"

Anthony frowned. He released the brake and rolled through the gate.

They drove down a long, manicured drive, over a ridge, then parallel to the sea, past a little boathouse. Anthony parked on the gravel drive.

It was dusk. The sea was dark. The swells were about three feet high. Several white racing keelboats were dry-docked in front of the boathouse, and the wind knocked their halyard shackles against their masts, like cowbells. Anthony put his keys into the glove compartment, and led Trip down to the fixed docks.

The boats were moored by size. On the far end were the larger, more impressive yachts. Closer in were the smaller weekenders. Anthony marched down one dock to a modest little yellow boat. The *Zephyr* had a blue racing stripe that ended in several short, curved lines, suggesting a soft wind.

Anthony grabbed a line and stepped aboard. Trip put one foot onto the deck and hesitated, his other foot still on the dock. "Trip, step on," Anthony said. "You never want to straddle the water like that!"

"Sorry." Trip stepped on.

Anthony began to unwrap the mainsail. "Help me. See how I do these." He undid a toggle. Trip stood watching as he undid another. "Come on, don't just stand there." He undid the rest of the toggles, then tossed the sail cover at Trip. "Fold this."

Anthony worked quickly, uncleating the dock lines. "Can you untie the mooring and haul the fenders over?" he said.

Trip was confused. Anthony sighed. He went around unwrapping the mooring lines from the cleats and tossing them onto the deck. He lifted the fenders over, unclipped them, and stored them under a set of seats.

Annoyed, he moved around Trip, then took the helm.

He dropped the outboard motor into the water and began steering them out past a long line of red buoys.

The swells had looked calm from the shore, but once they were out on the water, it was like they were on a pony. Trip felt sick. When he looked at the ocean, the feeling lifted a little.

"Put this on." Anthony tossed him a life jacket. He put a sleeker one on himself.

Trip started to slip one arm into the life jacket, then got distracted and let it fall onto the deck.

"I'm going to motor out past the buoys, but then I'll need you to wake up," Anthony said. "There are no passengers on a sailboat. You'll be manning the jib."

"What's a jib?" Trip looked at the jacket.

Anthony pointed. "Oh, you'll catch on." Then he thought about it a minute and said, "Actually, maybe we'll just motor over. It's not far."

He steered them out of the harbor past the grand boats. Trip looked at them with longing.

"Nice boats." Anthony turned to smile at Trip. "Hey, get your life jacket on! Here, I'll help you. It's tricky. Hold on."

He shifted the motor down into neutral, slipped the jacket over Trip's head and clipped it in the back. He pulled it a little, so it fit, nodded, then turned back to the motor and powered up, chugging past the floating pier.

"Man the helm for me for a sec." He passed Trip the tiller.

Trip took hold of it, and the boat immediately turned

to the right. He wasn't sure what to do. He tried to correct the steering by turning left, but it only went farther to the right.

"Whoa! Whoa, hold her steady."

Trip let go of the tiller.

"What did I say? No passengers on the boat. Take a hold, let me show you. Hold her steady. There you go. You see that outcropping? Just keep the bow pointed at that outcropping. If you want to go left, push it to the right. Vice versa."

He looked at his phone. "I should download some nav software. Let's see . . . Hmm . . . No cell service." Anthony glanced up at the coast and frowned down at his phone. "Doesn't seem right. You'd think we'd have a phone signal in sight of land." He held his phone toward the shore, then looked at it again and put it in his pocket. "For the best. For the best. We can see the coast, after all."

"Can I check my email?"

"No, Trip! We don't have service. What did I just say?"

"Can I just look and see? I read these new phones do satellite."

"This is not the Ukraine, Trip. Your generation with your phones. Look at the . . . nature."

The sun was low, the sky orange. On shore, a couple of dogs nosed the body of a seagull in front of a boarded-up beach restaurant with its neon sign switched off.

"Let's raise the sails," Anthony said. He hoisted the mainsail, then unfurled the jib and tied off the line.

Trip looked down at the outboard motor, still chugging away in the water.

"I heard my father-in-law has a safe on board where he keeps a pair of pantyhose for his mistress to go around in," Anthony said. "He never takes this boat out of sight of land. If she were mine, I'd take her somewhere far away."

The mainsail luffed, but Anthony didn't seem to notice.

"You want to know the best Hemingway daiquiri I ever had?"

Trip looked at the outboard motor, still chugging away in the choppy water, then up at the mainsail, which had begun to flog. It whipped back and forth in the wind.

"In Delhi, at the Ashok Hotel. It's not a great hotel, not a country known for cocktails, but it came to me icy in a classic martini glass and I drank it outside, in the darkness, the smog, and the heat."

Anthony adjusted the sail. On the coast, the condos became houses, then the houses had pools, and the gardens became larger and more manicured. Hedges replaced fences, the grass gave way to artful orchestrations of nature, mansions with uncurtained windows and bright interiors, people inside their homes watching television, or sitting in chairs looking at the ocean.

"My father-in-law used to sit like that," Anthony said. "His favorite joke was to say, 'I wonder what the poor people are doing.' And then my wife would say, 'Dad!'"

The homes began to recede farther from the ocean and one another, with rolling, private beaches and long stretches of grass, and then it was just green and blue, the water and the lawns.

They went slowly around a bluff, and Anthony said, "Here we are." He pointed to the blazing lights of three mansions on a cliff. On the terrace of the largest house, twenty or thirty people stood talking. A long staircase led from a lower balcony down to the inlet and a long dock, where a dozen small yachts were moored. As Anthony drew closer, he said, "This boat is actually the perfect coastal cruiser. I'm not an environmentalist, but I say a sail and the wind are all you need." Trip glanced at the motor. "All these other huge, tacky beasts are more suited to crossing the Atlantic. Though I'm sure half of them don't have the appropriate gear. The other half are probably geared to the teeth with things nobody can use, least of all the owners. People die out here every summer, in sight of land."

He pulled up toward the dock, slowed, and sliced past an open slip. "Fuck," he murmured, gazing up to check if anyone at the party had noticed. He looked down and began a second approach.

A tall, thin old man stepped out onto the dock and watched. He had dyed black hair and wire-rimmed glasses and wore white pleated slacks and a striped golf shirt.

"Shit," Anthony said. He missed the dock again.

When Anthony began his third pass, the man on the dock stepped out into the light and waved solicitously.

Anthony recognized the man as he nosed the boat toward the slip.

"Lancaster," Anthony said.

"Anthony, sir."

Anthony attempted to execute a forty-yard infinity-sign to come to a stop in the slip. Lancaster chuckled when he missed it again. Impulsively, Anthony steered the boat directly toward the dock.

"Whoa," Lancaster said. He spread his legs to brace himself. "Whoa, whoa."

The boat slammed into the aluminum dock with a boom. It was as loud as a car crash, knocking Trip over.

"Lucky it's covered in foam," Anthony mumbled, pointing to the foam-wrapped edges of the dock as he busied himself tying up the boat.

"A smooth landing," Lancaster said. "You have the sails up and the motor going. Not to mention the sails are wing on wing, Anthony. Dangerous."

"Yes, thanks," Anthony said. "Surprised he has you out here." He pulled the motor up and switched it off and began tying up the sails.

"I'll handle all that. Nice to see you, Anthony. Mr. Garabedian didn't tell me to expect you."

"I see you're working the docks."

"I requested this job. I like to be with the boats, on the water, speaking to the guests as they arrive. I see you have a guest, too. Let me help you. Stepping on." He took hold of a line and hopped onto the boat. He flipped open the seats for the fenders and began to tie them on, then paused to introduce himself to Trip, saying, "I'm Lancaster. Please go. Enjoy the party."

Anthony slipped past Lancaster onto the deck.

"You're a friend of Mr. Anthony's?"

Trip blinked.

Lancaster gave Trip a brief, appraising look, then turned back to Anthony. "Didn't expect to see you," he said. "Mr. Garabedian didn't mention it."

"You've said that," Anthony said. "Yes, he's a friend.

Come on. Trip, come on. Let's leave Lancaster to his labor. I want to show you the house."

Trip hopped off the boat and followed Anthony up a long ramp, their steps echoing under their feet, mingling with the sounds of the surf and the people above.

A pale blue shingled house was encircled by yellow buckeyes, mimosa trees, and azaleas.

A tent was set up on the lawn, lit by torches. Inside, party guests sat at round tables, eating from garishly lit towers of seafood. An old man in a white suit spooned caviar onto a potato chip, while a younger man in a pink shirt and three teenage girls with identical hairstyles waited.

Trip noticed a giant man on a couch in front of a swimming pool. The man raised his glass. He wore a dark blue shirt and a pale jacket and sat with a woman in white.

They walked through the grass, past the pool, past young men in white and groups of older people smiling and holding drinks, through the rear entrance of the house. The air inside was clean and cool and smelled like mahogany and lime. Anthony led Trip down a hallway to a great room crowded with people. The burgundy wallpaper matched the curtains but contrasted with a tablecloth the color of tarnished copper. A large portrait of a scowling young woman in a shirt and slacks hung on a bookcase, in front of the books piled sideways on the shelves.

A skinny older woman with long, straight brown hair and a large nose sat on a pale blue couch laughing with a woman in a gauzy white tunic. Standing behind them was an unusually tall, bald man in a jacket and tie. He wore large square glasses and had hands and lips the color of liver. He held an oversize half-full wineglass and spoke to a stoop-shouldered man in an open shirt. "I'm too old to live north of the highway," he said. The shorter man nodded. "You're too old to drive on the highway."

"Excuse me." A kid Trip's age with chin-length blond hair pushed by him, smiling apologetically. His friend, a taller, less attractive kid with bushy blond hair, frowned at Trip and looked away.

Anthony went to the bar. "Do you have any cans of Delaware Punch shaking around back there?"

"I think so," the bartender said. He was dressed entirely in white cotton. "Let me run back and make sure."

"I'd love a Lancaster. Trip, you've got to have a Lancaster."

"Is it . . . named after that nice guy on the dock?"

Anthony frowned.

The bartender came back to the bar. "All good," he said. "Let me just look up how to make it." He gave Anthony a thumbs-up.

"Oh, I can tell you. It's simple enough. An Arnold Palmer made with Delaware Punch from the can. The house drink." He turned to Trip. "They don't make Delaware Punch anymore, but Dick got a few dozen cases."

"Okay! Sounds good," the bartender said. "I'm on it."

Anthony opened a sideboard, glanced inside the drawer, then closed it. He opened it again, lifted the felt lining the base of the drawer, then half closed it. He touched the apples in a porcelain bowl and flipped one over, as if checking the price. The large-nosed woman on the sofa said, "The hospital in Saint Simon has the Cartier screwdriver. To the bracelet. They were tired of using bolt cutters," and the woman in the tunic rolled her eyes. "You can unscrew it with a fingernail." The short man was telling the taller man that his hyperbaric chamber had changed his life. "My digestion's done a one-eighty."

"Two Lancasters," the bartender said, holding out glasses on a tray.

Anthony took the drinks and passed one to Trip. "Cheers."

"Who is this? I don't think I saw him on the guest list!" The gigantic man from outside, the one in the blue jacket who had been sitting by the pool, slapped Anthony on the back and Anthony started. The man laughed and extended his hand.

"Dick Chambers," Anthony said. "Always a witty remark. You're looking healthy."

The large man laughed uproariously. "Sure, sure. Great to see you looking like a hunted animal. What are you drinking? Who is your friend this time?"

"This is Trip. He's a friend of my son's."

"Nice to meet you, Trip. I see you got a drink?" Trip noticed a thickness in his speech, and understood that he was drunk. The man held out his hand. "Call me Dick. Thank you for coming to our little gathering. What are you drinking?

"A Lancaster?" Trip held it up.

Anthony nodded.

"Oh, come on, no one drinks those anymore. You can't have a Lancaster in this. The storm is turning our way. Didn't you hear? You'll have to toast our storm. It's bad luck otherwise."

"We can toast with the house drink," Anthony said firmly.

"Tsk, tsk, it's bad luck. Come on, Anthony, we're all alcoholics here." He turned to the bartender. "Let's open a Petrus."

The bartender nodded and went down to the wine cellar.

"Now, you know, Dick, that's not for me," Anthony said. "I've been a friend of Bill's for more than a decade. And Trip is underage."

"Bill? I don't see any Bill around here, looking over our shoulders and sniffing our drinks. I think one glass of Petrus, in honor of the hurricane, is entirely in order. Thomas! Anthony, have you tried the Petrus? Are you going to have a glass?"

"I'll admit to some curiosity," Anthony said.

The guests nearby had gathered closer. They were trained on the host, like flowers to the light, or too-devoted lovers.

Dick said, "Anthony will tell you he attended the second-best business school in America. The University of Tulsa's is a great program. I attended Wharton, where we're obsessed with rankings. But I think if you actually look it up, Tulsa is ranked thirty-third, thirty-fourth."

"We can't all be Tom Buchanan."

The bartender came back up and stood waiting with the

Petrus. Dick turned to him and nodded, and the bartender opened it. He poured a half centimeter into a wineglass and offered it to Dick, who gestured to Anthony, saying, "Anthony, do the honors."

Anthony accepted the glass and tilted it by the stem. He looked at the color, swirled, tasted, and nodded. He did it simply, with the attitude of a person wiping down his kitchen counter. The bartender poured two glasses.

"And one for Anthony's latest friend. I forgot your name already."

"It's Trip," Anthony said.

"How could I forget. A toast to our fair lady wind. To Hurricane Amelia!"

They held their glasses up and drank. Trip had expected something like Hawaiian Punch, and was startled by the sour, bitter flavor. He grimaced. Dick laughed long and hard, then turned to Anthony, aware of the small audience that had gathered, and said, "Let's get some more bottles, enough so everyone can have a glass. Break out a case, Thomas!"

Anthony took a few quick sips of wine.

Dick said, "Should I tell them the one about your billboards?"

"I'm sure they'd rather hear the one about your regatta. That's one not everybody's memorized."

"Do I tell that story too often?" Dick looked around.

Several guests shook their heads. One said, "I'd love to hear it."

"But, yes, as you were saying, the billboards. So, Anthony had this novel idea of a smaller billboard. Less . . .

what was it, Anthony? What was it that you said at the time?"

Anthony was pretending not to hear.

"I believe it was less visual pollution. So, he went and—how many of those signs did you have manufactured? It was millions, wasn't it? He went all in. Small problem. From the road, nobody could see them. They were invisible. So—"

Bartenders came up with more bottles. One stopped beside Dick, who pointed to Anthony. "Let him, let him. I can't tell. I can't tell the difference between this and that. I don't know the tasting notes, never have. Dried raspberry, chocolate, spice, citrus, truffle in the background . . . it's lost on me. I'm just the wallet. Let him. He can do it."

The bartender opened a bottle, and Anthony went through the routine again and nodded. He seemed to be relaxing.

"So, Trip," Dick said. "Third in line! You know, Trip was often the name of the servant in eighteenth-century comedies."

Anthony's face fell. He was speechless.

Dick slapped him on the back. "Have a good time!" He shook his head and walked away, calling to another guest.

After the fireworks display, Trip followed Anthony to the pool, where a handful of guests were swimming in the light of the lawn torches. Anthony had a half-empty bottle of Petrus in one hand and a nicely poured glass in the other. He was loose and a little wild. Trip felt it, too. He felt sweet and embraced by the air and the sea and the people, like he could say or love anything. He wrapped his arms around himself.

"That guy wasn't nice," he said. "Dick."

"The aptly named."

Trip's eyes twinkled.

Anthony finished the glass of wine in his hand and dropped it in the grass. "Don't worry, I have a trick or two up my sleeve."

Trip laughed.

Anthony took a long pull from the wine bottle. "We're taking his boat." He dropped the bottle onto the lawn. "You wait here. I want to say goodbye."

Trip stood looking at the sky. He couldn't make out as many stars as he expected, because of the light from the house and the torches. He gazed for a while at Sagittarius A, the center of the Milky Way, then got distracted by the ocean. The swells were larger, bobbing the boats around. Even the yachts, farther out on mooring balls, moved with the waves.

Anthony came back holding two bottles of Petrus and a corkscrew. "Let's get moving."

They walked down the lawn, to the sturdy, aluminum-frame dock, where a forty-foot sailboat was hoisted five feet above the water on a lift. Several small portholes along the body of the boat were dark, reflecting the torches on the lawn.

Anthony was trying to open a control box. He struggled, finally prying it with the foil cutter of his wine-opener. He murmured to himself as he read the labeled switches.

"On," he said. He flicked a switch and the entire dock

began to vibrate. He looked back at the house, then glanced at Trip and waggled his eyebrows.

Lancaster was coming down the lawn toward them. He waved his arms in the air above his head and picked up his pace.

Anthony flipped a toggle switch, and the lift began to raise the boat. It rose a few feet, then vibrated in place and began to make a terrible whining noise.

"Anthony?" Lancaster broke into a run.

"Oh, down, down." Anthony flicked the toggle switch, and the boat began to lower toward the water.

Lancaster jogged down the ramp, speaking into a walkie-talkie.

Anthony hopped into the boat, hugging the wine bottles to his chest. He set them down in the cockpit. Trip stepped one foot onto the boat and froze.

Two uniformed men came out of the house and raced down the lawn toward the ramp.

A captain's hat hung above the helm. Anthony put the hat on his head and called out, "Trip, jump!"

Trip leaped into the boat.

Anthony nodded. He looked down, struggling to get the engine switched on.

"Get out of the boat, Anthony."

"Nice evening for a sail, Lancaster."

"Please get out of the boat, Anthony. You are not yourself, and the damages could be quite expensive."

"I give nary a shit," Anthony said. He looked embarrassed for a moment, then turned back to the instrument panel.

Lancaster had reached the slip. He was almost close enough to hop into the boat.

Anthony began to press different buttons and push knobs back and forth, cursing under his breath about bells and whistles as screens came to life and went dim, and the jib began to unfurl, and lights went on and off in the cockpit and on the bow and sides of the boat, but it didn't move, except for the rocking motion of the water.

"Anthony, I'm getting on," Lancaster said. He took hold of a grab line attached to the boat's side.

Anthony pushed a button, detaching the boat from the lift. They gunned forward, flipping Lancaster into the water. Anthony steered them out away from the house.

"She's not insured south of Saint Simon!" Lancaster shouted.

Anthony mashed the controls, and the mainsail began to unfurl, luffing in the wind.

"Bring *Valhalla* back! Bring her to me."

The mainsail caught and the ship leaped into motion. "Pull the jib sheet in." The captain's hat blew off Anthony's head. "Here, I'll show you."

He pulled in the sheet, taking a moment to adjust it and wrap it around its winch. The boat leaned toward the water.

He glanced back at Lancaster in the water, then looked at Trip, whose shaggy hair whipped sideways.

"She's heeling a bit. Can you tighten the vang down there?"

Trip was watching the uniformed men pull Lancaster out of the water.

Anthony pointed to the pole at the bottom of the mainsail. "This is the boom," he said. He pointed to the short diagonal line connecting the boom to the mast via a series of pulleys. "This is the boom vang." He was honking like W. C. Fields, but the words he said made sense enough.

Trip didn't move.

"And this is how you tighten it." He tightened the vang and the ship heeled farther toward the water. "Shit," he said, and quickly loosened the vang. The ship righted itself. "This is how you loosen it."

Trip wasn't listening.

"This is the cunningham," Anthony said, "And this is the outhaul. Can you tighten those?"

"Okay," Anthony said, tightening them himself. "Fine. We'll work on it later."

They were sailing along the coast, in sight of yards and private beaches.

"We're a little close in," Anthony said. He pointed the bow toward the open water, then adjusted the sails and looked at Trip. "Will you be okay for a second if I go down below?"

Trip felt uneasy and gazed up at the stars. He began following Cassiopeia's letter *M* to Perseus.

"Will you be okay for a second if I go down below?" Anthony said again. "I'll just be down a sec."

"Un mur mur murmure au mur."

"What's that?" Anthony stood at the companionway.

Trip found the star called Algol. "The demon's head," he said.

"Okay," Anthony said. "Good." He stood, unsure what to do.

Trip took the wheel.

Anthony said, "I'll bring back some hard alcohol."

17

I WAS BACK AT WORK. It was the middle of the night. The lights were all out, and no one was around. I looked inside the refrigerator in the lounge, then went back to my desk.

I logged onto email and noticed the picture of Trip on my desktop.

Then I was on the open ocean.

A boat skidded along the water, perpendicular to the coast. On the bow, a man held the mast and drank Wray & Nephew 17 from a pale pink tiki mug.

Crouched at the bow was a boy with his back to me. After a moment, I recognized Trip.

"Do you think they'll send someone out after us?" the man said.

Trip didn't move. He was looking at the sky.

"You know, I used to have a driver?" the man said. "A driver." He began to laugh. He laughed for a long time, in a slightly deranged way, like a person who might be having a breakdown.

"Dick might send someone," the man said at last.

"Lancaster might be coming after us right now in some kind of speedboat."

The man saluted and laughed some more. "Yes, sir, Lancaster, sir." He doubled over.

Trip was daydreaming about catching a fish. He envisioned himself in a fisherman's hat adorned with hooks and lures, and then he imagined the moment when a large fish caught hold of his line. He started to imagine reeling the fish in, but then he shifted, and the fish pulled him off the deck and into the ocean. He imagined breathing underwater, and remembered the mermaid tails girls wore in swimming pools when he was a kid.

The man began to vomit over the side of the boat, holding his cup off and to the side.

Trip sang the lyrics to a Baldi's Basics song in his head and visualized Baldi slapping his palm with a ruler.

The man stood and wiped his mouth. "I'm okay," he said. "Just a little seasick." The boat jolted, and the man caught himself on the mast, his tiki mug sailing overboard.

"Are you okay?" Trip said.

"Damn," the man said. "I'm fine."

Trip looked back up. He wondered if the kids at school had heard about him running away. He imagined stupid Maxwell, bitchy Bea. Then he listened to the water. He thought if he listened to it long enough, it would reveal ancient wisdom. He had an older friend in the twelfth grade who had taken some kind of special hallucinogen at the beach, who said that sometime in the evening, the ocean had told her a joke, but she couldn't remember what it was. He wanted to ask her sometime if it had waved. He imagined getting Anthony's cell phone so he could call his dad and tell him he was okay.

"Do you think they'll send the Coast Guard?" the man asked.

Trip looked at his thumb, squinting to see if he could see the little bite marks there in the dark. He imagined they were a portal that had brought him to the ship. He kissed his thumb, and said a quiet thank you to the Gila monster.

"What was your driver's name?" Trip said.

"What? Oh. David Nudell."

"I forgot I was listening to the water."

"Listening to water." The man nodded gravely, as if the comment made perfect sense to him.

18

VIC LAY ON the unmade bed. He lifted his head, flipped his pillow over, and lay down again, then curled onto his side.

He got up out of bed and walked down the hallway. He went to the bathroom and splashed water on his face. He looked up and saw himself in the mirror, then sat down on the floor, the faucet still running. He laid his cheek down on the tile and looked under the claw-footed tub. His eyes fell on Trip's old plastic Mount Rushmore, covered in dust. He reached under the tub and took it in one hand. It was a small replica, something we'd bought on a vacation we took to the monument when Trip was ten years old. It had probably fallen under the tub years before.

"This is going to make Maggie crazy," I said. "Leaving her with a dying dog."

"Misty isn't dying," Vic said. "Misty is fine."

"The dog is dying, Vic."

As we backed out of the driveway, the sunlight and

shadows on the garage door looked for a moment like the sword and rope, one closed eye, and the half grimace of black Fudo Myo-o, but then he was gone.

"Do you think we should stay home?" he said.

"No, we can't do that. The hotel won't let us cancel, and we promised Trip we'd take him to Mount Rushmore. I'm just saying that it's pretty inconsiderate."

Maggie was a family friend. She watched our dog for us when we traveled. She had divorced her husband and sold her house and set out wandering a decade before, and although she was available to help us, she was not a dog-sitter. She was a serious, well-organized adult. Also, she loved animals. Leaving her to care for a dying dog was sure to upset and offend her.

"I'll text her and let her know."

We drove on the interstate all day and spent the night in a hotel at the halfway point between home and the Black Hills. It was a chain, designed inexpensively in the style of a boutique hotel.

At the front desk, a very drunk person stood, begging to be allowed to return to the hotel's Tiki Lounge, which was off to the right, through a beaded curtain. The man had buckteeth and wore carpenter shorts and boots. His hair was clean and parted dramatically low on one side.

"I am going to be chill," he said, pronouncing it like *chee-el*. "I promise to be chill."

Trip ran back and forth in the lobby. When he saw the

curtain, he shouted and ran through it, then came back and stopped abruptly in front of two businessmen sitting in armchairs. They were glowing from recent showers, doing a passing impression of affluence, but in their faces I saw the question "What impression do I make?"

Trip shot off, back through the beaded curtain.

"Is that right, Mommy?" he shouted.

"You nailed it," someone inside the Tiki Lounge said.

I followed him into the lounge, which was hung with buoys and memorabilia, and lit with colorful paper lanterns. He stood at the corner of a circular booth of grandmothers in brunch suits, drinking zombies out of blue skulls. One identified me as Trip's mother and smiled, letting me know that it was all right to let him talk with them for a bit.

I took my phone out of my pocket and read a text from Maggie. "If it's okay," she wrote, "I would like to spend the nights with Misty. I'll bring bedding and sleep on the couch. We'll do a cool early-morning walk, and I'll spend the days with her, too. Thanks for letting me know that she is unwell."

Someone asked the bartender a question about one of the drinks.

A ball of flame caught my eye, and the bartender began to hold forth about the goddess Kali's girdle of severed human hands.

Another text rolled in from Maggie. "She has been eating grass."

I looked back at the booth.

One of the old ladies squinted at Trip. "I'm guessing you're, what, about eight years old?"

TRIP

"I'm ten," Trip snapped.

"I have a grandson who's eleven and has a foot on you."

"Are you very old?" Trip said.

The woman glared at me.

"Is your face yellow?"

"Trip," I said, making my way over to him, "let's head on back. I bet Dad is ready to go up to our room by now."

"Our room!" Trip said.

"He liked that," one of the old ladies said, laughing. Two others traded looks, apparently a little weary of me and my son.

"Come on," I said. "Let's leave these ladies to their cocktails."

Trip and I walked together back through the curtain to the lobby, where the check-in clerk was losing her patience with the drunk man who was still begging to stay. She said, "Sir, we have already asked you to leave."

Our room was small, with two queen beds, a tiny sofa, and a pocket door separating it from the bathroom. Trip was delighted. He stomped his feet and laughed, then got onto one of the beds and began to throw himself against the headboard. He leaped from one bed onto the other bed, then onto the sofa and back.

"Well, I guess it's okay," I said apologetically. "Not really a suite, but it's fine. A little small."

"It's not too small," Vic said. "I like it."

"I probably should have just put us over there." I went

to the window and looked across the river at the Hilton Garden Inn.

It was dinnertime, and the outdoor restaurant was full of life. People were drinking rosé and eating foot-long crackers.

Beside the restaurant, a few children played in a fountain. Water shot up from a dozen spigots at intervals, creating patterns of arches and minor segments through which they scampered, their hair and clothes soaked. On the outskirts, travel-dazed parents sat on park benches looking at their phones.

I suggested we go down.

A truck idled at the intersection before the access road, on the other side of a low wall that separated the splash pad from the freeway.

Trip was resplendent, soaked, his hair wet, his T-shirt stuck to his chest. He played with the other children, some ninja game they had started together, doing martial-arts leaps over one of the fountain's jets.

I was unconsciously appraising the other kids. The girl was normal. The boys had oddly shaped heads and arms, or maybe it was my imagination.

"Ninja!" Trip shouted.

He trotted through the fountain, then stood leaning on a pole.

I realized what I was doing—evaluating the children—and looked away.

We were sitting on a bench with our backs to the river.

I turned to look behind me at the water, where a small boat was slipping past. I was surprised to see it in the city, and wondered if it was allowed to be there at all. I got out my phone to check.

"Trip!" Vic shouted.

I looked up and saw Trip skipping over the low wall, heading toward the freeway.

"Trip!" I screamed. "No!"

He turned, looking confused, and hopped back over the wall. When he got back to us, we both put our arms around him and then we talked to him, while the other parents watched with a vaguely satisfied air.

Vic took Trip up to the room, and I went over to the tiki bar to see if they had food.

Two bartenders stood shoulder to shoulder, shaking drinks. One looked like Dennis Hopper in *Apocalypse Now*. The other wore a pink-and-orange brocade shift dress and had intricate blue lily tattoos covering both her arms. I sat at the bar and the man walked away, but the woman stayed there, shaking her mixer.

"Do you have room service?" I said.

"You can order from here and bring it up to your room." She set her cocktail shaker down, wiped her hands, and reached under the bar to get a short menu, which she handed to me.

"Do you have a kids' menu?"

"No. We don't." She adjusted her glasses and poured the cocktail into a large pink fishing boat.

I looked at the entrées. The fried-chicken sandwich would work for Trip. I could order it without pimento cheese. I flipped the menu card over.

"Could I get a glass of . . . Do you have a red wine?"

"I'll be with you in a second."

I looked back at the menu and frowned. I snapped a photo and texted it to Vic. "Any suggestions?" I wrote, then noticed the steak frites at the bottom and pushed the menu away.

Vic had answered Maggie, saying her plan of spending nights at the house sounded ideal. Maggie wrote back, "Great! Lotsa lovin from me. And please do send the vet info."

I started to look it up, but Dennis Hopper stopped in front of me. I asked for red wine. He looked confused. "Belle Glos pinot noir okay?" I nodded and ordered the steak for Trip, then went back to my phone. I opened Facebook, where a stranger in one of my parent groups had asked about her son, who had mooned his third-grade class at school and been carried out screaming, "I want to die!" over and over again.

The bartender set down my wine. I glanced around the bar and took a sip, then read some of the replies to the Facebook post. When the steak came, I paid and carried it up to the room.

We tore the takeout container in two and divided the food between the halves, then laid out towels on the beds and set one half in front of Trip. He ate a piece of steak and laughed, then launched himself across the couch. He came back and ate a piece of arugula, then flipped the food out of its container and onto the bed. We gathered it back up.

We left the television on until bedtime. Then Trip bathed, and I put him to sleep, the chorus from "Starships" repeating in my head as I watched him drift off in black and white, double vision.

Canvas platform tents were spread out in little groups on the mountainside, connected by gravel paths.

The lobby tent was C-shaped, with a check-in area on one end, a free-form lobby in the middle, and a bar on the opposite side, with snacks and canned cocktails served from coolers.

The attendant at the front desk was in her twenties. She had long, wavy brown hair, with a handful of thread-wrapped blond dreadlocks drawn forward and draped across her shoulder. She sat across from us at a slice-of-wood table, near an urn of cucumber water. She pushed forward an agreement on a tablet.

"This just says you won't bring food into the tent," she said.

"Oh. Right, darn. Okay." Vic signed it.

Trip wore his new binoculars around his neck. His chin-length hair dipped forward to cover one eye, and he held it back with a hand. "I want to see Mount Rushmore!" he said.

"We will. Let's just get checked in first."

"I want to see Mount Rushmore!"

I felt a text come in from Maggie. "Misty has been out back once, otherwise on her bed, usually sleeping. I bring water to her, and she drinks a lot, but pretty much just sleeps."

"I said I want to see Mount Rushmore!"

"That's the first thing we're going to do."

"You can't see it so well now because the sun is behind it," the desk attendant said and smiled at Trip. "At night, when they light it up, it's really cool."

"I want to see Mount Rushmore!"

Another text came from Maggie. "And I'm fine," she wrote. "I've been cleaning, which helps me stay present."

Trip walked to a nearby table, where three girls his age were playing a card game. He stood uncomfortably close to one of them, breathing down her neck, but didn't say anything. She widened her eyes and glanced at her friends, who weren't sure how to feel about him. He was looking very cute that day, and I could tell they noticed. They weren't sure if he was confident or unconventional.

Trip touched the girl's hand. Her friends seemed to recognize that he had selected the prettiest of them, and they were jealous. Because they were jealous, the girl seemed to decide to see it as an honor.

"Do you want to get some water?" Trip said.

The girl nodded. He led her over to the urn. He let go of her hand and took a plastic cup. He filled it with cucumber water and handed it to her, then filled a cup for himself and took her hand and led her away from us, toward the cocktail-lounge end of the tent.

Vic and I looked at each other. We glanced around and identified the girl's mom, who smiled and waved at us. A few minutes later, Trip and the girl came back. He brought her to the other girls, said goodbye, and came back to us.

"Wow," I said.

He looked me up and down. "Do you have a potbelly?"

When we were checked in, the desk attendant led us along a gravel path to a large wooden viewing deck. It was empty except for an old man who wore a sniper-rifle shirt that said NEVER MESS WITH A MAN WHO CAN END YOUR LIFE FROM A DIFFERENT ZIP CODE.

The desk attendant pointed at the mountain range in the distance. "That's it," she said. "You can see it better at night."

I squinted. "I think maybe I see it."

"No!" Trip said.

"It's there. I see it. It's small."

"Is it not really there? Is it pretend?" Trip locked his elbows and knees, shouting progressively louder.

"We're far away," I said.

The man with the T-shirt looked at Trip and stormed off.

Trip threw up his hands. "Is Mount Rushmore there?" he screamed. "Is Mount Rushmore there?"

"Yes, it's there, don't worry." Vic put an arm around him. "We'll see it closer up tomorrow."

"Not really!" Trip wriggled out of his father's embrace. "Is Mount Rushmore not really there? Is it pretend! Is it a pretend Mount Rushmore!" He kept shouting, but allowed himself to be steered off the deck.

Our tent was white canvas, with a roll bar on top that let you open a skylight and look at the stars. The attached bathroom had a working toilet and a propane-heated shower. A wood-burning stove was set up on a steel plate beside a hoop-shaped rack that held some logs, three fire starters and a book of matches.

"It's grubbier than the photos," I said.

Vic took out his phone and chuckled.

I got out my phone and scanned a text from Maggie. "She just threw up the grass she ate a couple of days ago. Her digestion is shut down. Not to insult anyone, but you may want to think about another vet opinion. She doesn't seem very responsive. She hasn't had a pee or a poop since I've been here. Sounds like renal failure to me. Not to be harsh."

Another text came in. "She's kinda knocked out on the bathroom floor. I think the retching took it out of her. Much love."

"Where's Trip?" Vic said. "Trip?"

Vic took two quick steps out of the tent and returned with our ten-year-old child in his arms. He quickly zipped the tent's screen.

"Is Mount Rushmore not really there?" Trip said. "Is it pretend? Is it a pretend Mount Rushmore?"

"What are we going to feed this kid?" Vic set him down.

"I guess we could go back into town."

"Let's clean up here, then go to Mount Rushmore, then eat, come back, and go to bed."

I showered first, then Vic, and last Trip. The water temperature wasn't adjustable. It was propane-heated, a little too hot, so I had to show him how to squat low, close to the floor, so he wouldn't get scalded. In the end, I came in to help, holding him close to the ground. Basically, I hosed Trip off, and Vic helped him into a T-shirt and jeans.

A walk lined with flags led to a balcony that overlooked an amphitheater and faced Mount Rushmore. Trip wanted to stay on the balcony a long time. He impressed the old people with all he knew about the monument and its construction.

At closing time, Trip asked a ranger to point him toward the secret chamber, and the ranger—charmed by the question—said the room inside the edifice wasn't open to the public.

The ranger dug through his laminated brochures for a map that showed the secret chamber and unfolded it for Trip, explaining that the chamber had been envisioned by Gutzon Borglum as a repository for documents central to American democracy.

Trip was rapt. "What is in the room now?"

"Oh, good question. Sixteen panels that explain how and why the monument was created."

"Borglum was an apprentice of Rodin's."

The ranger lifted his eyebrows and smiled at us.

We drove to one of a handful of tourist restaurants. It was like a saloon, with two-story-high ceilings, and art and memorabilia hung at eye level on the walls, making me feel like Alice in Wonderland, or a miniature person surrounded by disoriented old tourists the waitstaff was embarrassed for.

Trip wasn't getting cell service on his iPad, so Vic was linking it to his hot spot when a waiter came to our table and distributed menus.

"Good evening," the waiter said.

"Let's order for him now," Vic said. "Let's get him squared away while we have you here."

"Sir?"

Vic was jumpy from our day, and he had to make a conscious effort to communicate clearly. He looked away from the iPad, up at the waiter, and he pointed at Trip. "Sorry. I want to order for my son. We'll get the spaghetti and broccoli, and the chicken fingers and fries. And two salads for us."

The waiter took a beat to recover from his momentary confusion, then understood and wrote the order down.

"And I know my wife would like a glass of wine."

Vic picked a wine for me, and the waiter left, and I looked at my phone. Maggie had sent more texts.

"I've been playing Mozart," she wrote. And then, "Misty has always liked Mozart when I looked after her in the past."

Frowning, I wrote, "Sophisticated!"

"It's actually quite beautiful. Especially the choral works."

"I've heard he's good."

"He's had a following," she wrote.

I set my phone down on the table, wondering if we'd just had an argument.

When the waiter brought the food, Trip pushed both plates away.

I picked up a fork. I wound it in spaghetti and held it in front of Trip's mouth. His eyes were focused on a strange YouTube video that showed a character from one of his favorite cartoons in different environments. Trip ate. "Crammed . . . Jungle . . . High altitude . . ." I handed him a stalk of broccoli. He ate most of the woody stalk, then handed the floret back to me untouched. I glanced around, wondering if the other people noticed. They didn't seem to. I put it into my mouth.

Vic made an okay sign. He passed Trip a piece of chicken. Trip inspected it, took a bite, then dropped it onto the floor. He picked up a french fry, bit, and chewed, his face adopting a faraway expression.

My phone buzzed on the table. I flipped it over and read, "I got a little obsessive with cleaning your house. It's what I do when nervous. I cleaned your fridge as well. The outdoor furniture has been wiped down."

I looked at Vic. "Why is Maggie so crazy?" I said. "Why is everything so crazy?"

19

"You can trust me," Anthony said. "I'm not one of these gung-ho people who have never experienced an emergency. I know trouble. I've seen it, and it's not something I want to court."

They were in a southerly wind, staying in sight of the tiny lights of the coast. Wind-driven waves ran parallel to the shore, crisscrossing the ocean swell.

Trip felt sick. He sat dreading the moment when Anthony would tell him to unwrap and rewrap one of the ropes, which he called lines or sheets, speaking a foreign language.

"South it is, like it or not," Anthony shouted. "*Valhalla* is a great boat. A little bit of a pig, but you could live on her, take her around the world. I know it's bad luck to call your ship a pig, but the fact is, she's a little bit of one. She can steer herself, navigate herself. Once I figure out these controls. She's basically like being on land. Desalinator, refrigerator, gas grill with solar, television. Backup parts for everything. We could take her across the Atlantic. I bet you anything there's a nickel bag of coke on here somewhere. If there is, I'll find it. She is a little bit of a pig, though."

Trip glanced up at the sky and identified Alkaid.

"You've got that jib sheet wound counterclockwise," Anthony said.

He was tracing a line from Alkaid toward Messier 101. It should only have been visible with binoculars. He must have been confused.

"Unwind the line and wrap it the other way."

He could make it out, he thought. Maybe he was imagining things.

"Your jib sheet. Trip!"

"Sorry, sorry." He sat up, unlocked the winch. The sail unfurled, and the boat slowed and righted itself. "Sorry." He rewound the line and brought in the sail. The boat shot forward and heeled slightly.

"Take over here for a minute? Take the helm? Trip?"

Trip took the wheel. It really couldn't be Messier 101. The Pinwheel Galaxy.

Anthony came up with the second bottle from the party and a storm sail. "You've gone off course again," he said. He set down the sail and cradled the bottle on top of it. "You have the bow toward the open ocean. Not the place to be in the tailwind of a hurricane. Turn left. Your other left. Thank you."

Foam raced across the surface of the water. They began moving quickly, riding over waves and dropping heavily into their troughs.

The wind whipped Trip's face. His hands hurt from the ropes and winches.

"Hard to say how fast we're going," Anthony shouted. "This knot-meter tops out at ten. So, more than ten knots!"

He brought down the jib and hooked up the storm sail. It took longer than it should have, because he was sloppy and the lines were slippery in his fingers. The steering became more difficult once Anthony had managed to get the storm sail up and trim it. Trip focused on the wheel in his hands, but then he was distracted by the Pinwheel Galaxy.

"Better let me take the helm."

Trip passed him the wheel. He looked down at the ocean. They were moving at the same speed as the waves under the hull, so it appeared they were at a standstill. He felt like he was going to be sick and lifted his eyes to the horizon to avoid throwing up.

"Your jib," Anthony said. "Man the jib. The line—loosen it, then I'll—"

Trip unlocked the winch and loosened the rope, which shot out, releasing the small sail. It swung out and luffed wildly.

"No!" Anthony said. "Bring it back in! Sit down and grab the line! Grab the line! What are you doing? Stop. Take the helm."

Trip took the wheel and froze.

"I'll get that wrapped."

Anthony went back to the lines, murmuring that he spent more energy correcting Trip's mistakes than he'd spend piloting the ship by himself. He looked up and groaned.

"Trip, look," Anthony said. "Just look where you're steering."

Trip had put the coast behind them.

"Okay, executive decision. Prepare to heave to," Anthony shouted. "We can drop anchor for the night. Don't make that face. We're going to heave to for the night."

Anthony walked Trip through a series of steps, shouting at him and then stopping to open the second bottle of wine between his knees, the wine opener in one hand and the wheel in the other. The ship spun halfway around. Anthony took a long swallow of the wine and shouted, "Tiller to lee!" as he turned the wheel into the wind.

The boat rocked furiously. Anthony let out the sail, and the boat came to a stop.

"Magic," Anthony said. "Every time. Drop anchor for extra support. And let me show you to your chambers, sir. Actually, I can't remember if you drop anchor in the open ocean. I feel like you don't . . . Either way, it can't hurt. Come on."

He led Trip down below.

The cabin was clean and bright, lined with pale wood. It had a well-stocked galley kitchen, two benches that converted to a queen bed, and a bedroom in the bow with a short, triangular V-berth. "That one will be yours," he said. "You get privacy but I get easy access to the bathroom at night. Important at my age."

Anthony poured himself a plastic tumbler of wine.

"We could take her across the Atlantic if we had the nerve," he said. "I've half a mind to try. My father-in-law has a couple studios in Île de la Tortue. We could weather the storm there. Let's light candles."

The boat rocked, knocking Anthony off balance. He dropped his tumbler, spilling wine everywhere. "Whoa," he said. A look of wistfulness crossed his face. He found a towel. "That's all right," he said. "That's all right. Though, maybe candles are a bad idea. You take that V-berth, Trip. I'll stay out here."

Trip went into the small cabin and closed the door. He sat up in the darkness and braced himself against the wall. The boat rocked, slamming him into the bulkhead. He might throw up. After a few minutes, he heard loud snoring from the larger cabin.

20

"Now I have to . . . Unfortunately, this is important." Bart took a cocktail olive from behind the bar and put it into his mouth. "According to Karma Lingpa—or not just Karma Lingpa, so many others—there are one hundred special knots, or confluences in our channels, in our system.

"Now after you die, when the actual body and the actual veins are already dead, you'll only have the imagined ones, but these imagined ones also have confluences. In fact, this is why nadi—nadi and prana—the big portion of nadi and prana is the mind."[20]

He flipped his arm over and drew his fingers down the veins in his forearm. "These things, these greenish-bluish veins are just a very gross reflection of the most refined channels.

"So there are one hundred different knots, or confluences of nadi, and these one hundred knots will be projected. You will then experience the one hundred peaceful and wrathful deities. Now, you have extensive teachings on the hundred peaceful and wrathful deities in Karma Lingpa's thing . . .

"The moment I use the word 'deity,' I'm sure you're thinking in terms of like Tara, Manjushri, Shiva, Ganesh . . . Sure they are all very symbolic, they serve their purpose and we will always use them as symbols. But deity . . . What is deity? Well, it's luminosity. Deity is none other than the union of luminosity and emptiness. That's what deity is."[21]

"What are you talking about?" Jody said. "Union of emptiness and luminosity? What is that? It's just some made-up exotic language."[22]

"No, not at all," Bart said. "Union of emptiness and clarity—or luminosity—is just so important." He picked up a bar napkin. "Like this. Paper for me and you, human beings. For a spider, different kind of luminosity and emptiness. Not tissue. They don't think like that. For a hungry New Delhi cow, maybe something to eat. Every phenomena manifests differently for different things, and this is why this is none other than the luminosity and emptiness in union."[23]

Larry said, "Everyone? Let's get the drink order settled."

Bart helped himself to another olive.

"So, I'll see what, like, the Kurosawa *Dreams* thing where the little boy stole the cherries?"

"To you and me? A flash of blinding light. Looking at the sun. I don't know. Probably not even defined as bodies."

"Excuse me, that's fascinating, but I would actually kill for a strawberry daiquiri."

"She's been boiling Kate an egg for half an hour."

"I've heard it's good to order off the drink menu," Jody said. "Those are the ones she makes regularly." She flipped the cocktail menu open to the "Bartender's Selection" and ran a finger down the page. "Blood and Sand. Old-fashioned with coconut-washed rye. What does it mean when they wash it?"

"They pour warm coconut oil in, refrigerate it, and scrape it off."

"Why?"

Bart shrugged. "It enhances it."

"It's not so different from what we have now," Benito said. "Varied impressions continually arise. We mistake them for real."

"Emerald Fizz . . . I might like to try that," Jody said. "Vodka, cucumber, coriander syrup, sparkling—"

"Lost me at 'coriander.'"

"I was reading that in this new generation, everyone is drinking their martinis wet."

"Jody," Larry said. "Kate ordered an egg, and the bartender has been gone long enough to roast a chicken."

"Meaning?"

"Order beer."

"I have some noodle packets I brought from home." The neurologist laid a hand on his tote bag. "There's an electric kettle in the kitchen that boils water in about thirty seconds. It's kind of amazing. I'm happy to share, if anyone likes . . ."

"Who was it who always got his martinis dry?" Jody said. "I think it was James Bond. Or he liked his 'shaken, not stirred,' didn't he?"

"Do you eat meat?"

"I'm pescatarian."

"Oh, that's no good." Benito lowered his voice. "Meat eaters are choked, chopped, strangled in reverse."

"Please, Benito. Stop. I don't want to hear any more of this."

"What does that mean, to be strangled in reverse?"

"It's not good."

"Maybe a big-batch cocktail, like a sidecar punch."

"Last time I had a big-batch cocktail I nearly smoked myself to death with a pot of macaroni."

"What's a sidecar punch?" Renata asked. "I have to be very careful about my diet. If I get the slightest little bit thrown off, it's open season on the ody-bay. Not to mention my blood sugar."

"I'm getting horse-fucked by this algorithm. Nobody's seeing my posts."

"You get possessed, too?"

"No, I don't get possessed."

"Do we sue the hotel? I mean, not really. It's just one of those crazy . . ."

"What was that I saw somewhere about Daniel Craig liking to eat maraschino cherries?"

A man attached to an IV bag said, "Hey, hey. You. Lady. Hey. With the mouth."

"What?"

"You with the mouth."

"Me?" I said.

"Your face." He pointed to his own face. "All messed up."

I looked in the mirror behind the bar.

"You don't have a reflection, because you don't have a

body." He pointed at his mouth and nodded. "It's fucked up, though. Like, fucked up."

"Huh?"

"Huh?" He mimicked me. "You sent Trip to a facility?"

"A lot of parents do it."

Sylvia sat on a barstool beside the ramen neurologist, who went rigid and flushed all over.

Larry rattled off the ingredients in a sidecar, and Renata shook her head. "That would be a disaster for the whole surface of my skin and mucous membranes. I mean, everywhere."

"How about Flaming Blow Jobs?" Bart said.

Renata laughed.

"All right, Bart."

"What if we keep it simple?" Bercholz asked. He had groomed his beard and put on a collared shirt and a light gray linen jacket.

"What's simple?"

"Oh, you look nice," Bart said. "What's the occasion?"

"What's that supposed to mean?"

"Ordinarily, you dress more casually."

Bercholz blushed and frowned and turned to Renata. "Whiskey, straight up, is certainly simple."

"I don't do straight up."

"I wonder if that girl is ever going to bring me my egg."

The neurologist crossed and recrossed his legs. He took his packets of ramen out of his tote and lined them on the bar, then gathered them up and tried to fit them into his pockets.

The man with the chemo bag said, "No egg tonight."

The neurologist took the ramen out of his pockets. He stole a peek at Sylvia.

There was a loud crash. The bartender emerged from the back area. She had pink hair and wore a color-blocked T-shirt that said HERE COMES TROUBLE above a cat using a laptop computer.

Bercholz raised a hand. "Can I get a can of lager?"

"Sorry, ma'am," the bartender said to Renata. "No egg tonight."

"What?"

"I was the one who got the egg," Kate said.

"Ma'am. No egg tonight."

"Oh no."

The bartender opened a can and set it in front of Bercholz, who took off his jacket and folded it carefully, placing it on the bar beside him. He drank, narrowed his eyes, and scratched his neck under the collar of his shirt.

"Why can't you have whiskey?" Jody said to Renata.

"Renata is easily possessed by spirits," Bercholz said. "Something I understand, as I am sort of a medium."

"Okay. We're trying to coordinate cocktails."

Bercholz lifted his jacket and refolded it. He brushed it with one hand and took another drink, finishing his beer. He gestured to the bartender, and she set down a second.

Sylvia said, "Maybe we should randomly choose a few of the best drinks from the menu and hold it to a vote."

"What? Why? That's a terrible idea."

"We would need to establish procedure," the neurologist said.

"Like a vote on the vote?" Sylvia said, looking at him for the first time. Her eyes were ever so slightly crossed.

He nodded.

"Are you insane?" she said.

"No. I don't think. Ha ha." He touched his packets, then glanced at the ceiling.

"Can you get me anything to eat?" Kate asked the bartender.

"Crisps, madame."

"Fine, I guess."

The bartender poured chips into a small bowl and set it down in front of Kate, who took one and ate it glumly.

"How about we all have whiskey sours?" the neurologist said.

"What do you do again?" Bart said. "I mean, I heard you have a real job, not this professor crap like the rest of us."

The neurologist said he was a physician, but he pronounced the word so softly and quickly, it sounded like *fusuhsuh*.

"Fusuhsuh. Okay."

"What do people think of Gin and Sevens?"

"I'm a horse," Renata said. "I can't drink any kind of soda, anything with bubbles. Gastroenteritis."

"Bubbles give you gastroenteritis?"

"They upset my stomach. Does anybody have a light?"

"You can't smoke in here."

"Then why do they have ashtrays?"

"Do you mind smoking outside? There's a table."

Renata lit up.

"I just don't understand what happened."

"I mean, she slipped on a fucking hairbrush and face-planted into a marble counter is what happened."

"Right, but . . . is that fatal?"

"Please," Bercholz said. "Everyone, please. Some respect for the dead."

"It's not like she can hear," the neurologist murmured.

"I can hear," I said.

"They can't hear you," the man with the chemotherapy IV said.

"Some of them can." I pointed at Bercholz. "That's what he does for a living."

The man scoffed. "He's heard a few dozen people, but tens of thousands have gone unheard screaming in his face."

"Well, what do I do?"

"Give up, move on. It's too late."

"Would you like to try a Golden Shower?" Bart said to Renata.

"What's in it?" Renata exhaled a column of smoke.

21

Anthony held a gooseneck kettle, his hair pressed flat against his temples.

"What happened?" Trip said.

Anthony put a finger to his lips and mouthed the words "Six, five, four" as he poured hot water in slow, steady spirals over the ground coffee. He counted, poured, waited again, then streamed the coffee into two mugs and added milk. He offered one to Trip and sat across from him on the bench.

"The bad news is that we were dragged out into the open ocean last night. I don't think the anchor helped matters. I don't blame you, of course. But it is unfortunate, because I have spent all morning with it, and I've determined that the battery is out, or something. We have power in the cabin—we have lights and all the kitchen appliances are working—but the navigation equipment is dead, and I don't know why. Even the radio is out. It's a glorified coastal cruiser. I figured we had to have a backup, but if we do it's well hidden. I can't even find a go bag or an EPIRB."

"What about your cell phone?"

Anthony passed the phone to Trip. "No cell service, no charger. It's a brick." He sipped his coffee and grimaced, holding a hand to a spot on his cheek that looked slightly swollen.

"Maybe there's a charger on board somewhere."

"Not much use without cell service. You millennials really don't understand anything, do you?"

"I'm not a millennial."

"Sorry. Don't suppose you know how to navigate by those stars of yours? I'm joking, of course. Though this is no time for humor. But as to why Dick of all people has one of these . . ."

"Stars?" Trip squinted.

Anthony pushed a wooden box toward Trip. He opened the lid, and Trip gasped and reached for the instrument inside.

"We are well stocked," Anthony said. "We could go into a shipping lane, if we knew where we were. I guess the thing is to go west . . ."

"Can I . . ." Trip paused, finding the right words. Sometimes they just slipped away at the moment he needed them. "Can I . . ." he said, repeating the words he had while waiting for the ones he needed to come into his mind. "Can I . . . ?"

Anthony nodded.

"Can I . . . Can I . . ."

"You want to go up with the sextant?"

Trip nodded once.

"It came with this, too," Anthony said. He passed a manual to Trip.

Trip nodded once. He picked up a pillow from the bench

and tucked it under his arm, thinking the deck would be a good place to sit. He peered through the sextant's telescope and pressed the squeeze trigger. The arm snapped into the handle.

Anthony jumped.

"Trip, I hope you understand what I'm saying to you," he said. "I have no idea where we are. We were caught in hurricane winds last night and blown out to sea, probably southeast. My first instinct was to motor west, but what if we run out of gas? So I thought, Head east, stay with the wind, but it might make more sense to go west, motor, and then tack back to land. I keep changing my mind. In some ways, what I am saying to you is that we are as good as dead on the water. No navigation equipment, except that toy."

Trip nodded, his body still turned toward the companionway.

"Rudimentary sailing skills. Caught in the Gulf Stream heading east. Though I think it might make more sense to head east. Then I'm thinking west."

"I'm going to take this up," Trip said.

"You understand we need to decide, east or west, but you want to play with the sextant . . ." Anthony blew on the surface of his coffee. "Nostradamus saw it all. He said, 'The red enemy will become pale with fear, putting the great ocean in dread.' Well, that's obviously nuclear submarines. The steps head clearly to nuclear war, but we want to reform our trade relationship with China. We are living in degenerate times."

Trip shifted his weight and hugged the pillow and the

sextant to his chest as Anthony spoke about the relative ease of death by drowning, the possibility of jumping over, the Mayans, the pyramids, and colloidal silver.

"The Serenity Prayer!" Anthony gasped. "It's on the pillow you're holding." He pointed and read the text on the pillow quietly, then frowned down into his coffee. "It always seems to appear in times of need. Don't run off. How many days sober did you have before last night? Please, sit."

Trip grimaced and sat.

"Sure, sure, that's not something you need to share. I'm sorry, you know. I'm sorry I dragged you into that. I was going on the big ten. A decade sober. My first few years, I had it down to the minute. I was that guy. Thirty days, eleven hours, and ten minutes since I last got high. Getting the thin laughter, until one day Jim was like, 'Nobody cares.' My sponsor, Jim. What's your poison, if you don't mind my asking?"

Trip set the sextant on the table.

"I'm heroin and alcohol. Ten years. Double winner. How are you doing, by the way? I imagine you'd like to be touching base with a sponsor. There might be one around." Anthony's eyes sparkled.

Trip reached for the sextant.

"It's a dragon quest," Anthony said. "A couple weeks ago, my dealer must have opened his third eye, because he showed up at my door. Just a polite hello in a thunderstorm. Ten years sober, but I came very close to buying. I saw some chocolate around here while I was looking for a way to save our lives." He stood and opened a few cupboards. "Ah, yes." He took down a box of strange-looking chocolates. "It's got a little bit of a bloom, but still quite nice. Only the best for Dick."

He held out the box. Trip looked at the half dozen chocolates spread between forty empty paper cups and chose one wrapped in foil.

"Hmm," Anthony said. "I stick with the squares. Usually caramel."

He took a chocolate. "There's no finish line. Just a daily accounting, a daily remembering. That's what people don't understand. Without the meetings, we somehow forget who we are."

Trip bit into his chocolate, and cream and syrup burst into his mouth, startling him.

Anthony nibbled his square. "Maybe you and I should have a meeting right now. Two addicts under one sail. We could start our own group. The Dead Men. No, The Remainers. More auspicious. The Remainers."

Trip swallowed and looked at the box of chocolates in Anthony's hand.

"Here, take the rest of the chocolates. We could meet right now, you know. We have all the materials. Dick's library has some of the literature, and what he doesn't have is here." He tapped his skull. "What am I saying, you just woke up. Let's get oriented, take stock. I'm cuckoo. Tonight I should be able to figure out what direction we're heading, choose a course. What if we just sailed with the Gulf Stream? Go where the wind blows? Wait until tomorrow, the meeting. I'll serve snacks."

"Is there a radio?"

"If you know how to build one out of coconuts. No,

we're probably just in the Gulf Stream. Ride her into a shipping lane. You'll navigate with that."

Anthony pointed at the sextant.

"I don't know how."

"You'll learn! It's a glorified protractor. We'll ride her to the Azores. Africa, maybe. I've always wanted to see Nairobi. It's an adventure. Of course, it might be more practical to head west. Easy enough to head east, just steer into the morning sun, out of the afternoon light. If you have supplies. We'll run into someone. It's not the Dark Ages. People are moving things all the time."

Trip touched the device.

"I feel good," Anthony said. "I needed this coffee."

That afternoon, Anthony laid out a squeeze bottle of witch hazel, two steaming cups of green tea, and a large wooden serving platter of peanut brittle.

"God grant us," he said coaxingly.

"God grant me." Trip hesitated.

Anthony spoke over him, reciting the prayer in a fulsome voice. When he got to the end, he said, "In NA we say 'God grant us,' not 'God grant me.' I guess that's one refinement we have made. Not an improvement, but a change. This is not an NA meeting. This is an AA meeting, because wine is your poison. I'm a two-time loser so I go both ways. Mmm."

Anthony winced with pain. He reached back into his mouth and withdrew a piece of cotton. He soaked it with witch hazel and tucked it back in. "Toothache." He smiled.

"Hazards of life at sea. What do you think if I read the preamble, and then you can read the twelve steps and the twelve traditions, and then I'll read a daily prayer."

He launched into a recitation from memory of the preamble, paused, lifted his cheek three times as if in a half smile to adjust his cotton ball, then opened an ultramarine leather edition of *Twelve Steps and Twelve Traditions*. "Could you please?"

Trip read carefully, conscious to read ahead so he wouldn't stumble.

Anthony raised a hand and interrupted him. "Excuse me, Trip, there's a prayer we should insert here." He looked up at the bulkhead and took a breath, then began to speak from memory. "May I be a guard for those who are protectorless, A guide for those who journey on the road. For those who wish to cross the water, May I be a boat, a raft, a bridge."[24]

"So do I keep going, or . . . ?"

"No, no, that's fine, Trip." Anthony lowered his gaze. "Why don't you start."

"Sure. Let's see."

"You forgot to introduce yourself." Anthony smiled strangely down at the book, then took it and set it on the galley countertop. "So, as you know, you would begin by saying, 'Hello, I'm Trip, and I'm an alcoholic.'"

"I'm Trip."

"And . . . ?" Anthony raised his eyebrows. "Traditionally, under more formal circumstances, we'd say, 'And I'm an alcoholic.' I think we should adhere to the format, to give us a container."

"And I'm an alcoholic?"

"Hi, Trip."

Trip locked his knees. He wondered if he should lie about something like that.

Anthony waited.

Trip turned to Anthony. "Hi," he said.

"It's fine. You're doing fine. A two-person group is new for both of us."

Trip bared his teeth and opened and closed his jaw. He did not stim often. Only when he was very upset.

"Okay. You know, that's just fine. Good. That's a good first-day-back share. It's a first day back for me too, come to think of it. Thank you. Thank you for that, Trip. Thank you for sharing. Hi, my name is Anthony, and I'm an alcoholic and a drug addict."

Anthony waited. He glanced at Trip expectantly. He nodded once, then said, "Normally, you'd greet me. So, you'd say . . ."

Trip grimaced.

"Ordinarily, you would say, 'Hi, Anthony.'" Anthony waited. "So, we'll go again. Hi, my name is Anthony, and I'm an alcoholic and drug addict. Double winner."

Trip blinked.

Anthony frowned and said, "Hi, Anthony," and launched into a long recitation of his life story, then came around to his struggles with addiction.

"Since you're a booze guy, let me tell a booze one," he said.

Trip assumed Anthony would talk about the party they had been to, but he didn't. The story he told seemed like one he had told dozens of times before. He went on for quite a long time, and Trip was having trouble following him.

Anthony said, "The real low was at a wedding of a childhood friend, a direct descendant of William Whipple, a lesser-known signatory of the constitution."

"Declaration of Independence."

"What?"

"William Whipple. He signed the Declaration of Independence."

"Yes," Anthony said. "He represented Portsmouth in the Provincial Congress, I believe."

"All of New Hampshire."

"Sure, sure. This means a lot in certain circles, but the family had fallen on relatively hard times. They'd spent what they'd inherited and were being forced to sell the Whipple house and move to upstate New York. I was one of a few people invited to a small party at the home, the night before the larger wedding ceremony."

"He freed his enslaved servant, Prince Whipple."

"No cross talk, please, Trip."

Trip kicked his legs out and smiled.

"No interruptions."

"Oh, right. Sorry. My dad tells me that a lot. I interrupt people a lot."

"Cross talk. Trip, please. I was careful not to drink too much, but you know how that goes. It got ahead of me, and the next thing I knew, I couldn't walk. They made me a place in the Whipple study on an elaborate daybed, the sort of thing that's handed down in great families. When I woke up early in the morning, I had—well, not to put too fine a point on it." Anthony laughed, but his voice had begun to wobble. "I had shit all over everything. Of course, this happens from time to time with heavy drinkers, but when it's you in the Whipple daybed, I think you could say it's a bit more vivid."

Anthony raised his hands to cover his eyes. His shoulders shook. Abruptly he was completely sincere. "In spite of the fact that I dislike what I am and find self-condemnation painful, still I have never given it up completely. When I begin to give up, I feel I'm losing my occupation, as though someone were taking away my job. There's nothing to hold on to . . ."[25] He dropped his hands and looked at Trip, as if waiting for an answer.

Trip grimaced.

Anthony wiped his eyes. "This has been helpful, Trip. Thank you. I was worried I was going on too long. But the old gears." He pointed at his temple. "Should we discuss some minor housekeeping?"

Trip tensed his arms and legs.

"First off, there's the question of the wet bar. With two alcoholics on board, strictly speaking, the safest thing would be to throw it overboard. However. Under our particular set of circumstances, when anything could happen, with both of us meeting in good faith, I propose that we keep the wet bar under lock and key. Metaphorically speaking, of course. What do you think?"

Trip grimaced.

"So, it's settled. Now, when should we meet again? We could meet twice daily. It's not as if we have much else to do. Of course, of course. You're right. Twice daily is excessive. I'm an old meeting . . . I like my meetings. Let's meet every day."

He took hold of Trip's hands and said the Lord's Prayer. Then he swung their hands back and forth. "Keep coming back, it works if you work it, so . . ."

22

Vic unwrapped a hard candy. He logged onto his Gmail, looking at the chat window. Above the little blank space was his last chat, telling Trip that he was worried about him, that he needed to reach out.

He had been typing messages into the chat window since the day Trip ran away.

"Hey," he typed into the chat.

He waited.

"I miss you," he wrote.

"There's something that I need to tell you."

"It's about Mom."

"She had an accident in Nepal. I guess she fell in the shower. I'm trying to call you. Please call me. It's important. You aren't in trouble."

"Mom is dead."

He tried to figure out how to delete the chat, then shook his head and closed the laptop.

He was not doing well. He was arguing with himself, giving the reasons why he needed to stay alive, but he could not help thinking it would be better to kill himself, find oblivion, put all his problems and concerns to rest. He knew how he would do it. He was thinking that over, wondering if he would do it that day, then arguing with himself, saying that he couldn't at this time, that Trip would need him. The problem was, it was unbearable, not knowing what had happened to his son.

He got up. He put on a shirt and shoes. He put his vape in his pocket and got Misty Two on her leash. Often when he felt this way, all he had to do was stop eating sugar and go walking, sometimes for a long time. Things, he knew, would seem different by the time he got back. Less heavy.

He sat on the floor. He was kidding himself. It did not get any heavier. He unwrapped another candy, thinking of oblivion.

"Let's talk about Trip."

Vic and I were in a nondescript, windowless conference room, sitting at an oval table, surrounded by the administrators from his middle school. Our son was thirteen.

The guidance counselor extended a bright bowl of hard candies, and I took one.

"I've read the reports from the school, and Sandra's emails, but I'd like to hear it from you now that we're face-to-face."

"He got angry with his best friend," Vic said. "I don't think he threw the first punch, actually, but he swung a bat, and his friend required stitches."

I said, "You know, Trip has been bullied at school a lot

of times, and I don't recall there being any meetings like this. I saw just the other day, out on the basketball court, he asked a kid for the ball, and the kid threw it right at his face. Trip asked for the ball again, and the kid rolled him on the ground and twisted his arm."

"Well, I didn't see the incident. Whenever you see something like that, you need to tell us."

"I did. I emailed you. I described the whole thing."

"Well, I don't recall that. But isn't it fair to say that Trip didn't require stitches?"

Vic scoffed. He irritably resettled himself in his chair.

"What are his grades like?" the principal said. She was white-haired and wore jeans and a chambray shirt, and had turquoise rings on several of her fingers.

"Mostly A's and F's," the guidance counselor said. "Trip's a bright kid. His attendance is poor. I've talked to him, and he told me he likes to watch reality television. He said he wants to be a plastic surgeon."

Vic and I traded looks.

"I guess he thinks that would get him close to celebrities?" the guidance counselor mused.

Vic shrugged. "I'm not aware of that as one of his career goals. But I have a thought. I know that Trip hates having gym first thing in the morning. I wonder if it would be possible to schedule it later in the day?"

"No," the principal said. "At this point, no. Schedules are all set. Everyone's schedule has been set for weeks."

"Okay. I just thought maybe that's one obstacle we can remove. If we can remove obstacles, the ones we can control—if we can accommodate him on the little things, maybe that'll help with the bigger, harder-to-pinpoint things. Like his poor attendance."

"Sure," the special ed coordinator said. "We appreciate that input and we do take that into account. Vis-à-vis the attendance, there's a name for that, which is school refusal. The Japanese call them *hikikomori*, a whole generation of children living in their bedrooms."

She seemed overmedicated. Her speech was slurred, and once she got started talking, she talked too long.

Vic adjusted himself in his chair again.

The special ed coordinator said, "I even found a treatment center in Oregon that specializes in school refusal. Of course, you have to be careful with these centers. A lot of them are just random dudes milking the insurance companies for money. So . . . you don't want that."

The principal nodded. "I'm interested in hearing what Sue has to offer."

"Sure." The behavior coach nodded. She said, "I can advise the parents, but sitting here, I've got to say I'm dubious. With teenagers, it takes a certain toughness."

"They've even got licensed therapists who come to your house in the morning and shoot your kid with water guns," the special ed coordinator said. "I put Trip on the waiting list for that, but it's . . . not cheap."

"What you have here, in my opinion, is a behavioral issue being masked by a diagnosis," the behavior coach said.

"He needs boundaries," Vic said. "We know that."

"It's a little late in the day for boundaries," the coach said. "We need to surprise him. Get him out of his comfort zone."

"Meaning?"

"You take away Trip's things."

"As in?"

"As in take away his furniture, his clothes, his phone, and his bed. Get him a steel-framed bed, get two outfits from the thrift store."

The principal nodded.

"I think I saw that on Montel Williams," I said.

"Well, okay. Another thought I had," Vic said. "He seems to be having difficulty with algebra. Maybe if we could move him to pre-algebra."

The principal shook her head. "We're nearing a point where Trip meets the legal definition of incorrigible, and at that point it's my duty . . . I would have to hotline him, and kick this up to the state."

"What's 'hotline'?"

"Child Protective Services. I'm afraid it's the law. It would be my legal obligation. Mom and Dad, we called this meeting to present you with a choice. We're giving you the option of taking the behavior coach's advice and restricting Trip's access to some of his possessions, or taking this up with the state."

"Legally, I don't think you can do that," Vic said. "That's part of what his IEP does, is protect him and us from that kind of thing."

The principal looked frustrated. She said, "Sending a boy to the hospital for stitches isn't covered by Trip's IEP."

"You can't take my phone," Trip said.

We had taken him out to a coffee shop to tell him, because we wanted to avoid a scene.

"It's how I talk to my friends," he said. He wore an oversize hooded sweatshirt and a gold chain.

"We don't have a choice," Vic said.

Trip stood up and walked away, toward Vic's car.

Vic took a sip of his drink. "I'll call to get his phone switched off."

He got up and paced while he talked to the phone company.

At the table across from ours, two girls Trip's age were sitting in front of open laptops, talking about celebrities and their veneers. Whose veneers were good, whose were not. For a second, I longed for that for my son.

Vic came back to the table. "It will take a few days."

"Thanks," I said.

His phone rang. He looked at the screen and said, "It's Trip." He answered the phone with a stern voice.

"We're waiting for you," he said, trying to sound parental. "No, we're not coming to the car."

He put his phone on speaker.

Trip said, "Can we just have the meeting like this? I'll gladly do the meeting like this."

"Fine, Trip. You can phone in."

"What?"

"You can do the meeting remotely."

I said, "You're not doing the minimum of your responsibilities, so you're only going to get necessities."

"Why are you talking like that?"

"Let's move on to the next thing," Vic said. "Money. You're not getting any more money—no allowance, no money from Grandma, nothing. I'm taking your debit card."

"Hold on, I'm coming back to the table."

"Okay."

He came back to the table and sat down. His phone was visible in his hoodie pocket. We didn't mention it.

"These are the ways you can earn some of your things back," Vic said. "These are just things we agreed on. I happen to have written them down. First is . . . let's see. Ah, yes. We'd like you to work with your therapist."

"I do work with my therapist. I see Dr. Cathy once a week."

"But you haven't been talking to her."

"I do talk. I talk a lot."

I rolled my eyes. "The second thing you can do is get good grades."

"I have good grades!"

"The third thing you need to do is follow a normal schedule. Wake up at a decent time, go to sleep at before eleven."

"I do that anyway."

"Trip, you don't."

Then it was extremely bright. Difficult to see, impossible to describe. A woman with the head of a horse exploded through the coffee-shop scene, brandishing a human torso. I turned away, toward a soft and smoky light, a more familiar group of therianthropes who were gathered around a single candle.

"Volunteer now, or I'll pick someone," an owl-faced lady said.

A desquamated head, perched on a pile of reproductive organs, cleared her throat. "I can go if no one else is ready to go. Do I need to give the history, or?"

"No, I don't think so. For now, let's just try to dump our brains!"

"Right. Okay. So, what? I guess I'll just say it. I think of Harvey Weinstein when I masturbate."

The creatures howled.

"Nineties? Or circa jail?" a pretty dog's digestive tract shouted.

"I know," the desquamated head said. "I'll tell you what, though, he definitely had the lowdown. He knew what he was doing, as far as that goes. In that particular area. I mean, he was a great fuck. I guess I'm the only woman who slept with him because I wanted to."

"That's why we're here," the owl-headed woman said. "Now, who's ready to go next?"

"I guess I could go," said an indescribable creature surrounded by flames. Her voice was nasal and soft. In flashes, she appeared to have a cow's face, but then she went back to being a soft, confusing light. She said, "Blake and I got back in touch about a year ago during the holidays. I told him I'd miscarried our child without knowing what it was. 'Not that it's your fault,' I said."

The pretty set of dog entrails laughed derisively.

The indescribable creature surrounded by flames turned to look at her.

"No cross talk," the owl woman said.

"Sorry," the entrails said.

"No cross talk."

The dog guts flashed the okay sign and readjusted herself against the wall. "I just feel like I've heard this one before."

A black pyramid in a tie-dyed headband stood. "My misery is undefinable," she said. "I feel stupefied, physically dirty and lethargic. I rent a room from an old man. He is a hoarder, and I sleep in the room where he keeps his boxes. I never graduated from college. I don't tell anyone my age. I date men who are in their late teens and early twenties, and this doesn't add to my social standing, which is poor. I am at the very bottom of a group of dusty thirtysomethings who drink heavily in bars. All of them get nervous when I bring Josh around. Every night, I compulsively pick a huge scabby booger from my right nostril. I worry about it, because that's how Francis Ford Coppola's grandmother lost her nose."

The black pyramid looked around nervously. "He said she was scratching it with a knitting needle, but I don't believe that."

23

PEOPLE IN FORMAL WEAR milled around, smiling and introducing themselves to one another. A woman I thought I recognized wore a navy gown with a silk wrap around her shoulders. She had her hair back-combed at the crown to give it height, and she wore a string of pearls. She had a nice smile. Her teeth were not white or straight, but they were clean and well cared for. Her eyebrows were arched like pleasant half-moons. She extended her hand and introduced herself. "I'm Ann."

"Ann," I said.

I knew that I was supposed to tell her my name. I could remember the basics of ordinary social interaction. I knew we were people, that we were at a gala or something. I knew what ordinary behavior under the circumstances was, but I couldn't remember my name, and I wasn't sure if I was a man or a woman.

The woman's brow wrinkled. "And you are?"

"Oh . . . Trip!" I said. "I mean, that's not my name. Trip is my son!"

She frowned and tilted her head to one side.

A small, frightened fish was making its way deeper into the water. I turned, and the white hull of a boat was several inches from my face. I started to panic, paddling toward the surface of the water.

Trip and the man were at anchor in the doldrums, below the equator in the South Atlantic, far from land and any other boats. There was no wind. The water was like glass. It was very hot and sunny.

Trip was sitting on deck with a sextant and a manual. He looked through the telescope directly at the sun. It burned, and he quickly moved his face away from the lens.

He lowered a few green shades over the telescope.

He lifted the telescope to look at the sun. It was green and eerie. He aligned the lower limb of the sun with the horizon.

He split the sun into two, one larger and one smaller. He adjusted the arm to keep the smaller sun visible. He rocked the instrument back and forth, and the sun traced a semicircle above the horizon. He adjusted it until the lower limb of the sun touched the horizon at the bottom of the arc.

He lifted his eye from the telescope, not noticing that the man on the boat with him had poked his head out of the companionway.

"Enough with that, please, Trip!" the man said. He went up the stairs onto the deck. "I can't bear to watch you clattering around with it anymore. Give it to me. Now, please."

The man held out a hand. When Trip didn't give him the sextant, he pried it out of his fingers.

The man held the sextant in one hand. He lifted his other hand up in the air. "Wind! We welcome you! Join us!"

Trip thought about a video game he liked. He visualized the different characters, saying their names in his mind. Berserker, Obliterator, Mutant, Ravager, Dual Launcher. He imagined that he was home again, and that we were all together.

The man let his hands fall. He said, "The wind is coming, Trip. Don't worry."

Trip stood and went down into the cabin. He dug through drawers in the galley.

He opened and closed several storage compartments. He found a tool drawer. He lifted and dropped gears and rubber hoses, then found a zippered bag full of cables. He brought it up to the man on deck.

"Right," the man said. "Wires."

"It's a cell phone charger."

"Well, I can plug it in, as you know, but what we need is wind."

24

Renata swam the breaststroke without lowering her head under the water.

Bart sat in a lounge chair under an umbrella. He was on a Zoom call. He wore swim trunks and AirPods Max headphones, and he had his computer on his lap. Every now and then he paused, turned ever so slightly to the right, relaxed his jaw, and pursed his lips. Then he went back to frowning and grimacing.

A few chairs over, Jody and Sylvia were bent over a Ouija board from the hotel game room. The planchette was missing from the set, so they had cut one from thick paper.

"Yeah, the poporo. That's right," Bart shouted. "It's a gourd. I call it a ball, and inside they have a mash of burned seashells and cocoa leaves. When they put it in their mouths, the lime from the seashells activates the stimulant in the leaves. Yeah, that might have had something to do with it. No, but they were very elegant men. Very beautiful. Skin lit from within, dressed in immaculate white from head to—well, not quite toe. They don't wear shoes."

The hotel's rear garage was visible from the pool area. Inside it, the property owner kept an antique carriage under a tarp. On the soil underneath the carriage, its former driver was resting his eyes. Though human at one time, he now looked like a rumpled blanket.

"They define *reincarnation* as the rebirth of the soul in a new body," Sylvia said. "*Reincarnation*, in English—I looked it up in the dictionary. It says 'Rebirth of a soul in a new body.' Then immediately I had to ask: What is the definition of *soul*? Again in the dictionary: 'spiritual or immaterial part of a human being or animal regarded as immortal.' With this definition we have a problem."[26]

"Sandra. Sandra Vernon. Sandra, we want to talk to you," Jody said.

I was startled. I came close and said, "I'm here."

"It's like that play," Sylvia said. "Some women are sitting in the courtyard of a medical clinic, talking about a book. In it, a pirate rapes a girl and throws her into the sea. The woman in the play says that, according to the book, we're all the pirate and we're all the little girl."

"Okay."

Bart lit a cigarette. "I told them I want you to take me with you, right? Up to the secret mountain."

I reached down and tried to move the planchette, to speak to Jody and the other woman, but I couldn't. Just like in the movies and cartoons, my fingers passed through it. The problem, of course, was that I didn't have hands. I only had the memory of hands, the habit of thinking they were there.

"So I asked them, you know, take me to the secret mountain. They sat there awhile. They worked their sticks in their balls. The older one says, 'We'll ask the spirit.'"

I tried again to move the planchette. I even tried to move it with my mind, but I couldn't do it.

Out in the shed, the former carriage driver, the being that looked like a rumpled blanket, rose through the soil and into the carriage seat.

Sylvia said, "In the play, one of the women says that even if she were born into the pirate's life and endured all of his privations, she still wouldn't rape a girl and kill her. And I wanted to say, there isn't a you."

Bart leaned forward, speaking a little louder than necessary. He said, "I assumed the men would go away and send someone back with a message, but the older man goes, 'We need a room to contact the spirit.' I'm like, 'A room, okay, we can do that. Any special room you have in mind?'"

The being living under the carriage skidded across the dirt and concrete toward the Ouija board. It resembled the carriage seat for a moment, perched on Jody's right shoulder.

I said, "Jody? It's me. It's Sandra. Can you hear me?"

Bart exhaled a column of smoke. "So, we take them to Nigel's office. Exactly. The man is a little too proud of his books. I want to tell him, 'Look, they are sold at bookstores. You are not the end-all just because you read them.' Anyway, the Kogis took a look in Nigel's office and immediately said it was unsuitable. They were taken to a few more faculty offices and then to some classrooms, but every room they saw was quote unquote 'unsuitable.' Unsuitable for contacting the spirit."

"Really, to talk about reincarnation, you have to talk about emptiness," Sylvia said. The being sat on her hand.

"But even if you have a glimpse of realization, understanding emptiness is difficult."[27]

The being slipped onto the planchette.

"So what I'm saying is, in order to talk about reincarnation and karma, you have to talk about emptiness. Shunyata. If you separate those two, you can't talk. But, this is difficult. To have even a glimpse of understanding—forget realization—of shunyata is difficult, because the moment we talk about emptiness we skid into thinking we are talking about nonexistence. When we talk about shunyata, it's difficult to think in terms of, 'She is also talking about the nonexistence of nonexistence.' This is difficult, and you'll find in most of Indian philosophy and especially Buddhist, every time we study nonexistence of something it's easier, but when we talk about nonexistence of nonexistence, it's always difficult to understand."[28]

The being jerked the planchette abruptly to the right to the letter *M*.

"Shh," Jody said.

She and Sylvia focused on the Ouija board.

"Yes, yes. Yes. Yes! Ha ha! So now the provost is basically—"

"Bart!" Jody said. "Shut up, please!"

He couldn't hear through his headphones. "The Kogis asked if they could look for a room on their own and, oh, in about ten seconds flat, they took over the ladies' restroom. They said it was suitable."

"Bart!"

"Yes, the ladies' restroom. I stood in there with them for a bit, but they were sitting on the floor, working their sticks in their balls, and sometimes talking to each other. After twenty minutes or so I felt bored and left."

Jody stood abruptly and walked over to Bart. She lifted one of the headphones off his ear and said, "Bart, please! Lower your voice. We are doing Ouija."

She sat back down.

Bart looked baffled and irritated, but quickly got off the Zoom call.

I had the thought that the being might be able to help me speak to Jody. I could ask it to move the planchette for me, and we could give Trip and Anthony's coordinates to her.

I said, "Excuse me?" I reached out to tap the being on the shoulder.

The being jerked up to face me. "Your son will die ironically."

"What?"

"Of thirst, surrounded by the water. Ha ha. Irony. That is . . . irony."

"I won't let it happen."

"There's nothing you can do except forget."

The wind lifted and caught the Ouija planchette and flipped it into the swimming pool.

The being from the carriage howled. "I have waited two hundred years!"

It exploded in a flash of darkness and rage.

"Shit," Jody said. "We had someone there. Renata? Do me a favor: Can you hand us that planchette?"

"Sure thing." Renata was on the other side of the pool.

She began to slowly make her way toward the paper planchette on the surface.

"Let's just make another one." Sylvia slipped the playing-card-size pool menu out of its plastic displayette and set it on their Ouija board. "This should work."

She and Jody put their fingers lightly on the pool menu and sat, looking around, waiting.

Bart put his headphones around his neck. "You do know they've scientifically proven you're moving that thing unconsciously."

"Thanks for that, Bart."

"You are welcome, Jody."

"Who's presenting this afternoon?"

"Me." Renata climbed out of the swimming pool and handed Jody the soaked planchette. She stood, dripping wet, in her black one-piece. "The being who was moving the planchette is gone."

"How do you know?"

Renata shrugged. "It's an educated guess."

"What are you presenting on?" Bart said.

"Just talking about what it's like to be possessed."

"When you are possessed, can you see what's happening?"

"It's kind of like . . . have you ever gotten blackout drunk?"

"Sure," Bart said.

"Okay, describe that. Be precise."

"I forget some stuff, some of it I recall as if in a pinhole camera, and some of it's just disparate images."

"It's like that." Renata picked up Bart's cigarettes. "I

didn't know they still made Kamel Reds. I used to smoke these in the nineties. They're so dorky, aren't they? I can't believe we thought this was cool. Still, brings back memories."

"Be my guest."

"I shouldn't . . ."

"Yeah, no, we get it," Sylvia said. "You are a horse, and if you eat fried food or smoke cigarettes, ghosts are able to ride you."

Jody laughed.

"Glad someone thinks it's funny." Renata took a cigarette from the pack and lit it. "Ghosts rape my soul. Har har. What a gas."

She and Bart traded meaningful looks.

"See, I don't believe in a soul," Sylvia said.

25

THE CANDLES FLICKERED, making strange patterns on the walls. Through the porthole, Trip saw the endless black glass of the ocean in the doldrums at dusk.

Anthony was deep into his share.

"My MBA is from the second-best business school in the South." He picked up a slice of apple and turned it in the flickering candlelight, then popped the apple slice into his mouth, winced, and switched it to the other side. "My credentials didn't mean anything. Word had spread. No one would touch me. I was radioactive in Manhattan. Have some apple."

He held a platter out to Trip.

Trip looked at it.

"You really must. It's delicious."

Trip blinked.

"I don't know how you can pass it up. But I love apple." Anthony set the platter down. "We moved back to Saint Simon. My wife's family opened all the doors. They had a party to welcome us, and it was, you know, beat out the old coonskin. Impress the redneck muckety-mucks. My wife ordered whatever *Vogue* magazine and the local wives told her she should wear that evening. I don't mean to insult my wife's appearance, just her conventionality. She was a pretty girl, but she absolutely kowtowed to expectation.

"So, the day came, and I took her to the best salon. She didn't drive. It wasn't because she was a submissive woman. It was because she had let her license lapse while living in the city and had never renewed it. Submissive, no. Quite the opposite. She wouldn't even do oral."

Trip looked away nervously. He picked up the charged cell phone, turned it on, and tried to dial 9-1-1. The phone had no connection.

"Pass that to me." Anthony held out a hand. "Really, it's not the time. Your generation. It's like a pacifier for you. Anyway, she told me to wait outside, because she didn't know when she would be getting out, and she didn't want her hair and makeup to melt in the humidity.

"I've had oral, of course, just never from my wife. Would you like more brittle?"

Anthony held out another plate.

"I find that my interests in sex are very ordinary, if you will, but then when it comes to porn, I'm more adventurous. I know this is a bit off subject, but I feel we can speak about these things?"

Anthony nodded once and set down the platter.

"I was waiting out front, good little capon, when I realized the salon was a couple blocks from the place where I'd scored heroin in the past. So, naturally, wanting to *be polite*"—he spoke with exaggerated emphasis on those words—"I drove over to say hello to my former dealer."

Anthony folded his hands in his lap and smiled. Trip

didn't understand the joke. He was confused. He kept his face completely still. The story, which Anthony had told him versions of before, made him feel like crying. He didn't know why.

Anthony frowned. "Well, my dealer wasn't home. I wondered if he even lived there anymore. It had been years. I got back in the car, thinking I'd go back to the salon, but then I thought, Maybe he's out. I don't want to be *rude*."

Anthony folded his hands and smiled again, waiting for Trip to share the joke with him. After a moment, he sighed.

"I sat in the car for one hour, two hours. I had been waiting long enough, I knew I wanted to score."

"Oh," Trip said.

"No cross talk. By this time, my wife had gotten out of her appointment. She waited in the salon, then she went downstairs to look for me. Unable to find castrato and car, too embarrassed to go back into the salon, she stood in the parking lot with an elaborate updo and makeup, hiding from her hairdresser. Meanwhile, the prize gelding despaired. I waited three hours, four hours. And lo, the miracle! My dealer returned. We fixed up together, like old times, got to talking."

"What were you guys talking about?" Trip asked.

"What?"

"You and your old dealer."

"Oh, right. Doesn't matter. Dealer things. Shooting the breeze. I think he had an idea for an invention, and so it was a lot of oohing and aahing on my part. The point is, I picked up my wife near sunset, seven sheets to the wind, high as a kite. To be honest, she looked like hell. There was no question of missing the party. The party was in our honor. Anyway, that was the first time she asked me for a divorce."

Anthony sighed.

"If I had it to do again, I'd demand oral. From the very first night, I'd say, 'You're going to do this for me.'" Anthony nodded assertively. "'You don't have to get on your knees, but this is a part of our life together. This is something I require.' My college friends are all CEOs, CFOs. Me, I'm . . ." He gestured down at his feet. "Lost at sea in a stolen boat. Last year, she called me and said she wanted to quit her job. I said, 'Don't quit, take a vacation.' She makes an excellent living. Frankly, it would be tricky to make things work without her income. I said, 'We can go to Bali together. I'll arrange everything. Don't lift a finger.' I bet you wonder why we live apart. Trip? Do you wonder why we live apart?"

"Oh."

"Please look up, Trip. It's just an ordinary courtesy. Let's do this properly. As I was saying, we're not divorced. You thought we were divorced. No, not even officially separated. Yes, paperwork has been drafted. But we haven't even made it through my pretrial motions. Actually, the day I met you, I was coming from her office in Arizona. We had been exchanging letters. Old-fashioned letters, with the stamp and the envelope. She had said she could use someone like me out there, so naturally, I thought there was an offer in place. I believed it *was* an offer. I drove out to accept in person. The grand romantic gesture. She took me to the canteen to tell me. No job."

Trip bent and picked up his cup from the coffee table. He drank the last sip.

Anthony raised his eyebrows. "Can I offer you another cup?"

Trip shook his head. "No!"

"No? Sure I can't tempt you? All right. As I was saying, Bali. First morning, halfway up the mountain, she has a mental breakdown. And it's my fault. If she'd bothered to read the itinerary, we could have canceled the hike. It's essential to summit at dawn! Otherwise, there's no point in climbing it at all. But it all comes back to communication and mutual respect, what I was saying earlier about oral."

Anthony's mouth turned down and his forehead creased.

"That night, she said, 'Why don't you run my father's AirBnbs in the Keys?' She didn't want to call it a separation, because then she'd have to talk to me. And I asked her then, even though I knew better, 'Will you please do oral one time before I take on the rentals?'"

Trip thought, Maybe this is a dream. Maybe there is no hurricane, and I will wake up at home, and it will be time to go to school. I will get into Mom's car, and I will go to class, and everything will be ordinary.

"She spent the rest of the vacation at the hotel. Something she could have done . . ." He paused for a moment. "Do you hear that?"

Trip kept his face still.

"Trip, did you hear that?"

Anthony stood and ran up the companionway. Trip followed him.

Above deck, less than a city block away on the port side, a pod of whales swam parallel to the boat, just visible in the moonlight.

"Let's use a little gas. This is a special set of circumstances," Anthony said. He started the engine and motored toward the whales. One slipped into the wake, swimming behind the boat. It was black and gray, weather-beaten, with teeth marks visible in its ragged fin.

Anthony blew the horn and the whale slipped out of the wake. He blew the horn again and the whales dispersed.

"Damn." He slowed, circling the dark water. He turned off the engine.

The pod of whales began to gather around the boat. They moved slowly and gently, raising their heads, then showing their tails. One whale lifted its head and seemed to smile. It slipped under the boat and turned its belly up and floated there beneath them, occasionally brushing the hull gently with a fin. It rolled back over and lifted its head out of the water.

Trip pointed. Anthony gasped. He turned on the engine.

"I'm just going to tap her." He motored toward the whale, tapping its side.

Its manner changed abruptly. It had been in a daydream, but it awoke. All the other whales disappeared underwater. It stayed. It looked directly at Anthony. After a moment, it disappeared. Trip watched the way the moon ran across the black water.

"Maybe we better get out of here," Trip said. "I have a bad feeling."

TRIP

"These are Southern right whales. They love people." Anthony held a finger to his lips. "These are highly intelligent beings, Trip."

There was silence, then a loud crash. The boat lunged forward ten feet. Trip toppled onto the deck, and Anthony caught himself on the rigging.

They heard the hull creak, then the sound of water trickling into the cabin below.

Anthony panicked. He gunned the engine, shooting off in one direction for a few minutes. When he stopped, they were both afraid it would happen again, but the whales left them alone. That was the end of the attack.

"Jesus Christ," Anthony said. "Jesus Christ. That bitch cracked the hull. Don't worry. I've seen YouTube videos on how to fix this. Before I get out the kit, though, I'll need a drink."

They went down, and Anthony got himself a tumbler of ice, then opened a storage cabinet and brought out a bottle of vodka. He poured himself a tall glass and drank.

"I need that just to lower my heart rate. I thought we were done. Don't let my bad example influence you. You're doing splendidly with your sobriety, Trip. Me and my relapsing . . . I guess that's what we old alcoholics do. Even Bill W. called for whiskey on his deathbed, you know. Of course, the motherfuckers didn't give it to him."

26

BERCHOLZ SQUINTED AT his reflection in the window of the hotel's tiny gym as he passed.

He suspected that his beard was purple. His colorist said it was in his mind. The beard looked better when it was clean and freshly combed, he knew that for sure. Sometimes he caught himself in a mirror and thought, My beard is purple. That's just all there is.

Inside his beard's reflection, Sylvia jogged on one of the treadmills. Her frizzy hair held by a drugstore elastic, she stomped loudly, rattling the machine's arms. She was the most attractive woman at the conference. Everyone wanted to bed her. She should be wearing support socks, though, Bercholz thought.

He turned to trudge up the hotel's rickety stairs, past portraits of the royal family, into his suite. He sat on his bed and opened his laptop.

"David," I said, thinking it was worth a try. "Hey, David."

He murmured to himself as he opened his email and searched for a link. It took him a few tries to get his Zoom up and going.

A dainty man in an absinthe-colored shirt appeared on

his screen, staring blankly. He saw David and brightened. "David. How are you?"

Bercholz waved. "Hi, Dr. Searle. I don't know. Days and nights reversed. I'm about to fall asleep sitting here."

"Oh, that's inconvenient."

"It's exhausting."

"Well, how's Nepal otherwise?"

"We've had a death, as you know. She was a . . . seemed like a nice person. Maybe a little neurotic. A little pinched. Something . . . melodramatic in her gestures. A certain coarseness. She was not intelligent. The wordiness of the stupid . . ." Bercholz tightened his lips. He looked out the window, down at the hotel grounds, then back at his psychiatrist on the screen. "Like many homely women of a certain generation, she seemed apologetic for her physical being. Thick of thigh. Gauche and drawn."

"Could you close the shade so that I can see you properly? You've got the light behind you there."

"She had a big nose." Bercholz stood to close the curtain. "The nose is important on a woman."

Down below, an SUV with a flashing yellow siren pulled up the private road. The driver stopped and honked twice.

Bercholz sat.

"Ah, thank you," his psychiatrist said. "Nice to speak to a face. So, how are you feeling about presenting?"

"Fine. This is what I do, though with all the fakers and Facebook stalkers, it's complex."

"Sure, sure. So no anxiety. That's good. And when do you go up?"

"What? Oh, next week."

"Who's presenting this afternoon?"

"I don't know. I'll be fast asleep."

"Sometimes it's best to stay awake and power through. Maybe you could try that today? Drink a few espressos. Exercise. Do what you have to do to stay awake once. Go to the talk, whoever it is?"

"I can't. It's too sad. I don't know how the others are doing it, with their Ouija boards and doing the whole give-a-paper thing. Life is so ugly. It's so cruel. Benito eating sausage and eggs and saying how bodies and minds are the same thing. Arm is a thought, apparently, oh, delicious sausage. Oh, by the fucking way, a woman is dead. She may not have been graceful eating with a knife and fork, her clothing may have been all stretch fabrics, but she is dead. Died alone in a toilet. No sense of personal style and an unusual number of flyaway hairs, but . . . At least Bart is offering something. Feeding the dead. I would think she would appreciate that. Unlike Benito, who's all talk. Apparently, Larry thinks he's a genius."

"Remind me, who's Larry again?"

"He's a world expert on death and the afterlife. I missed his presentation. Slept right through it."

"Can I say something, even though it may be difficult to hear? I want to suggest you stay awake today, even if it's hard, and go to a talk. Get in the spirit of things. No pun intended."

Bercholz's face fell. "Unbelievable," he said.

His psychiatrist shrugged.

"I need a refill. That's what I've been needing to ask

you. If you can email it to me, someone at the hotel can run out for it."

"That'll work?"

"The pharmacists just need something. It's not like ten years ago, but it's still pretty loose compared to the U.S."

"I can do that," his doctor said. "I want you to do something for me: Go to the presentation on, uh, what was it? The woman who interested you?"

"Renata? Yes, she's got something very few women these days do."

"Yes, that's it. Go and ask her a question."

"Sex appeal."

"I'll write that prescription."

"Good taste. That was a joke. It's grace. Grace. All right, then."

Bercholz closed his laptop, crawled onto his bed, and fell asleep.

27

Donald, Sylvia, Horace, and Larry weren't able to see the old waiter sitting at their table. He was staring at me, pantsless, wearing a white uniform jacket, his arms and legs just a trail of smoke.

Donald said, "I tell my students it can happen quite easily to someone who is startled. When I was a kid, I was hit in the back by a firework, and my mind shot up overhead."

Larry nodded absently as he flagged the waitress and ordered milk tea and *papad*.

The dead waiter pointed at me. "Haven't I seen you around here before?"

"Nothing for me." Donald shook his head.

"I'll take a gin and tonic," Horace said.

Sylvia nodded. "Make it two."

"I do know you."

The waiter gathered the menus and walked away irritably.

The dead waiter nodded. "You sent Trip to a facility."

"Some people hear that story and tell me I dreamed it," Donald said. "It was all my imagination. I say, Go ahead and believe that, if you want to believe that stupid thing."

"Some of the professors at Sarah Lawrence use nitrous a lot," Horace said. "They call themselves the Crazy Crew. They say they get out-of-body like that."

"Nitrous? And this works?"

Sylvia shrugged. "So they say."

"Wait, really?" Donald said. "I'm surprised everyone doesn't try it. I might like to."

"Someone in the seventies started it. He wrote about it in his book, but he disguised the fact that he was using nitrous, because he worried that people would discredit his research."

"He was a businessman who got his nitrous from his dentist. He accidentally discovered this shortcut through recreational use," Sylvia said.

The dead waiter pointed at me. "You could do that."

"What? Get out-of-body?"

"Go in, dummy."

"I can't even move a planchette."

He shook his head. "Don't you remember the first night?"

"What?"

"He told you exactly how to do it," he said. "You go into somebody, like that woman who's a horse. You call your husband. You tell him where Trip is. Zip zap zup. I mean, give a general idea. Your husband doesn't even know he's on the water. Or if you can't talk, maybe you can walk. A lot of people can just walk—that's what they call zombies. So if you can just walk, you go to your husband and do a lot of pointing at old pictures and bodies of water. They have those things now with all the words. I see them sometimes at parks."

"Communication boards? They're not exactly common. How long have you been here?"

"Here . . . ?"

The living waiter set down a basket of *papad*. Donald snapped off a piece. He bit into it and winced, then sat bolt upright, his hand to his mouth.

He held his napkin to his mouth and gingerly spit out both halves of his upper bridge. He examined them.

"Damn it. Not again."

"Donald, what happened?"

Donald looked up at the others and smiled, revealing that he was toothless.

"I guess I might have an opportunity to try this out at the dentist tomorrow."

"What?"

"That *papad* snapped my bridge."

Renata was on the phone with room service. She was sitting on her bed, holding the landline receiver, listening to canned Ravi Shankar.

A recording of a woman's voice periodically interrupted the music. "All the lines are currently busy. If you want to keep the song, press any button."

She thought the recording was encouraging her to push a button and download a song onto her laptop. It was just where her mind went in that moment. She wasn't really paying attention.

I tried to remember everything the man had said over dinner that first night. If I had been alive, it wouldn't have been possible to jump right in, but I was not alive, and my mind was sharp and clear.

When I focused, my memory was perfect. I went over what the man had said.

"I got a vessel and placed it on a platform marked with the diagram. I think I have it here. Yeah, here it is." He had turned his phone toward Larry, and though I was not conscious of it at the time, it had faced me for a moment, and now I could see the diagram and read the word perfectly. "You can set the vessel down like a cup and write the word inside it with a piece of chalk, or you can flip it over and write it on top."

There was a clicking sound, and a woman from room service said, "Yes, good morning, ma'am."

"Oh, a real person," Renata said. "Finally."

"I'm sorry we kept you waiting, ma'am. What would you like to order?"

"Classic English breakfast with tea. No toast!"

I pictured the platform and the diagram. I was surprised. When I was alive, my visual imagination had not been great. But in death, it was detailed.

"You want classic English breakfast tea?"

The diagram faded.

"No," Renata said. "I want the classic English breakfast breakfast, no toast. No toast!"

"Ma'am, I'm not getting you."

I pictured the diagram again. I imagined setting the top of the vessel on a platform. It rolled onto its side. I imagined righting it. It rolled onto its other side. I took a deep breath and imagined flipping it over.

"What would you like to order with that?"

"Tea."

The picture was gone. I had to begin again.

"I went down to breakfast this morning and no one was there. I had to walk down the hill to get chai from the stall, and the sugar in it really got my apertures permeable. I am a horse. May I speak to someone else? I need somebody who can speak English."

"I'll call you back."

"No, don't call me back. Put me on hold."

"Okay, hold, please."

I pictured the diagram and the vessel. Now I just had to write the word on it with a piece of chalk. I opened my eyes.

Renata sat on her bed and leaned back on the pillows. The Ravi Shankar had resumed.

A man came onto the line. "What would you like to order?"

"Classic English breakfast with tea, no toast," Renata said, "and an Indian breakfast with *idli* and coffee."

"That's two breakfasts, no toast, ma'am."

I closed my eyes and imagined a piece of chalk in my hand. I wrote the word.

I felt a strong wind. I was blown by this wind through an aperture in Renata's cranium, down into her body.

The interior of Renata's body wasn't like a drawing in a medical textbook. It was its own cosmos, with its own style and order. It was a nautical culture. The inhabitants spent their entire lives at sea. I was drawing closer to the surface of the water. Flecks began to distinguish themselves as watercraft—yachts and speedboats, pontoons and container ships. And then I felt what I could only describe as a profound "no" phenomena, and the winds reversed. I was shot up out of the aperture, and I landed on the duvet beside Renata.

"What would you like to have with your classic English breakfast? Any juice?"

"I mean, orange. Whatever. I really don't—I've got a spirit in here trying to possess me."

The man paused. "Orange juice. And how would you like your eggs?"

I closed my eyes and pictured the diagram. I pictured the vessel.

Irritated, Renata stood and went to her suitcase. "Scrambled," she said, rummaging for something.

"And would you like the gluten-free bread basket to accompany that?"

I got the chalk, and I wrote the word. I felt the winds blowing.

"Aha." Renata pulled a teal beret out of her suitcase. She separated a sock that was attached to it by static and put it on her head. "Let's keep it simple," she said.

The man laughed. "No bread."

"I've got my hat on now. This hat was blessed by some powerful sorcerers. You won't be able to get through the hat, so you might as well move along to greener pastures."

"Ma'am, I'm not getting you."

Renata hung up the phone.

I pictured the diagram and wrote the word. I felt the wind, but the hat blocked me, just like Renata said.

I wondered who I could possess. I considered possessing the man on the boat, but that would not do any good. Trip and I would just be stuck together. I thought of Vic, and remembered the graduate students who lived next door to us.

I found them in their kitchen, standing at the counter near the stove, staring at a steaming beef bone on a cookie sheet.

"I think, can't you just push it out?" the girl said. "I feel like when I've had marrow before, it's just kind of pushed out."

The boy frowned. "I think that's osso buco. This is different."

"I feel like I've had it with a special spoon."

"That's osso buco."

The boy opened a drawer and took out a rolling pin. He swung it at the bone, which shot off onto the floor. The girl went and picked it up. She got a pot holder and gripped the edge of the bone. The boy paused, looking at her. She nodded, and he swung.

I tried to jump into the boy, but I was thrown back out.

"Let me try," the girl said.

I jumped inside the girl, a strange landscape of red light and horses. Yes, this is going to work, I thought, but then I kept going down, down, until I was pushed languidly through her legs onto the kitchen floor.

The girl swung the rolling pin and the bone splintered. She got a second pot holder from a hook on the wall and grasped the bone in both hands and twisted.

"Get the toast," she said.

TRIP

I tried to enter the boy again, and I was in an Italian restaurant. Two middle-aged men were having a drink at a bar.

"I've got to get my car fixed," one said.

The wind shifted, and I was out again, sitting on the floor by my neighbor's loafers.

28

A BLOODY SAFETY PIN, bent out of shape, sat on the small ledge under the bathroom mirror, next to a few wads of bloody toilet paper. Anthony had lanced the abcess above his bad tooth the night before. Trip peed and lifted the gray lever beside the ship's toilet. He pumped it ten times to drain the bowl. He clicked the valve on the left-hand side to allow fresh water to come in and pumped the lever ten more times. He knew there was something else he had to do. He looked at himself in the mirror.

In the galley, the bilge pump wheezed. They had tried to seal the cracked hull with underwater epoxy, but it wouldn't set properly. Anthony found a repair kit, but its poppet was missing and he couldn't inflate it, so he covered the crack with duct tape. It seemed to work, but the tape had come off in the night. About an inch of water sloshed around the cabin where Anthony was passed out in his bed.

The last apple sat on the counter. Trip picked it up, took a bite, and dropped it. He looked around for a mug but couldn't find a clean one. He drank water from the distiller in one cupped hand. Anthony was snoring, and Trip thought about shaking him awake, but instead he got the sextant and took it up to the deck.

He looked through the glass. It was soothing. He found the sun, split it in two. He brought the little sun down to the horizon, rocked the sextant. He got a reading, checked his watch. He crept back down to the cabin and began to look for a map.

Anthony slept through most of the day, and Trip sat on deck, working with the sextant.

Late in the afternoon, he heard a string of curses.

"Trip," Anthony said as he came up. "May I speak to you? You left the toilet valve open again."

He had a slight lisp, from speaking around the toilet paper wadded in his cheek.

"I have told you again and again, you must close the valve after flushing. You let in sea water. It was overflowing, must have been for hours. That along with the hull crack, and we have a few inches of water down there. This is life and death, Trip. If we hadn't had the bilge going, it could have really done some damage to the ship. It could have sunk us. Do you understand that? As it is, I woke up to water sloshing around the cabin."

Trip drew an '*X*' on the map.

Anthony went down the companionway. After a moment, he came back up. "Did you take a bite out of the last apple?"

Trip was deep in thought.

"I will take that as a yes."

The mechanical bilge pump wheezed in the darkness. Trip had grown accustomed to the sound. He sloshed through ankle-high water in the cabin, past the small berth where Anthony slept curled on his side, to the companionway. He raised his head out, looked for ships, and lowered the hatch.

He walked back past the small berth where Anthony snored fitfully, like a puppy. A woven bag of lemons and oranges swung lightly from the ceiling in the galley. Trip touched it, wanting unconsciously to steady it, and he felt Anthony's cellular phone in the net.

Anthony blew out through his lips.

Trip slipped the phone out of the net.

"It's pot-au-feu," Anthony said.

Trip turned. Anthony was sitting up in bed, eyes open. He blinked, then turned and buried his head in the pillow. The bilge wheezed.

Trip went up to the deck. He turned the phone on, went to settings, and scrolled down to "Emergency SOS via Satellite."

The phone screen was black. In the middle was a large gray circle, surrounded by smaller gray circles. The phone said, "Looking for a signal. Turn right to find a satellite." He walked around the deck, moving the phone right and left. A gray arrow connected the smaller gray dots.

It locked onto something. The circle began to swipe green. It said, "Keep pointing at the signal."

Then all at once the green cleared. "Not connected. Next satellite available in one minute."

After a few minutes, the phone caught another satellite. The upper ninety degrees of the circle turned green, and a circle with a dash on either end, representing the satellite, hovered on the outer edge of the ring of small circles.

"Connected. Keep pointing at satellite to send and receive."

"Help," Trip texted.

"This is the USAFRICOM. What's your position?"

"Can satellite determine position?"

"I can't determine it from here. Do you have access to Google?"

"Hmm," Trip wrote.

The phone was not connected to the internet by cellular data. It was connected by satellite. He opened a browser and searched, "What is my latitude and longitude."

The answer came back: -3.243993, -27.735565.

Trip got distracted, realizing he could check his email. He logged into his account.

A chat from his dad caught his eye. He scanned a few lines, then came to one that startled him. It said, "Mom is dead."

That was a really weird thing to write.

He opened some other emails. Sometimes I don't understand subtextual meaning, he reasoned. The other emails offered condolences. His guidance counselor from middle school wrote, saying he was so very sorry for his loss. He opened an email from a girl at school. "I heard your mom is dead. Are you okay?"

Pinpricks went down his spine into his stomach. It wasn't possible.

Anthony's phone began to ping wildly in his hands. He looked down and saw hundreds of texts rolling in from Lancaster.

Something flew past him, and he started, dropping the phone. It bounced off the edge of the deck, down into the sea.

Trip could see it as it sank, like a little luminescent fish diving for the bottom. He watched it for what felt like a long time, the light disappearing downward. Then it flickered out.

He hadn't sent the coordinates when he had the chance. His mom was dead. Everything was quiet except the bilge wheezing below.

29

DONALD HAD TAKEN a long car ride to the nearest town to see a dentist recommended by the hotel manager.

Her examination room had white walls and a chair like you'd see in America, but her ceiling was painted emerald green, and at the foot of the chair was a built-in shelf full of paperback books and personal effects—a tribal headpiece, a beaded Smarties box, a line drawing of a pair of saggy boobs.

She palpated the fistula above Donald's tooth with an ungloved finger. Clean and well groomed, with short, unpolished nails, she wore a calf-length skirt, a blue surgical mask, and a pair of glasses with external magnifiers.

Donald wore a paper bib over his chest. His bridge was on a tray beside the chair, in two pieces.

The dentist picked up a metal scaler and tapped the tooth below the fistula with its handle. Donald gasped in pain.

"Sorry." She set the instrument down and lowered her glasses to look at the X-ray.

"I see some bone loss under this old root canal. What I suggest is we go back in."

"I really just came in about the bridge," Donald said. "Is this root canal something to address when I get home?"

"Better not to wait. This could flare up anytime. I'd recommend we start now."

Donald sighed.

She got him numb and put sunglasses over his eyes. She put on gloves, cranked him back, and swung her Leica surgical microscope over his mouth. She rolled her chair forward, positioning his head between her thighs, and gazed down into the viewfinders at the tooth. She started to drill. In a moment, she was jamming, totally confident, rattling away inside his jaw.

Donald began to weep. The cave, Sandra in the bathroom, a broken bridge, and now an emergency root canal.

The dentist paused. She did not crank him up. She handed him a tissue and said, "Would you like nitrous?"

He blew his nose and balled up the tissue. "Yes, please."

"Let's do it." She held up a wastepaper basket and he tossed the tissue in.

She set the bin down, took off her gloves and threw them in, and reached behind Donald for a gray rubber mask. She placed it gingerly over his nose, got it in place, then leaned and cranked the dial. "We'll just give that some time."

Donald wiped his tears with his hand.

The dentist slipped on a new pair of gloves and picked up Donald's bridge. She rolled over to the sink and examined it.

"This is good work," she said. "Of course, we can't use it now."

She murmured to herself as she looked at it more closely, apparently unable to decide whether it was worth keeping.

She rolled her stool back to Donald and demonstrated that his bridge was beyond repair by poking it with a finger. "Shall I throw it in the trash?"

The nitrous was strong, and Donald was having a little trouble connecting to what she was saying, though he understood perfectly.

"Here, you keep the bridge and take it home with you to the States." She tucked it into his shirt pocket.

Donald was quiet.

"Where was it made?" She rolled back to the sink, took off her gloves, and washed her hands.

"In China." Donald began to giggle. "Chinese . . ."

"So, you were in China. Do you know how to fold a dumpling?"

Donald shook his head and shrugged.

"I can make samosas, but I don't really like them. Too greasy. Nepali food is all so greasy."

"Oh," Donald said. He forgot himself and let his toothless smile show.

"Every now and then, at teatime, if I've missed lunch and the samosa is very small . . . I can enjoy one. Otherwise, I prefer sushi."

"Well . . . I'm through with you."

The dentist threw her head back and laughed.

"I mean it. I'm through with you."

"You can let me fix your teeth, but you can't talk to me as a friend anymore."

"Ya." His voice sounded a little strange, a little nasal, because of the mask.

The dentist moved her exam light in front of Donald's mouth. "Open."

Donald opened his mouth, and she felt his upper gums.

"Will you get a load of these two," a voice said.

A man floated down from the ceiling. He was in his fifties, nice-enough-looking. He wore a dark suit and an off-white turtleneck sweater. He was conservative looking, except that in place of one of his arms, he had a dull black crow's wing.

He peered into Donald's mouth. "Looking bad," he said. "No teeth left there. Barely." He fluffed his feathers.

The dentist grabbed Donald's remaining upper molar with her fingers and pressed, then bore down firmly. "We can keep this tooth," she said, breathlessly. "This tooth is extremely strong."

"She seems like a nice person," I said.

"Yesterday she installed a molar sideways," the man said. "I didn't even think it could be done. And she's giving bad advice."

"What?"

"You save the tooth today. In five, six years, your friend is having a root canal. A few years after that, someone is extracting it. I can see it all. I can read his teeth like . . ."

"Are you a dentist?"

"No. I'm a travel agent."

He handed me a business card. I looked down. The characters were Chinese, but I read "Guanzhou Xingyun Travel Company" and his address and name.

"Sorry, bit difficult. I'm right-handed." He pointed at the wing. "You'll see. After about three weeks, your old habit of viewing your body in a certain way and thinking you're you dissipates. In my case, I am turning into a crow, so my right arm often looks like this."

He fanned the black crow's wing.

"How can you tell Donald will lose a tooth?"

"You can just see it. Look for yourself."

I looked down into Donald's mouth at the tooth in question, and I could see it. I could see the root canal taking place in five or six years. I could see the fingers of the endodontist who would perform the procedure, and I could see the dentist extracting the stub a few years later.

"I handle executive travel all around China. Better than A&K. I took some Kodak executives up the Chang last year. I can show you the Silk Road, People's Park, Army for the Afterlife. Actually could be quite interesting for you."

"Are you okay with more nitrous?" The dentist turned the dial. "You can kiss the sky. I'll give you a little extra."

Donald breathed deeply. He closed his eyes and began to drift. I could see this too. I could see that Donald flew high.

"Whoa." The travel agent nibbled at his feathers. "He is so high he can barely move. I bet you could get into his body."

"What?"

"Robert A. Monroe–style. You know?"

I nodded. "I think I do, actually." I told him about Trip and the man on the boat, how they were out on the ocean off Florida. I told him where they had been the last time I saw them.

"Shame." He shook his head. "I wish I could have helped arrange it. I can charter yachts. I do the whole crew."

Donald opened his eyes. He saw me and sort of lifted the corner of his mouth. "San nah."

The dentist chuckled. She brought her surgical microscope back into place and resumed jamming.

Disoriented, Donald executed the mental activity to roll onto his side and get up out of the chair, but his body didn't move. It stayed right where it was, and a second, chimeral version of Donald rolled over and stood, unaware of the body behind him.

Donald executed the mental activity to walk. Again, his body stayed on the chair. But his second self, the light-Donald, took a few steps and paused in the middle of the dentist's office.

"Sandra," he said.

His body was still lying in the dentist's chair.

Bewildered, his light-body looked around. "I'm confused. It occurs to me . . . I don't understand what is happening."

"Not to worry," the travel agent said. "You're, uh . . ." He snapped the fingers on his human hand. "Frustrating. It's on the tip of my tongue."

"Donald," I said. "I'm going to borrow your body." I pointed to it.

He turned and saw his actual body on the dentist's chair. "That's not . . . something I'm up for."

I pictured the diagram, the vessel. I could feel the travel agent watching me. I turned.

He was imitating me. He held a piece of chalk. In front of him was a vessel, resting on a diagram like mine, but much finer, with more depth, in richer colors.

"What are you doing?" I said.

He shrugged.

"Are you visualizing it, too?"

"I might like to have a body again," the travel agent said. "The truth is . . . you know . . . in life, I never experienced the things I wanted to. I have some regrets."

"Why does yours look like that?" I said. I turned back to my diagram, which looked like a child's drawing.

He shrugged. "I was always good at art."

I felt a strong wind pulling me and the travel agent in through the top of Donald's head.

30

DONALD AND I saw each other just as I was passing into a follicle on his scalp. We were distracted by each other then. It happened at a glance, just a moment before I passed into his body.

We were in an antique mahogany bed with a large and elaborately carved headboard. A hand-stitched velvet quilt was pulled up over our laps.

Donald said, "I would like you to pee in my mouth, then tie me to the staircase and go out and find a different man. Bring him back here and fuck him right in front of me." He paused. "That's normal these days, right?"

Donald wanted to scramble eggs for me in the morning and wait under the table so that he could eat me out while I had eggs and said specific things that degraded him.

The kitchen was a sunny room in the rear of the house, with a banana shrub growing outside the window behind the sink, and expertly hung polka-dot wallpaper without any pattern overlaps.

We were in a dry landscape, everything white, waterless, shale. He lifted the cover on the cistern and ladled green water.

I walked up the narrow servant stairs off the kitchen to the bedroom. I flopped stomach-down on the floral-printed duvet, then grabbed a decorative pillow and tucked it under my chest. During all this, we were hovering above Donald's scalp. It took a fraction of a second but felt like weeks. I stared at the wallpaper—loose lavender blossoms—and felt my heart rate slow.

Donald wanted to get down on his knees. He wanted to eat me out with clips on his nipples, attached to each other by a chain. He wanted me to put a small weight on the chain. Afterward, he wanted to be held down and raped. He wanted to wake up in the morning, get on his knees, eat my ass while I washed my face and applied creams or whatever. Flossed. While I went about my morning routine, he wanted to stay beside me on his knees. He wanted another couple to come over, and he and the other guy would eat me and the other woman out, taking turns. Then he wanted me to take him and the other man to the bedroom. He would kneel on the floor and watch while the other guy fucked me. Afterward, I would wipe myself off in Donald's hair.

The upstairs bathroom had two tubs. One was a larger-than-average porcelain tub, and the other was a smaller antique sitting tub, big enough to sit cross-legged in, with an odd faucet you worked by lifting a metal plug upright, then turning it clockwise.

The window was lavender-and-green stained glass—a white vase with a single broad purple stripe, full of cuttings from a green tropical plant. I opened the cabinet. There were all kinds of toiletries—soap, toothbrushes, toothpaste, lotion, tooth powder, floss—four or five of each thing, lined up.

Donald didn't like the bathroom's layout. From an energetic perspective he said it was wrong. The toilet was directly facing the door. He said that allowed positive energy to escape the room, and trapped negativity. He also disliked that the mirror faced the toilet, which, he said, aside from the obvious, created a loop.

I reached for the toilet paper, felt something strange, looked down, and saw a long, glowing tentacle in place of my right arm. I grabbed it and hugged it to my chest. I closed my eyes, then opened them and saw my right arm.

Donald said, "Look, if you must stay in there, at least let me hang some nice pictures. Arrange some succulents."

"Whatever is fine."

I explained that Trip had always liked cars, but after seeing the Disney movie *Cars*, his interest in cars became more *Cars*-specific. By the time he was five, it was sometimes easier to reach him, conversationally, if one spoke in the voices of his favorite *Cars* characters. There was a period when I went into revolt and refused to talk in those voices, but Vic kept doing them, and it was around that time that Trip switched. He had always been more my child, but when I stopped talking to him in the voices of the cars, he began to love Vic more.

Donald had me take him to a jewelry store. We rode together in a *tuk-tuk*. He wore a ball gag in his mouth. I had him open his pants and take out his dick. We drove through the streets. At the jewelry store, I picked out different pieces, had the salesman put them on Donald, who modeled them outside, walking in front of the store. We did something sexual in the jewelry store. It was starting to blend into everything else.

It was late. I was sitting up against the headboard of the bishop's bed, my legs tucked under the covers. I rubbed my eyes with my hands.
    I said, "Do you remember how you died?"
    "I'm not dead. I'm just getting my teeth done."
    "Oh, right."
    "We're passing by each other."
    "There are things I never want to forget."
    "Like what?"
    "About Trip. The web of red veins on his eyelids, and the bluish patch on his forehead above the bridge of his nose. The furriness across the back of his shoulders, two pencil-dot birthmarks on his left cheek. The pulse in his neck. A crease that runs from his shoulder to the upper part of his chest. The little flat, parallel lines below his fingernails.

Dancing with him and Vic when he was a kid. The jokes he wrote. The stories he told. His intelligence. The way he sometimes seemed to know things he couldn't possibly know. The three dimples at the base of his middle, ring, and pinkie."

"You'll forget those things, too. You'll forget everything."

I felt a strong wind. It blew us down, deeper into Donald, and circled us back up.

And then I was sitting in the exam chair at the dentist's office.

31

Anthony was passed out below.

Trip had not moved from the deck. The ocean was calm. He lay on his tummy, watching the water. There was no moon. The blacknesses above and below were indistinguishable.

A pale light moved toward the surface, dazzling him for a moment. It moved gently through the water, a blue neon cap with a dozen long tails, reminding him of *The Gaurea*.

He watched the jellyfish awhile longer, then went down and got the sextant.

32

I WAS INSIDE Donald's body.

The dentist swung her surgical microscope out of the way. She took her hands off Donald's shoulders.

"We were worried," she said.

I was looking at the green ceiling. Donald's body felt energetic—healthy. I tried to sit up, but his back seemed to lag behind my impulses. I wanted to touch something, but when I moved my arm, I was only able to kind of lift it and let it drop.

"The nitrous really knocked you out. You should have told me you might have that kind of reaction. I have other options for anesthesia. The procedure went very well, otherwise. I put in orders for your bridge, so we'll get you back in next week. Until then, soft foods, baby your remaining tooth."

I tried to stand, but my control of Donald's legs was limited. They moved like Jell-O underneath me.

"You're still groggy from the nitrous."

The brush of her hand on Donald's skin distracted me, and I lost control of his body. The dentist office receded, and the marshy interior of Donald's insides began to waver in my peripheral vision.

"Do you think you can stand now?"

The other world inside Donald dissipated. I said, "Rgh."

"Let me get someone to assist us."

She and another dentist in the practice helped me to the doors of the clinic, where I could see Donald's driver parked out front in a little car. The dentist opened the door. As they helped me into the back seat, the beige upholstery appeared to be made up of a million points of multicolored light.

"Climate is good, sir?"

"Margh."

"Back to the hotel, sir?"

"Grrble."

Donald had a cell phone in the back pocket of his jeans. I pressed down into the floor of the car with my right heel to lift Donald's right hip.

"Sir, is there a problem?"

"Blar."

I pressed the heel in and wedged Donald's knee in against the driver's seat. I shook the thigh back and forth, kicking the seat with Donald's knee.

"Sir?"

I spent the entire drive home trying to get the phone. When the driver came around to open the rear door, I still hadn't gotten it.

"Saa!" I said.

"Let me just help you," the driver said. He tried to take a hold of Donald's arm.

I said, "Saa! Saa!"

The driver stepped back, regarding me.

I said to the driver, "Ka? Ka. Ka."

The driver frowned.

I lifted Donald's bottom off the seat and pointed it out toward the driver. "Ka! Ka!"

"You want me to make a call?"

I nodded violently.

He took the phone out of my pocket carefully. "What number?" He held up the phone.

I couldn't point. I didn't have that level of accuracy. The driver didn't know what to do. We needed a board with the numbers big enough to point to, but the driver didn't think of that. He apologized and returned the phone to me and helped me inside.

A bellhop laid me down on the bed in Donald's room. "You wait here. I'll get someone."

I was able to roll off and drag myself to Donald's computer. I spent a few minutes trying to get it open. But it was not something I could do, and I just kept pushing it around on the floor. Using the wall and the TV console, I was able to drag myself to standing.

I made my way to the bathroom and looked in the mirror. Donald looked terrible. His hair stood on end. He had no front teeth, only a molar. His pants were bagging at the knee, and there were deep wrinkles pressed into his shirt.

I tried to clean Donald up a little, then checked to see if he needed to go to the bathroom. I couldn't undo his pants. The mechanism was a bit too delicate for me. I heaved and tore them down, then peed all over the floor.

I couldn't get his underwear up. I kicked his legs out of his pants.

I was looking around for a pair of elastic-waist pants when I felt a wave of tremendous exhaustion pass through me. It felt like I had been without sleep for days. In the same moment, a shock went through me, and Donald's body fish-flopped onto the hotel carpet. I didn't know if I was being ejected or if I was dying. His body went out of my control, moving spastically around the suite, and then came back under my control.

I stayed on the floor.

I was taking some deep breaths when I felt another fish-flop, like a seizure. I was disoriented, slipping between the world inside Donald's body and the world outside of it, and when I opened my eyes, Benito, Renata, Jody, and several hotel employees were standing over me.

"His eye is open," one of the hotel employees said. I recognized David Cross.

Benito had his wallet out, ready to place it between Donald's jaws if he had another seizure. Renata was squinting at me, inside the body. She said, "I see what's going on."

"What's going on?" Benito said.

"Well, it's interesting, actually," Renata said, "though troubling. Donald has been possessed by two spirits."

"The man is having a seizure," Jody said. "Enough bullshit. Could we please stick with reality for a minute? We need to call a doctor. I'm going to put his pants on."

Jody got a pair of underwear and some wool trousers out of Donald's suitcase and knelt to dress him.

Renata ignored her. "Hello in there," she said. "You have lost control of Donald's body for the moment. You are tired, and you will rest. It is like sleeping. The problem is, Donald's body is now being taken over by a different being."

"So, like yours," Benito said.

"I'm a horse," she said. "There's a certain permeability. But I'm not a possessed body."

"So, what does that mean for Donald?"

"This is more bullshit than I can take."

"Well, that's what I'm explaining. Listen. Listen." She snapped in front of Donald's face. "When you wake up, you'll have control again, but while you're asleep, you and Donald will be very vulnerable to the whims of this other being. That's why we have to get you both out of there. It's no good, being in there."

"Eat shit," the other being said. I recognized the voice of the travel agent. He stood Donald's body up, walked to the door, threw it open, and began to run.

"Huh," Jody said. "That was surprising."

33

"Shit," the travel agent said. "He has been ill."

I blinked. The travel agent and I were inside Donald's body, in a large, expensive hotel suite. An embroidered privacy shade was drawn across a large picture window, filtering the view of squat glass buildings lit up in the night. I smelled vomit and diarrhea.

Donald's body lay face down on a white duvet.

THE OBEROI GURGAON was written on napkins, stationery, and pens. Cigarette butts, several half-devoured meals, used condoms, and empty minibar wrappers littered the room. It looked like the travel agent had had a party with Donald's body while I was passed out.

"I'm sorry," the travel agent said. "But I'm not going to say 'I'm sorry' anymore. I am turning into a crow. I don't know how long I have. Last night a couple of times, when I meant to speak, crow language came out. Hissing and things. I told myself I wouldn't apologize. I can't go through life that way."

I tried to sit up. "What did you do?"

He zeroed in on a fly on the windowpane.

"Where did you take the body?" I said. "Where did you take Donald's body?"

"What? Oh, sorry," he looked away from the fly, remembering himself. "I wasted my life," he said. "I was in construction. Sheet rocking. Then I got into the tourism industry. I wasted my life, then I wasted my time here. Next time, I'll do something of value."

"What did you do?"

"It was so stupid. I don't know why I did it. The thing is, you are going along, everything is normal, and then you look down and you are slipping a sock onto a set of claws."

I tried to lift one of Donald's arms. I wanted to see who had control.

"It's that stupid hooker's fault," the travel agent said. "He ordered a green salad, and so I assumed it would be okay to eat it. I wouldn't think a top-quality hooker would make that mistake. But in a fancy hotel, you would think they'd disinfect the raw items. Of course, you Americans are so fragile. I have already arranged your travel to Miami. To get your son. First class, all the way. Details are arranged. Hotel staff has everything. I took care of it."

"What will that accomplish?" I said. "What am I supposed to do in Miami?"

"It's near the ocean or whatever."

Someone tapped on the door.

"It'll be great. You'll see."

The person tapped again, then let himself into the room. "Excuse me, sir?" A short, thin boy in a flax-colored uniform and Nehru cap wrinkled his nose and said, "May I just?" as he started to gather up plates.

"Gar!" I said. "Gar."

I knocked the phone's receiver off the cradle and onto the ground.

The boy in the Nehru cap bent to pick it up. He took a moment to wipe it down, glancing pointedly at me.

"Marrrgula!"

He placed a call, holding the phone at a distance from his face. He spoke briefly, then switched on a harsh overhead light and sat on the bed.

"Someone is coming," he said. "Don't worry, sir."

"This boy is cunning," the travel agent said. "Much too cunning. What does he think he's doing? He can't adjust my light. Tell him to sit in the chair."

The boy turned toward me.

I waved Donald's hand in apology.

The travel agent said, "Don't make excuses to the boy." He hummed part of a song by the band Indeep. "I wasted my life."

A few minutes later, an elegant man slipped into the room. The boy stood abruptly, and the elegant man took stock of the situation, returning a key card to his jacket pocket.

"You see," the travel agent said. "What did I tell you? This is the proper way to behave, not switching on lights."

The elegant man squinted at Donald. "Start a bath," he said.

The boy scuttled off to the washroom, head bent forward.

I heard the bath start in the other room.

"You see," the travel agent said. "Proper respect. I am a top-tier travel agent. I book tours for ministers, police commissioners. But in my life, I have never left Guangzhou before today."

The elegant man knelt beside us, so he was at Donald's eye level.

"Sir, you have been ill," he said. "Your flight to Miami, with a stopover in Munich, departs today. I have it from the front desk that your condition causes you, at times, to have some motor difficulties, and then other times not. Is this correct, sir?"

The travel agent wrested control from me for a moment. He made a loud farting noise. I regained control of the body.

The elegant man nodded. "Sir, are you able to get yourself to the bathtub?"

I wasn't sure. I wondered what had happened the night before. There was ketchup and mustard all over Donald's wool trousers, and he had several new small purple bruises on his biceps.

"I am going to get you into the bath now. Is that okay?"

I nodded.

The elegant man called to the boy, and together they undressed Donald, throwing his clothing into a laundry bag. The boy winced at the smell and moved his body in such a way as to communicate masked disgust, but the man behaved as if he didn't notice.

"Sir," the elegant man said, "it is after midnight. I will try my level best, but I think it is unlikely we will be able to have your clothing cleaned before your departure. I have been given to understand you don't have a change of clothes. So. The hotel gift shop is run by an outside contractor and will not reopen until morning. I think I can help you, however, if you don't mind traveling in an Oberoi desk clerk uniform. It's quite presentable for travel. It is an inexpensive charcoal suit."

I nodded. "Glar!"

"Yes, sir. Very sensible, sir." The man spoke to the boy in Hindi again, then turned back to me.

"The charge will appear on your room bill. Stand up now, sir?" The man turned to the boy. "Help me to lift him, please. Good. Walk with him. We are doing fine. You see, the situation is workable. Already, we are making progress, sir."

They lowered Donald's body into the sudsy bathwater. The elegant man rolled up his sleeves and began to wash it with a washcloth, speaking as he did so. "Sir, I will assist you in getting clean. If you have any objection, please make a noise."

I was quiet.

"This is service," the travel agent said. "Oberoi is number one. I always tell my clients: Oberoi is the best hotel. Imagine if all this mess had happened at some Marriott. No, you pay for the service."

The elegant man washed Donald's hair, conditioned it, and combed it. The bath products smelled like bergamot and citrus.

He looked at Donald's fingernails and frowned.

He went to the sink and opened a small cardboard box. He came back with a nail brush and lifted one of Donald's hands out of the water and brushed the fingernails.

"Black cats, my mother used to call them." He dipped Donald's hand back in the water and squinted at the nails. Unsatisfied, he put more soap on the bristles and began to work them deep into Donald's fingernails again. It felt wonderful.

"The everyday practice is simply to develop a complete acceptance and openness to all situations and emotions, and to all people, experiencing everything totally, without mental reservations and blockages, so that one never withdraws and centralizes into oneself," he said. "This produces a tremendous energy which is usually locked up in the process of mental evasion and a general running away from life experiences."[29]

He dipped Donald's nails into the water again.

"Ah, yes, there we go. No black cats."

He took Donald's other hand. "Clarity of awareness may, in its initial stages, be unpleasant or fear-inspiring; if so, then one should open oneself completely to the pain or the fear and welcome it. In this way the barriers created by one's own habitual emotional reactions and prejudices are broken down."[30]

I tried to follow what he was saying. He was making sense, but hard to understand.

The travel agent yawned theatrically.

"Can you call my husband?" I said to the travel agent. "When you have the body back, after your nap."

"Too tired now. I'll do it next time. What's the number?"

"Four, seven—"

"Ah, okay. Actually, I can't think right now. Write it down for me, eh?"

"I can't write it down." I repeated the number. "I need you to tell him where my son is."

He snored softly.

When it was time to lift Donald out of the bath, the boy came back and helped stand his body up while the man dried him and got him into his suit.

"I am afraid you'll have to—what is it one says? Go commando," the elegant man said. "I had thought maybe I could hand-wash your underwear and dry them with a hair dryer, but I'm afraid they're beyond saving. You don't mind?"

He got me into the pants, then he and the boy carried me to an armchair, where they sat me up. The elegant man put the white shirt on and did the buttons, fretting a little because it was on the big side.

"I don't think we have the time to size down," he said. "I am sorry, sir. And no socks. You do have a choice. We were able to find a new pair of dress shoes. Would you like to wear these dress shoes or your hiking boots?"

Donald's hiking boots were beat-up brown sneaker-style boots with red laces. The dress shoes were cheap, brand-new, dull black leather with shapeless round toes. I wasn't sure which would be more ridiculous.

I pointed to the boots.

"Yes, sir. I'm sorry the socks were beyond saving, sir. But I think if you look at the duty-free, you might be able to find a pair. These are good hiking boots, sir. You're right to keep them."

When Donald's body was dressed, gleaming from the hot bath, the elegant man got me into a wheelchair and took me downstairs to a hotel car.

"I will come with you," the elegant man said. "They will not let me into the airport, but I will get you to the doors, where an airline employee will take over. We've called ahead. You're in first class, sir. There won't be any difficulties. They'll have a chair for you at the airport. Please, try not to worry, sir. I'll put your passport and printed ticket just here, in your breast pocket. But at the airport, I will give them to the man who meets you. I'll speak to him. Not to worry, chicken curry."

In the car, the elegant man sat in front beside the driver, who adjusted his rearview mirror. "Professor," the driver said. "You're looking very well!"

The elegant man laughed gently. "He likes the suit," he said. "Suit is nice?"

The driver did a thumbs-up. "Climate is good, sir?"

"Maybe a little cooler," the elegant man said.

The driver smiled, nodded, and eased the car forward.

The elegant man made small talk with the driver, and I looked out the window. I saw signs for IGI airport. We must be in Delhi, I thought.

When the car pulled to a stop in the drop-off lane at the large international airport, the elegant man spoke to the driver, who got out and walked around the car. He opened the door beside me, letting in warm air, revealing a gray-black sky thick with fog. The driver reached across Donald's lap and unbuckled the seat belt.

The elegant man stepped out of the car. "Now hold him,

yes," he said. "Hold him like that, but strong. He's big, you must be strong. Yes, and I'll get the . . . You got him?"

The driver got his arms under Donald's and eased Donald's body out of the car. He got it stretched as if standing, and then he realized he didn't have a plan. He tried to sit Donald's body back down, twisting it into an awkward pose.

"Oh dear," the elegant man said. He got out and came over to help.

I tried to stand up. The driver let go of Donald's body, which began to fall over. The elegant man caught it. He was startled, and said, "Oh, shit!" He teetered left and then right, and then began to scold the driver. "Help me! Help me! The body is deadweight. Set him down. Set him down, and let's take a moment to get our . . ."

The driver took Donald's body from the elegant man and laid him face down on the pavement between the car and the curb. His legs were under the car.

"Oh!" the elegant man said, indignant and alarmed, but then he abruptly gave up. He had to catch his breath. He got a scarf out of his pocket and wiped the sweat from his face, then got a small bidi cigarette and lit it. He took a puff, filling the air with smoke. "I'm sorry to leave you like this, Professor," he said. He sat down unceremoniously on the curb beside me. "Life is strange."

"Argara," I said.

"The past is but a present projection, and the present itself vanishes before it can be grasped."[31]

He took a few more puffs, then extinguished the cigarette delicately and returned it to an inner pocket for future emergencies.

"In a moment, they will be coming with your wheelchair. This has been a long night for both of us, and it is a new experience for me. I hope you can understand."

I made a soft sound of irritable resignation and forgiveness.

A man from the airport approached us with a wheelchair. The elegant man waved at him.

"Okay," the elegant man said. "I think the first thing is, let's get him back in the car. Then let's get the wheelchair set up beside the door. From there, we can work better."

"If you are able to help me at all, sir, please try." The elegant man lifted Donald's body from under his arms and sat it back in the bucket seat of the car.

"Okay," the elegant man said. "This is how we should have proceeded from the outset. We should have waited for the chair." He repositioned the wheelchair, then sniffed as he locked its brakes and lifted the footrests.

"Now," he said. "Professor. Could you please hold on to this handle up here with your inside hand? Professor, if I take this hand and wrap the fingers around the handle, can you hold them closed? Very good. Professor, if you look that way, your head's going to be on this shoulder. Get things lined up. I'm going to squeeze your knees here. Okay, are you ready, Professor? First we're going to stand you up. One, two— Wait, wait, wait, we have to go together. One, two, and up."

With the help of the man from the airport, the elegant man lifted Donald's body, and I pressed down on Donald's heels.

"Okay," the man said. "Can you reach over, grab something. Grab something, Professor." He turned to the driver and hissed in Hindi. The driver quickly took one of Donald's hands and drove it into the elegant man's hair. I grabbed a fistful. The man did not seem to mind. He said, "Pivot, pivot. Put your bottom in there, Professor. Bottom in. All the way in."

"Watch. Watch the head," the airport employee said. "Mind the head."

"Built for comfort," the elegant man said. "Just kidding. Okay." He gently un-balled Donald's fist, removing the fingers from his thick black hair. "We did it!" he said. "Success, ah? Lower these footrests and you're all ready to go."

He reached into Donald's jacket pocket for his boarding pass and gave it to the airline wheelchair attendant, who pushed him through the doors.

At the check-in desk, I saw that the ticket cost twenty-three thousand dollars. Poor Donald. What had I done to him? He watched his money so carefully.

I was wheeled into the lounge. When Donald's flight was called, I was wheeled on board. The flight attendants walked through the cabin serving champagne and distributing menus, behaving as if they weren't alarmed to see a toothless man in a hotel uniform in first class. When a glass of vintage champagne was offered, I gurgled, and the attendant set it beside me. I was taking pleasure in the amber color, the little bubbles sitting immobile on the side of the flute, when she took the glass and held it to my lips. Human beings are not so bad.

After the plane took off, the same flight attendant fed me a three-course meal, then put noise-canceling headphones on my head and selected a Tom Cruise movie. She gave me a sip of cognac, then tilted my seat all the way back and put a quilt over my legs. I fell into a pleasant sleep, wondering if I might even dream.

I woke up when they raised the cabin lights hours later, and I couldn't move again. I looked down and saw that Donald's body was duct-taped to an economy seat in the back of the plane, in an empty row.

A flight attendant with a salt-and-pepper mustache stepped out of the rear galley. "Watch your mouth. What did I say to you, sir."

He was talking to me.

"What's the matter, cat got your tongue? Okay, that's it." The flight attendant went back into the galley and reemerged with a roll of duct tape. "Can I get some assistance back here with the unruly passenger?"

Three additional flight attendants marched back and flanked him.

"I'm afraid I have no choice but to gag you, sir," the flight attendant said. "We have warned you repeatedly, and you have not complied."

"Absolutely!" one of the additional flight attendants said. She was particularly angry with Donald. "Absolutely."

The flight attendant holding the tape hesitated. "Are you capable of being quiet, sir? This is your final warning. I mean, I don't want to hear a peep from you."

I gurgled.

The flight attendant looked at the three women who had come to help him.

"I say do it," one said. "He's been warned."

"I mean, seriously. The man he, uh, orally pleasured in first class was sleeping! That's rape. Cut-and-dried. And the curse words . . . I've had enough of his . . . behavior."

"I just hesitate," the mustached flight attendant said. "I mean, he doesn't have teeth."

"It's your section."

"You're lucky Jeff is nice," the angry one said. "I take over back here in two hours, and I don't have that problem. You need to shut your mouth. We've had enough out of you."

I frowned.

"Okay, that's it," she said. "Give me the tape."

She pulled a length from the roll. "Stuff something in his mouth. Give me a sock."

I made plangent begging sounds.

"Sherry?" the man said. "I'm not comfortable with the sock. He could asphyxiate."

"Not another word," she said. "Not one word. And I'm going to put a little tape right here on the back of this seat for you to look at, as a helpful reminder."

The woman put a four-inch piece of duct tape right across the television screen. "Don't make me use that," she said. "Fermez la bouche. When we land, you're going to jail."

"Do not pass go, do not collect two hundred dollars," the male flight attendant added. He turned to the women for approval, but they were embarrassed for him and looked away.

34

Trip had moved a blanket and pillow onto the deck. His V-berth was taking on more water than Anthony's part of the cabin.

He had spent the night charting their position with the sextant, orienting himself with Crux, and Alpha and Beta Centauri. He had marked a series of *X*'s on the map, just below the equator. He was pretty sure they were near a shipping channel that ran up the west coast of Africa.

Below deck, Anthony was splashing around the galley, just up, probably still drunk from the night before.

The wind blew Trip's hair across his eyes. He pushed it out of the way.

Anthony put his head over the edge of the companionway. "Hi, hi," he said. "Ugh, my head."

"Good news. The wind is back," Trip said.

"Huh," Anthony said. He stuffed a forefinger into his mouth and withdrew a wad of bloody toilet paper. "One problem. We don't know where we are and we don't know where to go. And please put away that goddamn sextant. How many times have I told you to forget about that. I don't know how we get out of this mess we're in. But it sure as shit isn't that thing. It's making me crazy, watching you play with that."

"Sorry." Trip set down the sextant. "Oh, sorry."

"What is all this?"

"Sorry, just a map I found."

"You have the map out?" Anthony came closer. He noticed the X's below the equator. "What are those?"

"That's us. Sorry, I wrote on the map."

"Trip, listen to me. Is that us?"

"What? Yes. Sorry I wrote on the map."

"That's us! That's us!"

"Sorry I wrote on the map. Sorry."

Anthony danced a crazy little jig, pumping his arms up and down. "Trip!" he shouted. "That's us! You crazy kid, you've saved us! You're a genius!" He tried to jump and click his heels in the air, but was heavier than he remembered. He smoothed his hair, embarrassed but still jubilant. "I'm just going to get a tiny drink."

Anthony ducked back into the cabin, and returned a moment later, steadied.

"Stay with us, wind. Please, stay with us. Trip, just keep out of my way. I have to be speedy, now. We don't know if the wind will hold."

Anthony pulled the halyard to lift the mainsail and set a broad reach. Like that, they were sailing. They cut across the line of low, quiet swells. Spray scudded across the deck.

35

THE HOLDING ROOM inside the Munich airport felt like a contractor's trailer. It had plywood walls and one small window covered by a set of mini blinds. I worried about missing my connection to Miami.

I had been waiting for more than an hour. I tried to stay calm. I didn't think Donald was in a situation that couldn't be fixed, but if I got tired and the travel agent took control, that would change.

The door opened.

A man in a cheap black suit settled into the seat across from mine. He wore a white shirt, and had an ID around his neck on a ball chain. He glanced through the papers in a manila folder.

"Sir. You understand why you're being held?"

I gurgled.

"Sir." The man flipped through his papers again and shifted uncomfortably in his chair. He took his badge and tucked it into his shirt, then removed it and wiped the sweat off the back of his neck with his hand. "You're being held for lewd and disruptive behavior, minor assault of a crew member, drunk and disorderly conduct, feigning a disability, provoking panic and creating a safety hazard, and theft of airline property aboard flight 2667 from Delhi to Munich. There is some question of whether or not you will be charged with terrorism and rape."

I shook my head no.

"You have caused extreme passenger distress and potential interruption of an international flight pattern, and just because the old man, the gentleman, whom you fellated is not interested in pressing charges at this time, that doesn't necessarily mean we are satisfied. The crimes you are accused of can come with jail time, and hundreds of thousands of euros in fines. There is also the likely scheduling interference."

I lifted my watch.

"I'm afraid it's a bit more serious than that. These are serious charges. I'm going to get one of my colleagues in here, and she's going to transfer you to a jail. Do you understand?"

I heard a crow sound. It was inside Donald. The travel agent rattled and clicked.

The man stood up. "I wish you the best of luck, sir. But drunk or no, you really should be ashamed of yourself."

He glanced at the blinds and went to the door, fumbling with the handle as he let himself out.

The travel agent cawed.

A middle-aged woman with a little straight line of a mouth let herself into the holding room. Her hair was pulled into a bun, with wild broken hairs all around her face, curling into little locks beside her ears. The buttons across the chest of her shirt parted occasionally, revealing a garnet bra.

"I'm Officer König," she said crisply. "I'll be taking you to Stadelheim, where you will be charged. I understand Officer Wolff has explained about your charges."

"Caw," the travel agent said.

"Sir, please answer my question with a nod or a head shake. Did Officer Wolff speak to you about your charges?"

"Caw!" the travel agent said. "Caw! Caw! Caw!"

I nodded.

"Caw! Caw! Caw!"

She made a note on her form.

"Caw!"

I irritably swung an arm over my head at the travel agent.

The woman stood. "Please place your hands on the desk, close together, so that I can appropriately restrain you."

I did as requested. The woman zip-tied Donald's wrists together roughly.

"Ah," I said.

The woman led me through a sparse and brightly lit room where people from all over the world sat on beat-up industrial couches looking discouraged. Some of them furtively used their phones, others tended to small children. We went through customs, where Donald was ogled by shocked travelers, and out of the terminal and to a passport-control-officer parking lot, where she put me into the back of her prowler.

She radioed ahead, then drove. It was early evening. She put on German talk radio, and two German men argued about something. On the freeway, the police officer was passed by a woman in a Volvo station wagon, and the two boys in the back seat made faces at me. I flashed Donald's gums, causing them to laugh uproariously.

The officer pulled off the freeway and up to the prison gate. She showed her badge to an officer inside the checkpoint station and parked in a line of other police cruisers outside a redbrick building that resembled a cathedral.

She got me out of the back, and we walked up the steps to the jail, where she nodded to a man behind a desk, who led me into a small cell with a kitchenette and a double-barred window.

"Sir, this is the toilet." The man opened an orange IKEA-style door to reveal an ordinary porcelain commode. "And this is your coffee station. Sir, hot water comes around at seven, I believe."

"Mgh," I said.

"If you have a legitimate medical diagnosis, sir, if there are prescribed medications you require, the staff can address that after the weekend. Until then, you'll be safe here. Okay, then. Until morning. Try to get some rest."

He locked the door and walked away.

"Well, he was nice," the travel agent said.

I lay down on the little bed, but I couldn't sleep.

Just after sunrise, a guard tapped on my cell door, then opened it with his key. He was a polite, fastidious man with orange eyeglasses.

"Just a routine check, sir," he said in English. "The

caddy will come shortly to brew coffee or tea. You could use that to indicate if you'd like hot water." He pointed to a switch on the wall.

I made the telephone gesture and pointed at my watch.

"This is the weekend, sir." He switched on my hot-water light. "The weekday staff can handle this kind of question. Tschuss." He closed the cell door and locked it.

The cart came around half an hour later. An inmate and a guard unlocked the door and filled my carafe. Irritated, I threw up my hands, and the officer brewed my French press. I sat at my double-barred window overlooking a grassy quad and contemplated how to proceed. Then I began to feel very sleepy.

All the cell doors were open, and the inmates were congregating in a rec area when I became conscious again.

"Hey, was ist mit deinen Zähnen passiert, du Fickfehler."*

The travel agent was circling several haggard-looking inmates who clustered around a Monopoly game. He hissed at a stoop-shouldered inmate with a wispy mustache.

"Du bist auch ein hässliche Drecksau," the man with the wispy mustache said. "Verpiss dich."†

The travel agent leaped forward, took hold of the inmate, and bit his ear. Then the travel agent toddled around him in a circle, walking straight-legged with a wide separation between his feet.

---

* Hey, what happened to your teeth, you fucking freak?

† You're an ugly bastard, too. Fuck off.

The man with the wispy mustache stood and shoved the travel agent.

"Caw! Caw!"

"Lass ihn in Ruhe. Verlasse ihn. Er ist verrückt. Sie werden ihn am montag in die Forensik verlegen."*

The man tried to shoo Donald's body away more gently.

Another inmate spoke up. He was an older man with intelligent eyes and wire-rimmed glasses. He said, "Letzte Nacht hörte ich ihn mit den Wachen sprechen. Er war ganz normal."†

"Caw! Caw!" The travel agent leaped nimbly onto one of the picnic tables, scattering the Monopoly pieces.

"Du wirst das aufräumen, Rumpelstilzchen."‡

"Caw!" The travel agent jumped up and down in place, then strutted back and forth, establishing his territory.

"Sei vorsichtig. Es ist der Nachtkrapp."§

Several of the inmates laughed, but a couple of them, the more sensitive ones, were nervous. They moved away and kept their eyes on him. I could see they had some understanding that something unusual was happening, even though they couldn't make any sense of it.

The travel agent was still strutting back and forth on their game, looking for something shiny. He darted a hand down and picked up a silver top hat, cawing loudly and triumphantly.

---

* Leave him alone. Leave him. He's a crazy person. They will be transferring him to forensics on Monday.

† Last night I heard him talking to the guards. He was completely normal.

‡ You'll clean this up, Rumpelstiltskin.

§ Be careful. It's the Night Madman.

The wispy mustached inmate said, "Wache! Wir brauchen hier drüben eine Wache, Mann!"*

"Caw!"

The spectacles on the older inmate caught the travel agent's eye, and he bent suddenly and snatched them off the man's face with his toothless jaws. He jumped up and down on the table in excitement, then darted back inside his cell, the glasses in his mouth.

"Pimmelfresse!"

"Pimmelfresse! Kreiz Kruzefix!"†

"Ich gehe nicht dorthin zurück, Mann. Das ist der Nachtkrapp!"‡

"Ich brauche meine verdammte Brille! Wachen!"§

I could barely hear them talking over the travel agent's endless cawing and jumping up and down on the bed in his cell. He hid the glasses and the Monopoly hat under his blanket.

I began to wonder what would happen to me. I did not have limitless time to help Trip. Like the travel agent, who had apparently become a crow, at least in his head, I would move on to another form.

I understood for the first time that there were fates worse than death.

A guard wearing rubber gloves entered the cell. Behind him was another guard, who stood in the doorway.

---

* Guard! We need a guard over here, man!

† You ding-dong! Jesus Christ!

‡ I'm not going back there, man. That's the Night Madman!

§ I need my damned glasses! Guard!

The first spoke. "Sir, would you mind having a word with me."

"Caw!"

"Sir, here in Germany, especially with Ausländern, we have—it's a systemic problem. It is one we are aware of. Often foreign nationals in need of psychiatric care are treated as criminals. This may in fact be the case here, in your situation. A mistake may have been made. We are awaiting a visit from a Betreuer to represent you. Advocate for you. In the meantime, we must take some action. And so this man, Officer Peters, behind me, has come to take you to the hospital, where they will do a comprehensive evaluation."

"How do you do," Officer Peters said.

"Caw! Caw!"

"I understand you have asked to speak to your embassy. Yes, that will happen as well. In fact, it may actually be easier to arrange from the psychiatric hospital."

"Caw!" The travel agent jumped up into the corner above his bed, flapping back and forth between the two walls near the window.

"Sir. If you could come down from the wall, we could do this quite easily, and there would be no need for any kind of restraint, physical or chemical. You are in a foreign country, in jail, being transferred. Anyone would feel a little nervous. Now, unfortunately, and I think this is really rather a bad policy, it is my duty to get you situated on this gurney for the transfer."

"Caw!"

"Sir? Sir, this is completely understandable, but it is

also outside of my area of expertise. Now please, if you could lie down on the gurney, then—"

The travel agent leaped from the bed toward the open cell door, smacking his head on the wall above the door and landing heavily on Officer Peters.

Abruptly, the two officers went into a different mode. They stepped into the cell and took hold of Donald's body and moved him onto the gurney, restraining him physically while Officer Peters injected Donald's arm with a sedative. In a few moments, Donald's body went limp, and the travel agent and I lay helplessly watching as the officers restrained his arms and rolled him down the hall.

"Du fickst mit dem *Nachtkrapp*,"* an inmate shouted as the gurney passed.

"Caw," the travel agent whispered.

---

* You're fucking with the Night Madman.

36

IT WAS NIGHT. Trip was on the deck, sailing with the jib, holding course with the Southern Cross and Pointers. Occasionally he held his hand up like an L, his forefinger and thumb extended, to check his position.

Anthony was down below in a hammock he'd rigged up, playing "Pictures of You" on repeat. The sea was black. The wind was behind them, and the ship moved evenly across the water. He could have been dreaming, but he felt very awake.

Something flashed on the horizon. He started. At first he thought it was the whale. He squinted and made out a trail of dim red, white, and blue lights. Was it the shore?

They were ships, he realized. He'd found the shipping channel.

37

THEY HAD MOVED Donald to an electroconvulsive therapy suite.

The technician placed electrode sensors on his temples to connect him to the electroencephalogram and the ECT machine, then put similar stickers on his chest to connect his body to the ECG machine. She Velcroed a blood-pressure cuff around his arm and slipped a pulse oximeter onto one of his fingers.

"Make a fist," she said. She looked for a vein and clucked her tongue, then frowned and picked up his arm.

"Okay," she said as she slid a needle into his forearm. "I got it now."

She picked up a syringe from a tray and set it on Donald's chest as she unscrewed the IV bag. She screwed it into the IV and depressed the plunger.

The woman finished injecting the medication, set the syringe on the tray, and took Donald's upper arm with her crooked, manicured fingers.

"You are getting electroconvulsive therapy," she said. "I gave you your propofol, and that makes you sleepy. It feels like a cocktail. In ten minutes, you wake up, and it is finished."

She patted Donald's arm and glanced down at her Apple Watch. Its face was black, the strap bright orange.

I tried to sit up.

"You startled me," the technician said. Her hand was cool. She removed it. "Just lie back and relax."

I felt myself drifting away from the woman and the suite. The technician waited, then turned to the table. She found a tube and slipped it under Donald's nose. "Oxygen," she said.

A doctor let himself into the suite, wheezing. He was obese and waddled a little bit on his unusually large legs, out of breath from the walk from the elevator. I could see that he was highly intelligent.

"I've seen this before," he said. "It's a mild form of psychosis. It's not as unusual as you might think."

The technician held up a second syringe, and the doctor nodded.

"I've seen it in Africa, Southeast Asia. ECTs can really help with this."

The technician screwed the syringe into the IV connected to Donald's arm. "Succinylcholine," she said.

"Two or three weeks of therapy, and the patient's everyday personality is back. It's remarkably effective. Usually there is no recurrence of the pathology." The doctor flicked open a plastic box and pushed an orange button.

Donald's eyelids fluttered. His right foot half pointed, with a slight tremor. The travel agent and I were shot upward, out of his head. We passed by Donald, who was going the opposite way, back into his body.

"Hey," I said. "How's it going?"

Donald scowled.

There was a loud whooshing sound, and we shot out of the top of Donald's head, past the doctor and the technician, into the wall. I looked around.

The nurse put a hand on Donald's socked foot. The ECT machine whirred, printing a receipt that showed a wavy line, a representation of the electricity that had been sent through Donald's body.

The travel agent, the crow, flew up into the corner, through the ceiling. He disappeared, saying, "Caw!"

Donald blinked. "Where am I?" he said. "What's happening?"

The nurse patted his foot. "You're still here," she said. "In Munich. You've just had your first round of ECT."

"That is round number one," the doctor said. "We do five rounds. We assess. Do maybe five more rounds."

"My phone," Donald said. "My friend. Sandra. She needs . . . she took my body after we made love in different places. Everything was changing. And a travel agent. Took me to the Oberoi."

"Please, sir. Lie down," the nurse said. "You had a major procedure. You must relax. There will be some disorientation."

Donald pulled lethargically against his restraints. He fell back, surrendering, and said, "Okay."

38

An orderly let himself into the electroconvulsive therapy suite. He pulled the sheets off the bed. He sighed, knees clicking as he knelt to pick up a pillow, singing the words to a German pop song.

Something about those clicking sounds woke me up for a second, and I understood that nothing had ever been wrong with Trip. Or with anything. I could see everything all at once. I could see the scholars, and Donald in the future, visiting Vic. I could see my future parents. I could even see the travel agent, the crow, heading out toward the water.

I stood up and recognized the scholars. They were having a talent show in the ballroom of the hotel.

Someone had rigged up lights and sound. The scholars sat on gold-framed banquet chairs with burgundy velvet cushions. On the dais someone was enacting the destruction of the *nadi* wheels.

A smoke machine coughed into gear. Multiple wheels of light shot around the ballroom. "*Nadi* wheel of the navel is destroyed," the scholar said into a microphone. "Subtle supporting winds begin to escape."

TRIP

The smoke in the room was thick. I am using the proper words for all the things that were going on, because it's the only way I can describe them, but actually, by this time, I didn't really know the words much anymore.

I was back in the house. It was a year into the future, early in the afternoon.

Vic was in front of an electric pottery wheel. He had his jacket folded on his desk, his sleeves rolled. He was fiddling with a piece. It was long and skinny, irrelevant, not the kind of thing anyone would ever buy, but he was consumed by it. His nails needed to be trimmed.

The doorbell rang.

Irritably, Vic switched off the wheel. He stepped back, wiped his hands on a cloth.

He went to the door and looked through the peephole.

Donald stood on the doorstep in a wool sweater and jeans.

Vic contemplated creeping away, but Donald's eyes seemed to meet his in the peephole. He unlocked the door and opened it.

"Vic?" Donald smiled, revealing a mouth of pearly-white implants. "I'm Donald."

"Oh, of course. I'm glad. I forgot it was today. My phone was supposed to remind me. Stupid Outlook. Come on in, come on in."

"I hate Outlook," Donald said, wiping his feet.

"Can I offer you a cup of tea? Trip usually gets home

from his robotics club around four or four thirty. He does it through the Y." Vic filled the electric kettle. "I'll have to head out to teach before then, but you can make yourself at home."

"I'll be fine."

"Is Earl Grey all right with you?" Vic set down the kettle and turned it on. "Not too late in the day for caffeine?"

"Earl Grey is fine," Donald said.

"Are you sure?" Vic held up a tin of peppermint tea.

"Positive."

"All right."

The kettle steamed and Vic swished hot water around in a teapot, emptied it, then spooned in tea. He filled the pot and covered it with a cozy and set a timer.

"Okay," he said. He pulled down two cups and filled them with boiling water. "Oh, have a seat, I'm sorry."

Donald sat on a stool. "I wanted to say, again, how sorry I am for your loss."

"Thank you." Vic touched the electric kettle, then looked out the window. He wiped his hands on the back of his pants.

"I was with her when she died. Around that time."

Vic looked back at Donald for a second, then turned and emptied the boiling water out of the cups and filled them with tea. "How do you take it?"

"Milk, no sugar."

"Me too. Actually, I'm going to have a spoonful of manuka honey. Would you like some?"

"I'll have a little."

Vic made the tea. He gave Donald his cup, and the two men faced each other.

Donald sipped. "The proverbial well-made cup of tea." He paused and looked at the teacup. "This is a lovely mug. I hesitate to call it a mug. Where did you get it?"

"Oh, I made it. Thanks. I made all of this. I mean, not the silverware, obviously."

Donald nodded, looking at the mug in his hands a little longer. "So, I think, when we spoke on the phone, I was explaining about my dental procedure, but I couldn't really . . . Are you familiar with a businessman in the seventies who wrote books about out-of-body experiences?"

Vic shook his head.

Donald nodded. "It's relevant to this discussion, but . . ." He took a sip of tea, and the two men were quiet for a moment.

Donald said, "I have something I'd like to tell Trip, about Sandra. I think it is something she would want him to know, and I think it would be meaningful to him also. Can I speak to you openly?"

Vic set down his cup.

"I was with Sandra for a while after she died. I mentioned the nitrous. I had an out-of-body experience, and Sandra used my body to try to get to Trip. It sounds crazy, but I was sort of . . . there."

Donald paused, trying to figure out if Vic thought he was insane. But Vic was listening.

Donald said, "She was thinking of Trip. He was the only thing she thought about. She loved him so much."

Vic nodded. "Yes, you should talk to him. That would be good. Thank you." He looked at his watch. "I mean, if he's open to it. I wouldn't force it."

"No, of course not."

"He might be very interested . . . If I had to bet, I would say he'd be interested. But you never know." He finished his tea. "I hope he tells me about it. I mean, I want to know, too. But I get the sense this is just between the two of you. And honestly, just now I really have to run. Why don't you wait here? I'll call him and give him a heads-up and remind him, so he knows to expect you."

I was still in the ballroom of the hotel in Nepal, and Larry was talking about the second half of the bardo, when one would be desperate for a place to hide, for a body, and might jump into anything. He was describing the visions that might precede birth in different realms and continents.

"If you are reborn in Japan, the Philippines, Indonesia, New Zealand, or Australia, you will see lakes and waters adorned with male and female swans," Larry said. "Think of renunciation and do not go there. If you are reborn there, your situation will be comfortable, but you should not go there, as the dharma is not easily available to you in those places."[32]

I could hear Larry talking about the importance of avoiding caves and gray light, and I could see Donald and Vic. I could even see the crow.

TRIP

He had ridden into the shipping channel on a cargo boat. He ate the food left out by the men during the day. It was quiet. He missed the crows from the harbor. He noticed a black thing bobbing on the horizon. The thing seemed to be taunting him, telling him he was not where he was supposed to be. It offered something vague and important, maybe another crow.

He was curious and bored. The black thing grew smaller. Its laughter at his cowardice felt more urgent, and so he flew the long way down to find an enormous many-colored propane tank bobbing on the surface of the water.

The crow was tired. He cawed two times to the other crow that might be there, saying, "I am here," though he knew he was alone. He sat on the tank, thinking he would rest his wings, then fly back to the boat. He closed one eye.

When he opened the eye it was night, blackness stretched out endlessly in every direction. He was completely alone. He cawed two times. The ocean lapped back at him. He stood and felt dizzy. He cawed three times, sending out a warning, then looked down into the water.

Here was the magic thing. A mystical and glowing orb of blue light just below the surface. The crow ducked his head into the water and lifted the thing out by its crown, dragging it up so its tentacles draped along the tank and trailed down the side.

The crow nibbled the jellyfish's head. The jellyfish trembled. The crow pecked again, changed his footing. The meat was water saturated, delicious. And then the crow became aware of something bad and enormous. The long tentacles, tangled around his feet and bottom, contained millions of venom-packed stinging cells. They were injecting him with powerful, painful toxins. The crow tried to fight back, entangling himself more deeply in the tentacles.

When the sun rose, he and the jellyfish were still there, hovering and confused, above the scene of their dead bodies entwined on the industrial fuel tank. The jellyfish was shriveled. The crow felt reluctant to leave his corpse, which still looked like it might rise up and fly away.

They stayed there together for a little while before moving on.

A woman lay in bed in a hospital gown, a white paper disposable hair cap on her head. Her legs were up in stirrups. A tech held an ultrasound wand to her lower belly.

A man sat in a chair beside the bed, holding her hand.

Beside him, a doctor looked at a computer screen at the image of the woman's uterus. She picked up a picture of an embryo. "Very good," she said. She handed the picture of the embryo to the woman, then walked around to the foot of the bed. She stood between the woman's legs, and lifted a sheet.

She cleaned the woman with some blue solution in a squirt bottle and a Q-tip.

"Does everything look good?" the man said.

"I'm just cleaning her up."

She put down the blue solution and threw away the Q-tip, then turned and picked up the embryo in a pipette. It took just a second to put the embryo into the woman's uterus.

"Okay, that was easy," she said.

"That's it?" the man asked. "We're done?"

"Yeah, that's it." The doctor nodded.

The woman took her legs out of the stirrups, and the doctor folded them and tucked them inside the bed. The woman pushed herself back onto the bed.

The doctor took off her gloves and threw them in the garbage. "The embryo is where it needs to be. You're welcome to stay as long as you like, but you don't need to stay lying down."

She started to let herself out.

"Wait," the man said. "Didn't you say you know the gender of the embryo? Because we got the genetic testing? I mean, could I ask the gender?"

"Do you want me to check?"

The man nodded, and the doctor let herself out.

After a few minutes, she came back. "Do you want me to write it down, or just tell you?" She was nervous about the couple asking the embryo's gender. She saw a lot of couples like them. She wanted them to be optimistic, but realistic, too. She said, "It's a . . ."

But I couldn't make it out.

Trip threw his backpack down by the doorway and went to the refrigerator. He didn't notice Donald at the bar until Donald stood.

"I'm Donald. Sorry to startle you. I'm Sandra's friend. I'm a friend of your mother's. I was with her after she died."

Trip turned from the refrigerator. He didn't look surprised. He lifted his headphones off one ear.

"What is it?" he said.

"Maybe we should sit down."

I closed my eyes and let go of my past.

I thought for the last time about how I had not diagnosed Trip early enough. How I had been impatient with him. How at times, I had sort of ignored him. I had taken the easy way out, sending him to therapists who would play with him, rather than doing it myself. I had let him look at screens. I had let him eat dyes. It was my fault for living in a house with lead paint on the porch. For feeding him meat. For not drawing him out sooner, over and over again, the very first time I wondered about him playing alone with his cars.

I let go of how, like one of his teachers, I had tried to argue my way out of it at first.

I thought of how it *was* a strange experience, speaking to someone who didn't tune in to you. It was like taking hallucinogens, and maybe I had dealt with the strangeness a bit too much by not talking to him. I mean, I spoke to get things done, but I rarely met him in his world and shot the breeze.

I thought about how shy it had made me, for a person to be different. How nervous, even angry.

How rigid, how conventional, how prescribed my expectations were. Because I had been a strange person, I hadn't noticed for a long time how much I looked at those around me and followed, and how much they did the same, how little flexibility we had, how someone who actually was a little different made us lose our minds. How it shook us out of the characters we were playing, disrupted our zombie flow, when someone did something as simple as refuse to answer our questions.

And I was happy to have been shaken out of it a little bit by my son, to have been made to feel disrupted, shameful, ungainly, awkward, and unsure. To have been made to stir for a moment in the everlasting sleep that had been my life. Sandra Vernon's life. Or whatever. Whatever. Whatever it was.

ACKNOWLEDGMENTS

I'd like to thank D., Clancy, and my mom. My editor, Mitzi Angel, and Susan Golomb, my agent. I'd also like to thank Dzongsar Khyentse Rinpoche, Sechen Rabjam Rinpoche, and Robert Thurman for permission to quote from books, talks, and teachings. My writing group: Brian Booker, Jake Hooker, Sarah Smith, Alena Graedon, Dave Astrovsky, April Lawson, and Casey Walker, for reading this chapter by chapter and remaining supportive. And the following people for reading drafts or individual chapters, or answering questions of mine: Sam Chang, Tom Gibbon, Jude Harris, Ben Nugent, Chris Bollen, Enrico Gnaulati, Alton Bozeman, Rinchen Palbar, Arthur Bates, Sanjna Singh, Brian Spinks, Paul Barnett, Noa Jones, Lorin Stein, Cheryl Burgess, Sam Stark, Kunga Rinchen, Arne Schelling, Patrick Cottrell, Ben Jasnow, and Anthony Madrid. I'd also like to thank Zeljka Marosevic, Devon Mazzone, Emma Chuck, Caitlin Van Dusen, Sasha Landauer, Janine Barlow, Liz Selig, Amber McCommon, Gwen Colman, Rachelle Terry, Mari Jacoby, and Jody Vernon. And finally thank you to my children, Ratna, Kali, Zelly, Margaret, and Portia. I love you.

SOURCE NOTES

CHAPTER 4
1. Used with permission of Dzongsar Khyentse Rinpoche.
2. Ibid.

CHAPTER 5
3. Used with permission of Ben Nugent.

CHAPTER 6
4. See more in Tsele Natsok Rangdrol's *The Mirror of Mindfulness*, translated by Erik Pema Kunsang, and Andrew Holecek's *Preparing to Die*.

CHAPTER 10
5. Adapted from a message Dzongsar Khyentse Rinpoche recorded to play for a longtime student and practitioner of Buddhism, when he was dying. The message was reprinted in Nalanda Translation Committee's 2022–2023 newsletter.
6. Ibid.
7. Ibid.
8. Ibid.

CHAPTER 12
9. See more in Gyurme Dorje's complete translation of *The Tibetan Book of the Dead* (Penguin, 2009).

CHAPTER 13
10. Used with permission of Robert Thurman. From his translation of *The Tibetan Book of the Dead* (Bantam, 1993).
11. Ibid.

SOURCE NOTES

12. Ibid.
13. Ibid.
14. Ibid.
15. Ibid.
16. Ibid.
17. Adapted from "Bardo," a talk Dzongsar Khyentse Rinpoche gave in Deer Park, in India, in May 2022.
18. Ibid.
19. Ibid.

CHAPTER 20

20. Adapted from "Bardo," a talk Dzongsar Khyentse Rinpoche gave at Deer Park in India, in May 2022.
21. Ibid.
22. Ibid.
23. Ibid.

CHAPTER 21

24. *The Way of the Bodhisattva*, by Shantideva, revised and translated by the Padmakara Translation Group (Shambhala Classics, 1997, 2006).
25. Adapted from *Cutting Through Spiritual Materialism*, by Chogyam Trungpa Rinpoche (Shambhala Publications, 1973).

CHAPTER 24

26. Adapted from a talk Dzongsar Khyentse Rinpoche gave on reincarnation at the Numata Center for Buddhist Studies at the University of California, Berkeley, in 2015.
27. Ibid.
28. Ibid.

CHAPTER 33

29. *Maha Ati: Pith Instructions on the Great Perfection*, by Kyabje Dilgo Khyentse Rinpoche. Used with permission of Shechen Rabjam Rinpoche.
30. Ibid.
31. Ibid.

CHAPTER 38

32. *Tibetan Book of the Dead*, translated by Gyurme Dorje (Penguin, 2009).

A NOTE ABOUT THE AUTHOR

Amie Barrodale's stories and essays have appeared in *The Paris Review*, *Harper's Magazine*, and other publications. In 2012 she was awarded *The Paris Review*'s George Plimpton Prize for Fiction for her story "William Wei." She is the author of the short-story collection *You Are Having a Good Time*.